CW00921751

THE LOVE ALGORITHM

CAMILLA ISLEY

Boldwood

First published in Great Britain in 2024 by Boldwood Books Ltd.

Copyright © Camilla Isley, 2024

Cover Design by Alexandra Allden

Cover Images: Shutterstock and Getty

A CIP catalogue record for this book is available from the British Library.

Paperback ISBN 978-1-83751-952-1

Large Print ISBN 978-1-83751-951-4

Hardback ISBN 978-1-83751-950-7

Ebook ISBN 978-1-83751-953-8

Kindle ISBN 978-1-83751-954-5

Audio CD ISBN 978-1-83751-945-3

MP3 CD ISBN 978-1-83751-946-0

Digital audio download ISBN 978-1-83751-947-7

Boldwood Books Ltd
23 Bowerdean Street
London SW6 3TN
www.boldwoodbooks.com

If you ever wished you could have a droid friend, this book is dedicated to you...

1

REESE

The email subject says, "Meeting request." It doesn't say *"Open me, and you'll end up making a sex tape in the office."* (The robotics lab specifically, but let's not focus on the details.)

Clueless to the drama the simple message would stir, I click on the bolded line and read the confusing text.

The president of Mercer Industries, Nolan Mercer, wants to see me in his office on Monday morning. At eight o'clock sharp.

The request is unusual and unexpected. Mr. Mercer and I may abide by the six-degrees-of-separation rule *in theory*—he's the boss of my boss's boss—but I've never spoken to the man in real life. Not even when I was first hired as a robotics systems product owner in the research and development division of Mercer Robotics, which I now lead.

Have I seen him around?

Sure, occasionally. Mostly as one of the thousands of employees listening to his end-of-year address to the company—he was a far-off figure, speaking on a stage, unreachable, untouchable. Once, I even crossed paths with him in the main hall. He was being fussed about by suits, while common mortals like myself were doing our best to scramble out of his way, flee elevators in case he needed to ride in one, or just stare awestruck at the multi-billionaire mogul.

So even if only three layers of managerial corporate crust separate us, in reality, Nolan Mercer is to me what Steve Jobs could've been to Apple Geniuses working retail. A myth, a creature of legend. Hence why it's super weird that he's summoning me to his office—let alone that he knows I exist.

My next reaction to the email is relief that his assistant let me know in advance. At least I won't make a complete fool of myself. I push my wheeled chair away from the desk and assess my wardrobe. Yeah, black baggy sweats and a hoodie that says, "*Dear Math, grow up and solve your own problems*" wouldn't cut it for a meeting with the big boss. Nor would the space buns on my head.

Even if it's Friday, my outfit isn't casual Friday wear. Informal clothing is par for the course for me and my staff.

In most companies, R&D engineers are lab rats. We're secluded away in our research facilities, where we live on a parallel plane to the rest of the organization.

I can count the times I've had to wear a suit to work on one hand. It's exactly two. One each for the two years I've been head of the department and had to present an advancement report to the CEO and general director of Mercer Robotics. Nolan Mercer, of course, wasn't present.

"K-2P?" I ask aloud to my droid. "Why do you think the big boss wants to see me?"

The robot replies in a mechanical voice from his position beside my desk, "I have calculated a 98.9 per cent probability that the meeting is related to the department's work."

K-2P is not part of my research at the company. He's an AI project I've been working on since college—even if now I think of him as more of a friend. Maybe my only real friend.

I stare at the compact, claw-armed tripod android. His face is a mass of buttons and switches surrounding twin radar eyes, one of which has its red light focused on me.

"That's a very unimaginative reply." I pull the chair closer to him. "We need to up your creativity drive."

I make to touch him, but he scurries back on his wheeled feet.

"Please leave my drives alone. My imagination is fine."

"Really? I asked an ironic question, and you gave me an ultra-boring, to-the-point answer."

"My hearing sensors could not detect the irony in your tone." The droid lets out an offended beep-beep. "You should probably review the empathy code Garrett uploaded to my CPU last week."

"Stop being distrustful of Garrett. You know he means well."

"I do not. Since he tangled with my operating system, my capability to interpret human behaviors has been clearly diminished."

"But not your creativity?" I give the droid a dry stare.

"My creativity is perfectly fine." K-2P swivels—the robotic equivalent of shrugging. "I answered your question straightforwardly. I could've given you a million sarcastic answers."

"Fine. Let's go over it again. Why has the big boss asked for a meeting?"

"Mr. Mercer wants to start a rocket division like any respectable multi-billionaire on the planet and wants you to lead it."

"Better." I nod, suppressing a smile. "I appreciate the scornful touch toward billionaires and their rocket measuring contests. Give me three other funny reasons in quick sequence." I snap my fingers.

"One. He wants you to steal the secret prototype of a revolutionary assembly robot code-named Project Nemesis. Two. He needs you to develop better weapons for conquering the galaxy after his rocket project becomes a success. And three, my simulations show the likelihood of him offering you a promotion is at 0.00000003 per cent."

A burst of laughter escapes my lips. "That last one wasn't funny. Now you're just being mean."

"My facial scan detects upturned lips and bared teeth, clear indicators of mirth. You're laughing at my jokes."

"Because I, contrary to you, can take jabs with irony."

K-2P lets out a series of electronic sounds. "You ruffled my circuits; it is not my fault."

I pat his dome. "I'm sorry, K-2P, I didn't mean to."

A low beep lets me know my apology has been accepted.

I stare out of my office's half-glass, half-panel walls at the dark prototype lab. Like every night, I'm the last one in. I don't have much of a life outside of work, and I'm mostly fine with it. I'm a bit of a lone introvert who needs a lot of time by myself. I've tried being in relationships before, but they've been nothing but a letdown. My family has always been absent. My father bailed before I was born. And my mother has always been a bit *distracted* when it came to me, forcing me to become self-reliant from a young age. Plus, I've never been great at making new friends, especially since I've always been on the fast track, skipping entire grades and outpacing colleagues, making it tough to stick with the pack.

But work has been a reliable constant. It has never betrayed me.

I let my gaze span over the massive research facility beyond the glass. The technology we're researching is state-of-the-art. And working here is my dream job. My career is the only aspect of my life that I have under control. My work is who I am. And I'm afraid whatever Nolan Mercer wishes to tell me *in person* can't be good.

For the first time since opening the email, my stomach churns with anxiety. I hope it's not bad news. They wouldn't fire me? Would they? And if the meeting were to fire me, I doubt Mr. Mercer would do it in person. He'd send an HR hit squad.

Still, it's Friday, 13 October, and an email like that lands in my inbox out of the blue? Can't help a shiver of foreboding from running down my spine.

I sigh. "Time to go home."

K-2P lets out a succession of pitiful beeps. "Can I come with you?"

If droids could make puppy-dog eyes, that's the expression he'd be giving me now.

I clasp my hands with his flat-fingered ones. "I've told you a million times, you can't come home with me."

Whining beep. "Why?"

"Because I can't be seen walking a droid who's not part of any Mercer Industries research project in and out of the office every day."

I made sure the IP for K-2P would remain mine by never using company equipment or resources on him. He was already complete when I brought him here after they promoted me to head of the department and I gained a private office. I did it because otherwise, I'd never see him. But he's also good for morale. K-2P has become the lab's unofficial mascot, and my co-workers have sometimes taken an active interest in his coding. But even when I or someone else in the lab work on him, I ensure it's in our break time and on a laptop I own that is dedicated solely to his upgrades.

Three disgruntled beeps. "It wouldn't be every day. Just for the weekends."

"Trust me, not a good look, either."

Low, dejected beep. "I understand."

"I promise Monday will arrive before you even notice. We'll be together again soon."

"No, we won't." K-2P lets go of my hands. "You're probably getting fired, anyway."

"Now you're being hurtful again."

With no further sounds, K-2P retreats to his portable charging unit. He plugs himself in and shuts down all his lights.

And I know droids don't have feelings, yet leaving him cracks my heart every single time. But keeping him at home would only mean spending less time with him, seeing how I practically live at the office.

"All right, little guy." I switch off the lights. "I'll pop in tomorrow, so you're not alone all weekend, okay?" I'm actually glad for the excuse to come to work even on my day off.

No response.

Oh well. Shrugging, I pull the door closed and plug my earbuds into my ears, blasting Fleetwood Mac at top volume and hoping Monday will be just a day like any other, that I won't get fired, transferred, or who knows what else.

2

THOMAS

"Come to the table everyone," my mom announces, entering the living room. I'm reading on the couch while my dad pretend-smokes his cigar in his favorite armchair. "The meal is ready."

Sunday brunch at my parents' house is an unmovable Mercer tradition that has existed since the dawn of time. No one is exempt from attending the family get-together, not unless gravely ill or not on Manhattan soil. So it's weird that Mom would call us to the table before Gabriel, my older brother, has gotten here.

"Shouldn't we wait for Gabriel?" I ask, noting how my brother is twenty minutes late. Very atypical.

"He isn't coming." Mom sighs.

"What? Why not?" Last I checked, he was in New York and able-bodied.

"He texted me earlier." My mom beams. "He and Blake got back together last night. I told him not to worry about us and to spend the day with her."

I set my fantasy thriller book aside and stand up. "Thank goodness. I couldn't have suffered his moping, beaten-dog attitude for another minute."

Mom shakes her head. "Ah, Thomas, one day you'll fall in love, and then you'll mess it up, and we will support your beaten-dog attitude because we love you. Now, let's go."

"Come on, son." My dad squeezes my shoulder affectionately. "There's something I need to talk to you about."

Uh-oh, no sentence starting like that ever ended up in a good way for me.

"No shop talk while we eat," Mom counters.

I frown. "You know what this is about?"

Mom nods.

I turn to Dad. "What—?"

"After lunch, son." His solemn tone doesn't allow for a retort.

I stare at Mom.

She shrugs.

Dad moves along, topic dropped.

Fine.

No point in asking again. If Dad said we'll discuss the topic after lunch, he won't give me any hints until the last crumbles of dessert are polished.

"Very well, then," I say. "Let's eat."

Delicious as the meal may be, I don't enjoy the food much. With the ominous "we shall talk" looming over my head like a dark cloud, I'm too worried about what's coming next. It'll be something work-related, I'm sure. And I won't like it, I'm equally positive.

The decision to join the family business the moment I graduated from college was a no-brainer for me. I didn't have the same drive my brother had to build a new business from the ground up. *One* family empire is enough for me. But sometimes, working for my dad, and him being the literal boss of me, is not the easiest.

By the time coffee is served back in the living room, I'm bouncing my knees so hard that even my mom can't stand the tension anymore.

"Nolan, please," she says. "Go to the study to discuss his new position. I can't stand to watch him break his kneecaps from jitters."

My ears perk at the words *new* position. I love my current role as head of corporate communications at Mercer Industries. I'm the group's spokesperson and media relations guy. In short, all I have to do is look pretty, charm investors, and pose for the cameras. I'm the face of the company.

If *WIRED* magazine wants to publish an article on our environmentally conscious approach to mining iron ore, I'm the guy to interview. If *Fox News* is doing a special on our innovative mental health initiative for employees, I show up. Company parties, retreats, public appearances, charity galas... I'm the family representative who attends all these events.

"Yes, love." My dad sighs, nodding to my mom. He rises and turns to me. "Let's move to the study."

I follow him out of the living room, wondering what sort of curve ball he's about to throw at me. My father turns right and enters the study. I get in behind him and close the door.

This is the only room in the house my mother had no say in decorating. The space is all Dad with its antique desk and wall-to-wall bookshelves, carrying enough books to sink the *Titanic*. The tomes sit alongside plaques and photos of him with other successful people—heads of state, Nobel prize winners, celebrities, innovators, athletes, other titans of industry—next to more low-key family portraits. And at the back of the room, a gorgeous view of the city below. As usual, Dad's desk is clean and orderly. Papers, pens, and other office supplies are arranged perfectly in the antique wooden tray next to his giant computer screen that's now off.

From the mobile wooden bar in the corner, Dad pours himself

a Scotch, raising another glass to me as a question. I shake my head and take a beer from the refrigerated cabinet.

We settle on opposite sides of the mahogany desk, and I can tell he's in an excellent mood from the way his white mustache bristles as he takes his first sip of the amber liquor.

I grip the leather armrest of my chair. Things are looking grimmer by the second.

"Well?" I ask, taking a swig of beer and bracing myself for the worst.

"Proctor is retiring at the end of next year," Dad says, skipping preambles.

Emmet Proctor is the current CEO of Mercer Robotics, a subdivision of Mercer Industries—the umbrella company to all our various businesses. We're a global leader in manufacturing advanced automotive components, specializing in electrification and automation for sustainable solutions across industries, including mining.

Proctor and I have crossed paths once or twice. He's one of the best managers in the industry and helped make our robotic division the leading automation company in the world. The man has a mind like a damned computer. He's an engineer, but gifted with a business-oriented brain capable of foreseeing where the market is going to be in five, ten years from now with alarming precision. He'll be hard to replace.

A cool shiver walks down my spine. This is monumental news. I hold my breath, waiting for Dad to go on.

"He will announce his decision to the board at the shareholders' meeting next week," Dad continues, "and we want you to be his replacement."

"Me?" I laugh at that. "You're joking, right, Dad?"

My father stares me straight in the eyes. "I'm not."

"You can't be serious. Mercer Robotics is our most technology-heavy division. You can't even set foot in their facilities without holding at least seven engineering degrees."

"Your great-grandfather funded this company with no degree at all. And your technical skills might be lacking, but you have a good grasp on how the business side of things works."

"My great-grandfather was living in a different century," I clarify. "When everything was growing and being smart was enough to seize an opportunity. A bunch of hardcore engineers will never respect a guy from communications as their leader."

"Come on, son, that's not true. Many industry CEOs aren't engineers. At that level, you're not required to be technical, you only need to have a general understanding of the technology's fundamentals and be able to analyze the numbers to make strategic decisions."

I pick at a loose thread in the leather chair armrest. "Well, my robotics knowledge is exactly zero." I make an okay symbol with my hand to emphasize what I'm saying.

"Which is why I'm not proposing you start in the role of CEO tomorrow." Dad's eyes glint, signaling he's got me exactly where he wants me. "We have roughly fifteen months to make you robotics savvy enough to guide the division. And I want you to start your training at the core of the business, in the R&D department. I set a meeting with the research and development director for tomorrow morning at eight—"

"Wait, you set the meeting already?" I drop my beer on the desk with a loud thud—I should've gone for the Scotch. "Before I even agreed to the career pivot?"

"I don't enjoy wasting time, son. We need to plan for the future, and I'm an impatient man. If you want to replace me as the next head of Mercer Industries one day, you can't keep being our poster boy until I retire, and then move straight from communications to the top job." Dad leans back in his chair, looking so much like a domineering CEO that I suddenly revert to being the awed kid who followed his hero father around the office. "You'll have to get your hands dirty at some point."

I stare at him, aware he hasn't left me much of a choice.

The silence stretches for a while until Dad speaks again. "Glad to see we agree. I'll see you tomorrow at eight, then."

"I can't tomorrow," I reply, taking another sip of beer and rejoicing in being able to deny him at least my presence at his little ambush.

"Why?"

"I have a ceremony at our facility in Newark."

"Can't someone else go in your place?"

"I don't know, Dad. Our longest-employed worker is retiring after forty years. I'm supposed to hand him a plaque. You're the one who always told me how someone from the family must show up for this kind of thing." I pin him with a stare. "So, you tell me, can I skip?"

"No, you can't. Anyway, no harm done. You'll have to meet with the department head on your own in the afternoon."

Another thought strikes me. "Who's going to take my place as spokesperson?"

"No one," Dad says. "You'll still do most of the public appearances."

Oh, so I'm not getting a *new* position, I'm getting a second job *on top* of the one I already have.

"Don't make that face," Dad chides. "You've had it too easy so far and you know it."

"I guess the new challenge will be good for me," I reply, irritated.

"That it will. You're always complaining you spend too much time on social events. Now you can put all your focus on what really matters—the core of our business."

"Sure, Dad."

I rise to my feet, ready to leave my parents' house—I've got a lot to process, starting with my new job title. I glance at my father and Dad beams at me, the stern captain of industry gone, the loving father back. "Don't underestimate yourself, son, you can handle the extra responsibility and a million other things if you put your mind to it."

"And now you sound like my third-grade teacher."

Dad laughs, standing up and coming next to me to pat my shoulder. "You've come a long way since then, haven't you? I'm very proud of you, son."

"Thanks, Dad. I love you, too."

He opens his arms and I embrace him.

Is this what they call tough love? I prefer to refer to it as inconvenient, pain-in-my-ass love.

3

REESE

To say I'm stressed on Monday morning would be an understatement. As I swipe my badge past the turnstiles to get inside the Mercer Industries headquarters, the pants of my suit chafe my thighs with every step I take. And the button-down white shirt I've stuffed down the suit pants is slowly suffocating me. I'm not used to wearing fitted clothes. How do the suits wear a tie all day and not die of asphyxiation?

My hair is even worse. The pins I used to lock my long mostly brown hair in a low chignon—to hide the pink tips—are prickling the back of my head like a thousand needles. I don't bother much with makeup or other beauty routines. I just wouldn't have the consistency to do it *every single day*. But pink hair is my cosmetic expression. I only need to retouch the dye about once a month. Maximum impact with the lowest possible effort—except when I have to hide the tips like today.

Besides wearing a downright torturing hairstyle and uncomfortable clothes, I'm indecorously early. I was so worried about being late that I arrived at the office two minutes before seven. A generous hour earlier than my usual check-in time.

Since I have a full hour to kill before I have to go meet the higher-ups on the top floor, I head to the basement where the robotics research lab is located.

The only other person already at work is Maria, my mobility team leader. She's a Caltech graduate with the personality of a sarcastic pixie, the face of a fairy princess, and the aesthetic of a gothic evil queen—monochrome black hair, clothes, nails, and makeup.

Presently, she's bent over a computer screen, puzzling over endless lines of code. K-2P, rescued from the loneliness of my office, is earnestly standing by her side. She's so intent on her work that she hasn't spotted me.

"Maria," I greet her. "Good morning."

She jolts, turning to me. "Boss, what are you doing here so early?" Then she does a double take and low whistles at my fancy clothes. "Did someone *die*?"

"No one died." I shrug. "The big boss has asked to see me at eight in his office."

"Proctor?"

See? When I say "big boss," Nolan Mercer is so far above us, we don't even compute him.

"No, bigger boss. Nolan Mercer himself."

Maria's Snow-White eyes widen. "Do you know why?"

"Your guess is as good as mine."

"You think it's a promotion?"

"K-2P calculated the chances of that are very, *very* low." I look down at the robot now. "Morning, little guy."

The droid gyrates, presenting me with his back. If his mechanical arms could cross, they would now.

I raise my eyes to the ceiling. "Whoever programmed his capability of getting offended should be iced."

Maria raises a sarcastic eyebrow at that. "You know it was probably you, right?" Then she turns and stamps a kiss on the droid's dome, leaving a black mouth imprint on it. "You're a grump, boss, and he's your little minion shadow self."

I knock on the plexiglass. "Hello?"

No response.

"The bitter-bot attitude doesn't look good on you. Throwing a tantrum won't get you anywhere," I complain.

"He can throw tantrums only because his programming is flawless," Maria cues, caressing his dome. "Plus, he won't stay offended forever," she adds. "He's just a little moody, and we love him for it."

Still, K-2P refuses to speak to me, so I concentrate on Maria.

"What are you working on?" I ask, dropping my messenger bag on the chair next to hers.

"Control theory for our autonomous vehicles line."

"To do what?"

"Improve throttle. I'm tweaking the transfer function of the PID control."

I stare at the formulas on her screen. "The error signal?"

"Yep."

I sit next to her, trying to study her work while in reality, the equations on her screen blur as I keep wondering what Nolan Mercer wants with me.

"Gosh," Maria says after a while. "You're thinking so hard it's distracting."

I stare at the computer clock: seven thirty-five. "I should go anyway. How long does it take to ride up fifty floors in an elevator?"

"Four seconds per floor," K-2P replies. "Which would add up to three point three minutes if you were to ride without stops. Considering an average stop time of eight seconds per floor, the total travel time could add up to eleven minutes if the elevator stopped at every floor." He emits a still-offended beep. "You should probably leave."

That conclusion doesn't sound properly mathematical. He's still being a sour puss—or a sour neural net.

"Thank you, K-2P, I'll go."

"I'd say break a leg," the robot replies. "But since luck is a supernatural belief for simple minds, I'll abstain."

"Thank you also for the philosophy lecture."

I drop my bag in my office, replace the battery in K-2P's portable charging station with the one I charged at home, and head back out toward the elevators.

For the first time since I started at Mercer Industries, I push the top-floor button. Even if the elevator doesn't stop at every floor, the ride still seems infinite. And when the doors finally open on my destination, the space is eerily quiet.

So much so that when a woman in her mid-forties greets me with a loud, "Dr. Campbell." I jump.

"Sorry," the woman says. "I didn't mean to scare you. I'm Monica, Mr. Mercer's personal assistant."

How did she know I was arriving at this precise moment?

As if reading my mind, she answers the question I haven't asked. "We get an alert whenever someone pushes the button to this floor."

Sure they do.

"Come with me." She smiles. "Mr. Mercer is waiting for you."

I discreetly stare at my watch as I follow her. I'm ten minutes early. No one could accuse me of having left the president of the group *waiting for me.*

"This way." The woman shows me inside a huge corner office with glass walls all around. The furniture inside is less modern, though, more English country. But I don't have much time to ponder on the décor as my gaze gravitates toward the white-haired man seated behind the gigantic desk at the back of the room.

Judging from his looks, Nolan Mercer must be in his late fifties or early sixties with a bushy, snow-white mustache and a strong jaw line. Even sitting down, he has an imposing presence. Dressed in an impeccable gray suit and wearing a watch that could cost more than my yearly salary, he carries himself with an air of authority and a firm, no-nonsense demeanor.

"Dr. Campbell," he welcomes me. "Please have a seat."

I take a step forward while the woman who guided me here says, "Call me if you need anything, sir."

I hear her retreating footsteps behind me, then the click of the door as she shuts it, leaving me alone with the tycoon.

Why am I so nervous? My department is one of the best in the country. I run a tight ship and I'm a competent, hard-working team leader. The performance of my floor is consistent, solid, and unreproachable. I should have no reason to be intimidated in front of a man whose only merit was to inherit a fortune as his birthright.

Still, that blue gaze of steel is unsettling.

I cross the room, keeping my chin held high.

"Good morning, Mr. Mercer." I take the seat across from him.

He scrutinizes me for a long moment before he speaks—probably thinking I'm younger than he expected. That's what everyone thinks the first time they meet me.

"Good Morning, Dr. Campbell." Nerve-jolting pause. "You're probably wondering why I've called you here this morning."

I make a non-committal grimace, acting as if I hadn't obsessed over it for every minute of the weekend.

And apparently, the wait isn't over because, instead of telling me what I'm doing here, Nolan Mercer pierces me with another significant stare and asks me a question. "It says in your file that you're not interested in developing your career to a more powerful managerial position?"

I blink, unsure of what he's asking.

He leans forward, resting his elbows on the desk and interlacing his fingers in a bridge-like shape. "In simpler words, you don't aspire to become the general director or CEO of Mercer Robotics."

"Correct, sir," I confirm, hoping he's not considering offering me either position.

"Why is that?" he asks instead.

"I love what I do. To design new products, to solve issues that seem impossible to solve, to build the future. Having to deal with the financial, commercial, and client support side of things would be a figurative nightmare for me."

Nolan Mercer nods in understanding, then leans back in his chair, crossing his arms over his chest. He's still observing me intently as if trying to read my thoughts. Is this some sort of test?

"What would a promotion look like to you, then?"

My first thought is that I'm going to stick it to K-2P and his 0.00000003 per cent probability of me being promoted.

Next, I give a concrete answer. "An expanded research budget, more independence on the projects my department may implement, more engineers on the floor." Then, as if it's an afterthought, I add, "A raise?"

Mr. Mercer chuckles. "That's quite the list, Dr. Campbell. It's good to have ambition."

I stare at him, still unsure about the topic we're circling.

"Proctor is retiring at the end of next year," Mr. Mercer finally cuts to the chase.

Dang.

A change in leadership is always a potential disaster. Especially when the guy leaving is a half-genius like Emmet Proctor. My brain is still shuffling through all the terrible repercussions his retirement could have—financial, technical, and human ones— when I hone in on the real issue: why is Nolan Mercer telling *me* this?

"Have you already picked a replacement?" My question comes out in a too-small voice.

"Yes." The big boss levels me with another of his penetrating stares. Please, *please* let him not offer the job to me. I mean, he wouldn't. We've established I'm not interested.

I'm still praying in my head when he drops news way worse than a job offer. "I want my son Thomas to take up the position."

I frown, trying to remember what the son does. Isn't he in some marginal department like *communications*? Is he even an engineer?

The president must read the consternation on my face because he asks, "Surprised?"

More *appalled*. I'm a fan of nepotism just as much as I appreciate balance sheets.

"I-I'm..." I honestly don't know how to answer.

"You're skeptical, as it's your right to be."

"I, sir, have no—"

"Please, Dr. Campbell, I know you must have reservations. I could take a good guess at what they are, too."

"Sir?"

"Thomas isn't an engineer. He doesn't understand the product or the technology. He can't possibly run the company as well as Emmet did..."

His words, not mine.

"All valid objections, but not ones I share."

Of course, it's *his* son.

At this point, I keep quiet while he explains to me why a guy with no engineering background would be an excellent choice to lead the robotics division.

"At the end of the day, what a great CEO needs to do is to make sensible business decisions. Look at the numbers you despise so much and steer the company in the most profitable direction, have a vision, a strategy."

I abstain from saying that to have a vision, one should at least know what he's *visioning* about. What the technology boundaries are. Or he could expect us to design a Terminator-like cyborg with a self-healing, flesh-bound endoskeleton in three to five years.

"But I agree with you that before he takes up the position, Thomas should gain a deeper understanding of the technology."

Did I say that last part aloud? I don't think I did.

"Sir, I never said—"

He raises a hand to silence me. "You didn't have to. I could read the objection on your face."

I blush. I'm going to have to work on my poker face.

"Anyway, the reason I've asked you here is that in the next fifteen months, I want Thomas to rotate through all the different departments at Mercer Robotics, starting with yours."

I swallow. "Why?" I didn't mean to blurt out the question so blatantly, but it just burst out of me.

"I want him to get a grip on the different products, assembly lines—"

"No, why start in *my* department?" Now that I've asked, I might as well obtain a legitimate answer.

"Oh, that. The moment Proctor makes the announcement of his retirement at the board meeting later this week, every other department head will start gunning to be his replacement seeing how the general director is also close to retirement. You're the exception, Dr. Campbell. I need to give the others a few months to adjust to the decision that *Thomas* will take over. Were I to send my son to production first, I'm afraid Briggs would try to stab a knife into his back and ridicule him if he makes a mistake, whereas I'm confident you'll give him a fair shot at learning the ropes without too much prejudice or resentment."

It sounds more as if my job will be to keep hand-feeding the family prince from his silver spoon.

I can't say what I think, so I just nod politely. "Of course, sir."

"Great. I'm sorry Thomas couldn't be here with us this morning, but he had a previous engagement. He'll drop by your office later in the afternoon."

I know when I'm being dismissed. "If there isn't anything else?"

"No, you're free to go."

I stand up. "I'll go back to work, then."

"You do that," Nolan Mercer says with a benevolent smile. "Oh, and Dr. Campbell?"

"Yes?"

"I'm sure it needn't be said, but I'm trusting you to keep this conversation to yourself."

I frown. "How am I to explain your son's presence in the lab, then?"

"Not that part, the part about my lack of complete trust in the other department heads. Their feathers will be ruffled already once we announce Thomas will take over. We don't need to stir up more trouble."

"Very well, sir. Have a good day."

I'm sure I won't.

4

REESE

On the elevator ride down to the basement, I bite my cuticles, wondering how earning a bachelor's degree in mechanical engineering, a master's in mechatronics, and a PhD in applied robotics has led me to becoming a glorified babysitter.

Once I reach my floor, I storm through the lab without talking to anyone and shut myself inside my office.

I sit at my desk, staring at the black screen of my computer, still nibbling at my poor fingers until a knock distracts me.

"Yeah?" I call out.

Maria pokes her head in. "Hey, boss, just checking how the meeting with the almighty went?"

"Terrible," I say.

"Oh." She shuffles in followed by K-2P. "What happened?"

"We're being invaded!"

Maria rounds my desk and sits next to my turned-off computer. "Barbarians? Oh, no, wait. Vikings?"

"Worse," I say. "Suits!"

"No!"

"Yep."

"How? Why? Who?"

"I'll have to make an announcement later anyway, but the gist of it is that Emmet Proctor is retiring at the end of next year and our president thinks his son would make a qualified replacement."

"Wait, doesn't Thomas Mercer work in HR?"

"Communications, I think."

"What else is on his CV? Major in college?"

With a shudder, I say, "I suspect *business*."

An equally appalled shiver runs down Maria's spine. "Pull up his resume on the company directory."

I turn on my computer and navigate the company's organizational chart until I locate his name under Head of Communications. I click on it.

A picture of Thomas Mercer pops up on my screen, and I find myself staring into the hazel-green eyes of an annoyingly handsome man with light-brown hair pulled back in an expensive haircut and a jawline so sharp it should be patented as replacement tooling for our lathes.

His qualifications read: Thomas Mercer, Bachelor's in Business Administration, MBA.

His work accomplishments are summarized in two single lines. Deputy group spokesperson and then straight to Head of Corporate Communications.

That's all he's done in the past seven years.

"Are you serious?" Maria gapes at the screen. "This will be our new boss?"

She must be as horrified as I am.

"It appears so."

Maria chews on her lower lip. "Well, I wouldn't mind working *under* him for a late-night session."

"Maria!" Apparently, her mind was on a totally different page than mine.

"What?"

"You can't say stuff like that about the new boss—or any of our co-workers, for that matter."

"Why not? I mean, look at him, he's almost *too* handsome," Maria muses. "You don't think he's hot?"

I press my lips into a thin line. "I care more about how unqualified for the job he is."

"No, you're right, he probably has a small pecker to compensate for the chiseled jaw, broad shoulders, and that cute little dimple in his right cheek."

"Ma-ri-a! We won't discuss the new boss's alleged small willy."

"Yeah, forget about it, Mercer Junior is probably not worth it," Maria continues unperturbed. "Even if he had a normal-sized penis, he's too good-looking to be any good in bed. The handsome ones never put enough effort into it."

That's when K-2P gives his two cents. "The chances of the new boss having a micropenis are very slim. The condition affects only 0.6 per cent of the male population worldwide. In the United States, only approximately 1.5 in 10,000 infants are born with micropenises."

Maria chuckles. "You think the new boss is well endowed, K-2P?"

"Up to 90 per cent of male penises are within an inch of the average size. While only 1 per cent of men have a larger penis between seven—"

"All right, that's it." I interrupt K-2P before he can deliver even more disturbing statistics. "Out! Both of you."

I shove Maria off my desk and herd her and K-2P out of the office.

Alone once again, I close Thomas Mercer's skimpy resume and pull up the remote diagnostic protocol for cyber-physical systems I was working on last Friday before the email of doom landed in my inbox.

I open the log file where I left off and start reading through my notes from the weekend, which I spent mostly working. I popped into the lab on *both* Saturday and Sunday, so I don't see why K-2P should act so offended. Maybe he knows I re-watched *The Force Awakens* trilogy without him.

Soon, I get lost in the improving of the feedback loop, losing sense of time and forgetting all about the hazel-eyed, dimpled, presumably brainless calamity that's about to rain down on me.

Three hours later, I'm so engrossed in my work, that I don't notice when the lab door opens.

"Hey, Reese."

I jump, startled by my colleague's voice. "Garrett, what's up?"

"Sorry for bothering you." The process technology team leader steps into my office, scratching the back of his head. "Everyone is heading out for lunch, and I was wondering if you wanted to join us." He blushes tomato red.

Garrett seems always over-nervous around me. Like now. Besides his flushed cheeks, his hands are trembling as he brushes a strand of hair away from his face. And all just for a simple invite to lunch?

"Sure," I tell him. "Where are we going?"

"TGIF."

On a Monday. Isn't it ironic?

I stand up and immediately get reminded how moving comfortably and wearing a suit are mutually exclusive. "Let me change into human clothes and I'll catch up with you at the restaurant."

"I can wait for you if you want."

"No need," I say.

"All right, see you there, then."

As he exits, K-2P rolls in. "That guy has a major crush on you," the droid announces.

"Shhh. At least close the door before you start gossiping."

K-2P fumbles with the handle, his flat fingers gaining a clumsy hold, and shuts the door.

"Just because he asked me to lunch and was a little flustered around me, it doesn't mean he likes me."

"Please. I bet the only reason he hasn't asked you out is that he's your direct report."

I join K-2P by the door and pull the blinds down. "Just because my ex dumped me the moment I got promoted to a better job than his, it doesn't mean all men aren't supportive of their partners' careers."

"I was talking more about the anti-fraternization company policy, forbidding romantic relationships between executives and their subordinates."

"Oh, that." I nod, glad the policy exists. Garrett might be an excellent engineer, but he's always given me the creeps. "But I'm not sure he's into me; he's weird around everyone."

"But he's only obsessed with you."

"How'd you reach that conclusion?"

Condescending beep. "I'm your droid and he tried to alter my speech drive to only say positive things about him."

I gasp. "He. Did. Not."

"Did too." K-2P swirls indignantly, his previous grudge toward me forgotten now that he has found a new enemy. "Here's a list of the catchphrases I had to self-scrub from my system: Garrett is a good listener, Garrett is a great problem solver, Garrett is the most reliable and hard-working person I know."

Laughter bubbles out of me. "You seriously had catchphrases about Garrett stored in your memory?"

"My operating system was violated and you laugh about it!"

"Violated? Now you're being dramatic, as always."

"I'd like to see how you'd feel if someone tried to force-imprint the following phrases in your brain: Garrett is an outstanding leader who inspires his team; Garrett is incredibly smart and has a great sense of humor."

"Okay, I get it. Please stop."

"No, I have several more to recite. Garrett is always on top of things, Garrett is reliable, Garrett is an inspiration, Garrett has a magnetic personality..."

Since K-2P doesn't seem intent on quitting his disclosing of all of Garrett's unique traits, I put in my earbuds and blast R.E.M. at top volume before I have to listen to a single other of Garrett's alleged admirable qualities. Swaying in time to the notes of "Losing My Religion," I begin unbuttoning my pants getting into the groove and shaking off the morning's worries.

5

THOMAS

The retirement ceremony for Mercer Industries' longest-standing worker starts at 10 a.m., but my schedule kicks off at eight as I have to do a tour of the factory—the production floor in particular, shake hands, compliment the workers, and chat up the middle managers.

Despite hating early mornings, today I made an effort to have time to talk to everyone. These people work for us, are loyal and dedicated, and we'd be nothing without them. The least I can do is show up early and make sure everyone I interact with has my undivided attention and feels properly cherished.

Tour over, the official tribute starts.

While someone else makes the introductory addresses, I check my speech one last time, adjust my tie, and wait for my turn. When it comes, I fold the written speech back into my suit's pocket and stand on the dais. I deliver my piece, awarding the retiring worker with a watch and a plaque for his distinguished service. Then I shake his hand for the cameras, pose for pictures with the staff, and go back to my seat to listen to the closing remarks.

A few good words from the CEO of our automotive division

himself, followed by a round of enthusiastic clapping from the audience, and the event is over.

On a normal day, I'd linger behind and share a few more words with the workers in an informal setting. But today, the applause still hasn't died down and I'm already halfway out of the door, heading back to my office.

Is this what my routine will become with the new job? Rushing from one commitment to the next? Not a fan, not going to lie.

Thanks to bad traffic, it's already lunchtime by the time I arrive at Mercer Industries' New Jersey headquarters, where the admin offices and R&D facilities of the robotics division are located. I could go grab a quick bite before I check out my new *tutor*, but I decide to see if the head of R&D is still in her office. Maybe I could invite her to lunch. Break the ice before we start working together by getting to know each other in a less formal setting.

I ask the receptionist in the lobby where Dr. Campbell's office is, and the unfortunate answer is: in the basement, within the robotic labs. Guess another perk of my new position will be being stashed away in a dingy, subterranean dungeon with no actual sunlight while surrounded by brainy nerds who will probably look down their bespectacled noses on a business major like myself.

I picture my light-filled corner office on the thirty-fourth floor and have to suppress a groan.

Thanks, Dad. Thanks a lot.

Before I head down to the torture chamb— err R&D department, I check with the security guard on the ground floor to see whether Dr. Campbell has already left for her lunch break or not.

The guard consults the log and confirms that she's still in the building.

All right, on to the dungeons then.

The robotics lab is a vast underground facility that gets just a teensy bit of natural light from awning windows lining the top portion of the walls along the entire perimeter.

Given the hour, the lab is empty. No one is manning the various desks, or tinkering with the miscellaneous electronic parts scattered over the workstations, or toiling with the actual robots of different shapes and sizes scattered all over.

Most of the space is divided into a handful of smaller stations, each equipped with state-of-the-art computer systems and innovative machinery. Whereas a massive robotic arm dominates the center of the room. Its practical application, I couldn't fathom.

Lining the walls are back-to-back racks of shelves laden with tools, manuals, and different mechanical and electrical components.

The only boxed-in office with a door is at the back of the room. As I meander through the various workstations, the Mercer Robotics screensaver—the company logo rotating on itself—greets me from all the darkened computer screens.

I reach the office door but can't see inside since all the blinds are pulled down. But the plaque next to the door reads "Dr. Reese Campbell". I'm in the right place.

I knock.

"Come in," a weird, almost metallic voice replies from inside.

With my hand on the handle, I hesitate, checking the laminate glass walls and wondering if glass can distort a woman's voice like a stormtrooper helmet would.

I shrug and open the door.

My eyes widen in shock at the sight on the other side.

A woman is shaking her—*pant-less*—booty to an unheard tune. She has her arms swaying up in the air, causing her black blazer to raise to her waist and leaving me an unobstructed view of her pastel blue cotton panties and firm buttocks.

I stare hypnotized as she slowly undoes the tight chignon at the base of her neck and liberates a cascade of brown locks with neon-pink tips.

I don't know what tune she's dancing to in her head, but I'm imagining something out of the *Fifty Shades of Grey* soundtrack.

For a moment I'm too shocked to talk or move. When I get my bearings again, I mumble a hurried, "Sorry." And I'm about to retreat and leave the lady some privacy when someone speaks to my right.

"She can't hear you."

Not some*one.* Some*thing.* A forty-five-inch-tall droid, who wouldn't look half-bad in a *Star Wars* movie, rolls toward me on his wheeled feet.

"She always listens to music too loud," the droid elaborates.

"Are office stripteases another habit?"

"No, but she's taken up Zumba lately and it must've gone to her head."

The dance the woman is engaged in doesn't look like any Zumba class I've ever seen.

My gaze flicks back to the dancing queen just as she turns and, hands grabbing either side of her white shirt, she parts the fabric in a wild jerk, flashing me a pale blue bra to match the panties, and a toned stomach.

Then, just as quickly, she screams, pulling the lapels of her black blazer together and crossing her legs, trying to cover as much of herself as she can. With her other hand, she removes her earbuds and shouts, "What are you doing here? Shouldn't you knock before coming in?"

"I wanted to invite you to lunch, and I did knock; you told me to come in."

"I. Did. Not," she responds, outraged.

"I invited him in," the droid clarifies.

We both stare at him for a second before the woman shouts again, "Well, get out now! Out!"

Technically, I've never even come in, I'm still standing on the threshold, but I refrain from being fastidious. I raise my hands, take one step back, and close the door behind me. Then I go and sit on the workstation nearest her office, and, crossing my arms over my chest, I wait.

6

REESE

Still in shock, I drag my hands through my hair. Then turn my rage on the only other being in the room.

"Why would you tell him to come in?"

K-2P swivels. "It's the polite thing to do when someone knocks on a door."

"No, it's not. Especially not if I'm getting undressed and am not wearing any frigging pants. Oh, gosh."

I rub my forehead.

Thomas Mercer has seen my butt. I flashed him my *boobs*. Oh, gosh, oh, goodness gracious, I'll never be able to look him in the eyes ever again. He's my new boss, and he's seen me half-naked.

I glare at K-2P. "How long had he been standing there before I turned?"

K-2P, who's programmed to log and measure all changes to his surrounding environment, gives me a punctual answer. "Ninety-three point two seconds."

I sag back against the desk, gripping the edge until my knuckles turn white.

"You'll have to come out eventually," a deep voice calls from outside.

Oh, good grief, he's still out there.

"In a minute," I shout back.

"Take your time."

His voice sounds like warm massage oil being poured over cool skin and then spread with big, rough, calloused hands. And the body that accompanies the voice is no joke either. In person, Thomas Mercer is even more impressive than in his picture, which didn't convey how tall he is.

I hate tall men. How they tower over me and the way they stare down their noses at me.

And his face? I scoff. If someone asked me this morning, I would've told them Thomas Mercer is a very photogenic man. If they asked me now, I'd say that profile picture looks like a crappy sketch made by a three-year-old compared to the real thing.

The big boss's son is the breathing, walking, talking personification of a *GQ* magazine cover.

Brainless, I add. Most probably an unintelligent, arrogant, spoiled, self-centered, vain, cocky moron. Let's concentrate on that.

"Ughhhh," I groan, and grab my sweatpants, hopping on one foot to shuffle my right leg into them. Keeping my back to the door, I remove my blazer and button-down shirt and pull on the plain white T-shirt and the white unicorn hoodie I'd prepared on my desk. Next, I pull my hair up in a messy bun.

Even when I'm fully decent again, I don't go outside. I remain entrenched in my office, hoping that if I stay locked in here long enough Thomas Mercer will just go away.

And why is he still hanging around, anyway? Does he plan on humiliating me some more?

"Maybe you should go ahead to lunch and we should meet afterward," I call to the man still outside my office.

In response, there's a pause. And then, "Nah, I'll wait. You need help with a zipper or something?"

That does it for me. I'm angry now. In two quick strides, I cross the office and fling the door open.

Thomas Mercer is waiting for me on the other side, casually draped on a desk, with his arms crossed over his broad chest.

His stupid, perfect hair is gorgeously tousled, almost as if, while he was waiting, he's been raking his fingers through it.

I stop dead in my tracks while his hazel-green eyes lock on me, forcing me to notice the speckles of gold in his irises. Thomas tilts his head and flashes me a dimpled smile, causing my breath to hitch in my throat.

Whatever remark I was about to make dies on my lips, so he takes the lead. "Dr. Campbell, all set?" he asks in a slow, indulgent drawl.

"Yes," I say, regaining my composure.

His eyes travel over my new outfit, and I do the same with his two-thousand-minimum dollar pinstriped suit. Gosh, the guy couldn't look more posh if he tried.

"Nice hoodie," he says eventually.

"Nice suit," I reply.

He studies me for a moment. "Why do I have a feeling that compliment isn't exactly genuine, Dr. Campbell?"

"I can't comment on your insecurities."

He tilts his head back and laughs.

My turn to cross my arms over my chest. "Having fun much?"

"I have to say, this is not how I expected the introductions with the head of robotics R&D director to go." He must notice the indignant rage building up in me because before I can reply, he raises his hands to stop me. "But let me start by apologizing for barging into your office, I had no way of knowing it was a robot who'd invited me to come in and not you."

"I am not a *robot*." K-2P shuffles out of the office behind me. "I'm a highly sophisticated, artificial intelligence machine programmed to interact with organics."

"Sorry, little guy, what should I call you then?"

"I'm an advanced kinematics precision pneumatics service droid."

I roll my eyes. "He's K-2P."

Thomas Mercer surprises me by offering his hand to the droid. "Very pleased to meet you, K-2P. I'm Thomas."

I watch in a sort of out-of-body experience as the lab's mascot and the soon-to-be new CEO shake hands.

Then Thomas Mercer looks up at me and offers me the same hand. "Thomas Mercer."

I hesitate.

"Just to make the introductions official," he adds with a wink.

I don't think winking at me is very professional, but I can't very well let him stand there like a tool with his hand outstretched, refusing to shake it. This is the man who will have the power over my research budget, my team, my salary, and my end-of-year bonus.

I close the few feet of distance still separating us and don't appreciate one bit how, with the reduced distance, I can smell his sexy, expensive cologne.

He smells like a dream you just woke up from and can't quite remember, but only know that it had been a *good* dream. A fantasy about something you desire with all your heart but can't have in real life. There might also be a hint of sandalwood and Bleu de Chanel mixed in there.

I take his hand and shiver at the contact, at the warmth that seems to flow from his palm to my hand, at the electricity that shoots up my arm. The current flows straight to my head, making my brain short-circuit. I forget proper social form and neglect to let go of his hand.

In a voice an octave lower than it has been so far, he says, "Nice to officially meet you, Reese Campbell."

The way my name rolls out of his mouth is indecent. It lands straight in my belly, warming me up from my core outward. That's when my gaze drops between our bodies and I notice he hasn't let go of my hand either.

7

THOMAS

The director of the R&D department drops her gaze to our joined hands and I realize I've been holding her hand for way longer than it'd be considered appropriate.

I let her go and scratch the back of my head with that same hand. This is not how I had expected the meeting to go. I knew the head of this department was a woman, but I'd just assumed she'd be a middle-aged person, not a hot brunette who probably isn't even in her thirties.

My gaze flits to the door of her office and the "Dr." etched before her name. Don't PhDs take ages to complete?

"How old are you?" I blurt.

She frowns. "What kind of question is that?"

The dick kind. I'm behaving like an idiot.

"Sorry, what I meant to say is, aren't you too young to already have a PhD and lead a department?"

She follows my gaze to the engraving on the door. "I'm twenty-nine, and yes, I'm too young. But I graduated a year early both from my bachelor's and master's degrees and completed my PhD in four years instead of six, saving four years of school in total."

I low whistle. "And how long after you started here were you promoted to the big chair?"

"Two years," she says begrudgingly.

"So, you're a genius?"

She throws me a sour stare. "I'm smart."

"Okay, Smarty, do geniuses eat? How about I take you to lunch, and we can get to know each other better?"

Her eyes widen in shock, so I raise my arms, adding, "Know each other *professionally*. If we have to spend the next three months working together, we should get comfortable with one another."

She narrows her eyes at me and if looks could kill, I'd be a goner. "Sorry, but I already ate. But, please, go have your lunch break and when you come back, I can give you a tour of the lab and the new products we're developing."

Nice speech. Totally believable. Pity that the moment she stops speaking, her stomach gives a loud rumble.

I raise my eyebrows in a silent "already ate?" question.

"I had a light lunch," she explains.

Sticking to her story, uh? "K-2P, did Dr. Campbell already have lunch?"

"No, she wanted to get changed first and then join the others at TGIF."

Arms crossed, head tilted, I'm all ears for some explaining.

She throws her arms up in the air. "I'm embarrassed, okay? My future boss caught me dancing half-naked in my office. Excuse me if I'm not exactly eager to go out to lunch with you."

I have to concentrate hard to push the image of her booty shaking and boobs flashing out of my head to keep my expression neutral.

"Could've happened to anyone, and I'm okay not mentioning the incident ever again if you are. Consider it erased from my memory." *Fat chance of that actually ever happening.* "And waiting to talk would only make things more awkward between us. So, what do you say we jump right back on the horse and share a meal while you give me the rundown of your department?"

"Fine," she snips.

* * *

I take her to my favorite Italian restaurant near our offices. If garlic bread and pasta don't soften her up, nothing will.

The weather isn't too chilly for mid-October in New Jersey. The sun is shining unchallenged by any clouds, but there's also a breeze coming in from the Hudson River that could make it too cold to have an entire meal outdoors.

"Is a table inside good?" I ask, keeping the door of the restaurant open for her.

"Sure." She shrugs and gets in before me.

The owner, Carmelo, greets me with his usual enthusiasm. "Thomas, great to see you, table for how many?"

I raise two fingers.

Carmelo's gaze shifts briefly to Reese before he grabs two menus and leads us to the front of the restaurant. With the sunlight flooding in from the wall-wide windows, it almost feels like we're sitting outside—minus the cold wind.

"Are you having the usual?" Carmelo asks, turning to me.

"What's the day's special?" I ask.

"We have a risotto today with almonds and stracchino cheese." Carmelo kisses his fingers. "Delicious."

"I'll get that," I say.

Reese closes her menu and nods at me.

"Two day's specials," I tell Carmelo.

"Anything to drink? I have this red from near the Vesuvio that's—"

"I'll go with just water." I look at Reese for confirmation, and she nods.

Carmelo leaves with our order and while we wait for our food to arrive, I take the time to observe the mysterious Dr. Campbell.

She's sitting in her chair nervously fiddling with the tablecloth, doing her best to avoid meeting my gaze.

I try to think of a way to draw her out.

"You know, if you keep avoiding eye contact with me it's going to be hard to break the ice."

Her brown eyes lift to mine. For a split second she glares at me, almost resentful, but she's quick to hide it. "Sorry, I'm still embarrassed about earlier."

"I sense your reluctancy to talk to me isn't 100 per cent due to the office incident. Why?"

Reese lowers her gaze guiltily.

"Come on, I can't fix what's wrong if you don't tell me."

Our eyes lock again, and she crosses her arms on her chest. "You want to hear it how it is?"

"Always."

"Okay." She leans her elbows on the table and grabs a garlic breadstick from a basket a server dropped off. "I'm not thrilled to have to babysit you for the next three months. I'm even less thrilled that Emmet Proctor an engineer with *cojones* is leaving the company and that"—she waves her hand, pointing the breadstick at me like a sword—"you, a man with zero robotics knowledge, have been selected as his replacement." Reese ends the speech and takes a giant bite out of the breadstick.

I take a moment before replying by unfolding my napkin and squaring it on my legs. "So, it's my business major that offends you."

Called it, Dad!

She replies, chewing with her mouth still half full. "If you were some kind of corporate rainmaker with experience running a company, it'd be at least digestible." She swallows. "But according to your online resume, you're just the boss's son with no experience except for looking pretty."

"Ah."

At least she finds me pretty.

The server drops our food in front of us, and I shuffle the rice on my plate, watching Reese out of the corner of my eye.

She only picks at her food, and I wait for her to annihilate me some more. "Too direct?" she finally asks.

"Nope," I say, taking a bite of risotto and not fully enjoying how good it is. "These are the same objections I presented to my father when he informed me of the decision—*yesterday*. You've met the man, haven't you?"

She nods.

"So you know he's not an easy man to say no to."

"For one of his *employees*, no. But for his son? I don't know."

"It's the same."

"If you say so."

Undeterred, I forge ahead. "Listen, Reese, we're in this together. Neither of us is particularly thrilled by the situation, but I believe that if we work together, we can make the best of the hand we've been dealt."

"How?"

"You teach me the ropes, and I'll work hard to unlock the division's potential," I say with a shrug. "I might not have a fancy technical degree, but I'm not an idiot."

She rolls her eyes. "You can't learn robotics in three months, or even fifteen."

I smirk. "Mmm, sure, it sounds hard, but not when I have a secret weapon."

"Oh, yeah? What secret weapon?"

"A genius teacher." I wink at her, and her cheeks flush.

8

REESE

Gosh. His secret weapon might actually be his charm. I'm doing my best not to like the guy, but I'm losing the battle. I've insulted him, belittled him, and he's still smiling at me—those insufferable dimples just adding to the affront.

And apparently, the smiling is infectious because my lips rebelliously curl up in a smile of their own, while my stomach responds to the wink by flipping in on itself.

"You're smiling," he says. "That's progress."

I stuff my mouth with risotto to wipe the smile off my face, and force myself to concentrate on eating.

Thomas lets me be for some time while we eat in silence.

When he speaks again, he almost makes me jump in my chair. "Have I earned the benefit of the doubt? Truce?"

I shake my head, conceding deceit. "You've at least one thing in common with your father."

He wipes his mouth on his napkin. "Really, what's that?"

"You're really hard to say no to."

Our eyes lock, and I've no idea what's going through his head, but his gaze seems suddenly more alert, more intent. And I don't like the way I'm responding to it. Still, I don't look away.

He breaks the eye contact, eventually, taking a long sip of water, which is not much better, as now, I've gone from obsessing over his eyes to finding myself staring fascinated at his Adam's apple as it bobs up and down in his throat. A sexy, manly throat that I catch myself wondering how it'd feel under my lips if I kissed it. Smooth or rough with stubble?

I stand up abruptly, making my chair scrape on the floor and dropping my napkin on the table, and excuse myself to the restroom. I enter the small room and lean my back against the door for a second before heading to a stall and locking myself in.

What is wrong with me?

I've never been sensitive to macho charm. In all my past relationships, I've always formed a mental bond first. Physical attraction came in at a distant second. Good looks never even factored in that much in my choosing of a partner. But Thomas Mercer is making me think things I never even thought myself capable of— like how easy it would be to pull him by his expensive tie into this stall with me and kiss the charming smiles right off his stupid face.

And if even bathroom stalls are eliciting prohibited fantasies, I should really get a grip.

Inhaling deeply, I exit the stall and head to the sink to splash my face with cold water. Next, I dab my neck and behind my ears. The coldness seeps into my skin, soothing my nerves.

I need to get a hold of myself and nip this unexplainable attraction in the bud before I do something stupid. I can be a professional. Be civil to Thomas Mercer, show him around the lab, teach him a few buzz words so he can appear more robotics savvy than he is, and then send him on his merry way in three short months.

Easy peasy robot squeezy.

I pull a few loose strands of hair behind my ears and head back to the table.

"We have a deal," I say, sitting down. "I'm going to teach you as much as I can about robotics in the short time we have."

He seems skeptical of my change in attitude. "And in exchange?"

I shrug. "It won't be bad to have the future CEO's ear in case my division's work needs support."

"See?" he says with an open smile that causes my heart to double its beat. "Win win."

When we re-enter the lab, everybody else is back to work, and most heads turn our way. Mainly curious glances with two glaring exceptions. Garrett is staring daggers at Thomas. And Maria is looking at me with a dreamy grin I don't appreciate one bit. She even mouths a "Wow" at me and pretend-fans herself.

I scowl at her in a "cut it" way and brace myself to make an official announcement. I clap my hands loudly. "Attention everyone, please pause your work for a minute and listen."

Once all eyes are on me, I present Thomas to the group. "This is Thomas Mercer; he'll be staying with us for the next three months as an observer." I'm not sure if I can already divulge the news that he'll become our new CEO to everyone—I can trust Maria but maybe I shouldn't have mentioned it to her either, so I keep the introductions vague. "Please give him full access to your current work and make him feel part of the team. We'll be making rounds of the various workstations now for you to meet him personally as we go by. Please return to your posts."

All the engineers and programmers scatter back to their stations, and I turn to Thomas.

"Word of warning, getting a rundown of all the products at once might feel overwhelming. We're working on a million different things."

He gives me a confident smirk. "Do I need to take notes?"

"That won't be necessary. I gave my presentation to the board on the state of the department only last month. I can forward you the PowerPoint, which summarizes pretty much everything. And you can also study the full report."

He leans in to whisper in my ear. "Will there be an interrogation afterward?"

His warm breath skims down my ear to my neck. In response, goosebumps run down my spine and arms, despite the heat in the room. I collect my wits and face him, whispering back, "From me, no. I'm the only head of department who doesn't want your job and the only friend you have here." I lower my voice still. "But you can bet Briggs will try to trip and humiliate you any chance he has."

"Briggs?"

At Thomas's confused frown, I add, "He's the head of production and heir apparent to the throne until you showed up." I poke his chest.

Bad move. My finger makes impact with a wall of solid muscle.

I pull my hand away as if burned and finish my speech. "So I suggest you take your time in R&D seriously and also that you familiarize yourself with the organizational chart of the company you're going to lead."

"Hey." He raises his hands defensively. "I was only appointed to the job yesterday. Give me time." He winks. "I promise not to disappoint."

My heart stutters in my chest. Because of the wink. For the way he's looking at me as he *promises not to disappoint*. And because of those darn gold flecks in his eyes.

I ignore all these reactions and move on to business.

"Come on, then." I walk to the workstation next to the entrance and gesture to the man sitting there. "This is Kevin. He's been with the company for the longest time on this floor and has been working on our arc welding industrial robots for the last three years."

They shake hands, Kevin gives us an introduction to his work, and we move on, going station to station and meeting everyone.

When we get to Maria's bench, she's waiting for us with a grin splitting her face cheek to cheek.

"Hi," she says, sounding slightly out of breath. "I'm Maria." She offers her hand eagerly.

They shake hands, and then Maria turns to me saying suggestively, "Strong handshake, I like it."

I roll my eyes and ignore the gratuitous comment. "Maria is our mobility team leader. She's in charge of automated guided vehicle systems, mobile platforms, and mobile robots—the mechanical arms on wheels, in short."

Maria looks at Thomas from under her long, dark lashes. Could be because he's so tall and she has no other option. But the way she's sensually biting her lower lip tells me the move is deliberate. "Looking forward to working together, Mr. Mercer," she purrs.

"Please, call me Thomas," he replies with a warm smile.

And before Maria can fully swoon, I push him forward to our next stop. We make our way through the lab in a semi-circle, going station by station, exploring designs, and talking to people. When we complete the first half of the circle and before moving on to the second half, I bring Thomas to the center of the room.

"This is Ari, our industrial robots team leader, she's in charge of"—I mimic the robot-like movement with my arm—"all our static mechanical arms like the big guy in the center of the room."

Thomas turns to study our biggest robot. "What's the development on this one?"

"We're trying to simplify his input system so that it will no longer be necessary to program space coordinates into the machine. Instead, we want to use AI-enabled 3D vision to perform location and mapping functionalities. In short, we want to turn it from a complicated numerical control machine into something even an idiot could use intuitively with no training needed."

"The new guy could probably help test that functionality." The grating comment comes from our left, suspiciously close to Garrett's station. I narrow my eyes at him while silence falls over the lab.

Thomas zeros in on Garrett as well. "Excuse me—I didn't catch your name, what was that you just said?"

Everyone stops working, and all eyes turn to Garrett. He's turned tomato red up to the tips of his ears, but he's staring back at Thomas with an air of open hostility.

You could cut the tension in the room as the two men square off with each other. I do my best not to roll my eyes at the measuring contest about to take place. That's why I prefer to work with women; we don't need to assert our dominance. But Garrett and Thomas look like two vicious wolves baring their teeth at each other, ready to fight for the role of alpha of the pack.

Just when I'm panicking the staring contest will never end, Garrett speaks. "I said..." He spits the words out in irritation. "I said..." Under Thomas's unyielding stare, Garrett caves. "Never mind."

Thomas waits another two full seconds, jaw tense before he acknowledges the other man's submission with a terse nod.

Garrett might be a good listener and a great problem solver, but an alpha he is not.

Crisis averted, Thomas turns again to Ari. "Apologies for the interruption," he says in a calm, friendly tone as if he hadn't just turned the lab into an episode of *Animal Fight Night*. "Why don't you walk me through the program?"

Ari explains how we're trying to make the robot follow simple pointing directions from position A to B, but also how the optic reading system is still getting confused, making the system unreliable.

"Do you think it's a hardware or software problem?" Thomas asks, proving maybe he's not a total idiot.

Ari sighs. "The hardware is state-of-the art; I'm afraid our programming isn't keeping up."

They talk some more, and when they're done, I check the time. We've been at this for three hours already. Guess we could all use a break and pause our tour of the lab until tomorrow. In reality, I want to avoid having to witness another incendiary interaction between Garrett and Thomas, since Garrett's station would've been next in our path. Both of them will probably need at least a day to cool off. So instead, I ask Thomas, "How about we finish the tour tomorrow?"

"Yeah, that seems like a good idea." He catches my drift right away. I imagine he was so hard with Garrett to let everyone know he wouldn't tolerate being made a fool of. But a good leader knows not to rub salt in the wound. A sour employee serves no one.

Begrudgingly, I award Thomas a mental gold star for empathy.

"Okay, I can share a web folder with you and put in the presentation and report on all our projects I was telling you about."

"Perfect."

Then another thought strikes me. "Are you keeping your office upstairs or are you moving down here?"

Thomas looks around as if he hadn't thought about it either. "I'd better move here. Get the full-immersion experience."

"Mmm, okay, my office is the only closed-off one. But I can leave it to you and transfer to a different workstation until you move on to your next rotation."

"Nonsense, I'll have a second desk brought in," he says with a sense of finality. "We can share."

9

REESE

Thomas leaves, to get a desk, to pack his stuff, to comb his perfect hair. Or do whatever it is rich, spoiled cover models do. I don't care. With him gone, I can finally let out a breath I didn't even know I was holding.

I cross the lab and shut myself into my office, enjoying the last few hours of peace before this space becomes a full-fledged co-ed.

What a joke.

It's incredible how much a place can feel different in just a short few hours. Work used to be my sanctuary, my happy place, and now it's a minefield. My preservation instincts should've kicked in, helping me to steer clear of Thomas Mercer's exceptionally powerful gravitational field. But, so far, the only impulse that's kicked in is the grab-the-boss-by-the-tie-and...

No. No. Nope. Good thing we have a specific company policy against such interactions.

Technically, he isn't your boss, yet, a malicious voice whispers in my ear. *There's no policy against peer-to-peer relationships.*

But he will be the boss in fifteen months—same thing.

I drop my head in my hands. Gosh, the next three months are

going to be hell. But then Thomas Mercer will be someone else's problem. Up until the point when he'll become CEO. Then he'll become a permanent complication. But at least then, we'll have an extra layer between us. Emmet Proctor and I sure don't talk every day or share an office. It'll be manageable. A few review meetings, the odd interaction, the annual Christmas party...

A very unpleasant kind of foreboding grips me. What if he shows up to the party with a beautiful plus one? Yuck. The idea shouldn't be disturbing, but it is. Heck, I'm not even sure if he's single right now—*and I'm not going to google it*. Better not to know. That Google probably has that information should be enough of a red flag. And he probably isn't single, anyway. How can someone with a face like that be single?

I shove the unsettling thoughts aside, dust my hands in a resigned move, and get to work. I create a shared folder for Thomas, find his company email in the directory, and grant him access. As I copy the presentation and report into the folder, I find comfort in the fact that it should take him a while to study them. At the very least until the end of the week, keeping our need for interactions to a minimum.

Honestly, he wouldn't even need to come here while he familiarizes himself with the projects. Thomas could study the reports alone in his private office. He *should* study on the upper floors—quieter there and easier to focus. Yes, I'll suggest it.

I've just closed the folder when someone knocks on the door.

My pulse speeds up for no reason. "Come in."

"Hey, boss." Maria pokes her head inside, and my heartbeat slows down.

"Maria, what can I do for you?"

She walks in followed by her sidekick, K-2P. "Nothing. I want to discuss Mr. Hottie McHunky."

"If you're referring to our future commander-in-chief, we've already discussed him enough this morning."

Maria crosses the office and takes her usual spot perched on my desk. "But that was before we saw the real deal; that photo didn't do him justice."

"Whatever you say."

"Why? You don't think he's more handsome in person than in his resume pic?"

"No."

Sure I do, but I won't admit it. If I give her rope, Maria will pull and pull and pull until the skin on both our hands is burned raw.

"Well, I think he is even hotter in person," she says, unabashed. "I like his eyes; don't you think they're smoldering?"

"Smoldering?" I shake my head. "You read too much smut."

"Smut is never too much, and I have no problem admitting when a guy is exceptionally sexy, broad-shouldered, very tall, with a tight butt that just begs to be grabbed and squeezed—"

"Maria!"

"What? You don't appreciate well-rounded buttocks? The way that suit was hugging his behind should be outlawed!"

"That is no appropriate way to talk about a co-worker," I deflect, trying not to picture exactly how well that suit hugged his behind. "And Thomas Mercer isn't my type."

"He's not, huh?" Maria widens her eyes in fake shock. "I never would have guessed."

"This isn't a joke, Maria. He's not my type and we shouldn't discuss his anatomy in any capacity. What if a colleague made a comment about *your* butt?"

"Fair point." She raises her hands. "And if he really isn't your type."

"He's not."

Maria frowns. "Hey, it's dark in here. Why are all the blinds down?" Her lips curl into a wicked smile. "Are you already planning to lure the boss into torrid desk sex?"

"What did I just say?"

She smirks innocently. "I wasn't discussing anatomy."

I roll my eyes. "I pulled the blinds down when I changed earlier." I don't tell her about the striptease and Thomas walking in on it because I'm still her boss. I need to maintain a shred of dignity.

"The new boss walked in on her mid-strip," K-2P rats me out. "It was hilarious."

I glare at the droid.

"Hubba hubba. Did he see you naked?"

I cover my eyes with a hand and drag it down my face. "He got a peek of underwear."

"Ah, now a lot of things make sense."

"What things?"

"Why he couldn't get his—*smoldering*—eyes off of you. You must've made an impression."

"Yeah, the impression of a dumbass who almost flashed her boss! And he wasn't looking at me in any way."

"I beg to disagree, boss. Thomas Mercer was totally checking you out the entire time. He gave you *the* look."

"He gave me *a* look because we were talking and to look at someone while they speak to you is the polite thing to do. No way he finds me hot." I point at my baggy hoodie as incontrovertible proof of my non-hotness.

"Agree to disagree." Maria hugs herself. "You're smokin' hot, even with lumpy clothes on."

"That's not what I need to hear right now."

"Just try to be cool, I'm sure he won't hold the striptease against you. The guy seems very laid-back for a rich dude. None of that snobbery, or looking down his nose at the rest of us. But he's also confident, self-assured." Maria fans herself with her hands. "Did you see the way he squared off with Garrett? My panties were about to drop from the sheer masculinity of it. Don't tell me you didn't find the staring contest hot as hell."

Even if I want to confess that, yes, I found the silent power play incredibly sexy, I'm not going to. I can't afford to entertain such thoughts about my future boss, let alone voice them out loud.

"Maria, stop," I chide. "He's going to become our boss next year, it's not appropriate to speak about him like that."

"All right, I'll stop if you admit he's even more handsome in person than he is in his photo."

"Who's more handsome in person than his photo?" a baritone voice asks.

Heart beating in my chest, I raise my gaze and find Thomas leaning his shoulder against the doorframe, arms crossed, dimpled smile fully weaponized.

I swallow. What are the chances he didn't hear us discuss his panties-melting superpowers?

10

THOMAS

The blush on Reese's cheeks is adorable.

"No one," she says.

I stare at the other woman with black hair, black clothes, and black lipstick, summoning her name and title from our earlier introduction. Maria, head of mobility. She stares at me with a saucy smile, not even a hint of color on her cheeks.

I won't get anything out of her, so I turn to my only ally in the room. "K-2P, who were the ladies discussing?"

"Maria was trying to get Reese to admit you look better in person than in your CV picture, and they were also trying to determine if you have smoldering eyes."

I chuckle. "Is that all?"

"No, this morning they were discussing how handsome you looked in your picture, but also speculating that to compensate, you probably have a small—"

With the reflexes of a ninja, Reese launches herself at the droid and flips a switch on his dome, silencing him.

"A small *brain*," she huffs, clearly rattled.

The droid rebels and wheels backward, emitting a series of

angry beeps. With his clawed hands, he flips the switch back on. "You turned off my vocal effector, that's rude."

"Repeating parts of private conversations you overheard is even ruder."

"No one had sworn me to secrecy."

"Don't play dumb now; you don't need to be told when something is private, K-2P."

I clear my throat to stop the human-machine argument. Reese's eyes snag on me again. A defiant flame burns in their amber depths. If that isn't the definition of smoldering, I don't know what is.

I drop the eye-lock and turn to the head of mobility. "Maria, would you mind giving Reese and me a moment alone?"

The brainy goth hops off the desk and, gazing at the floor—to hide an amused smirk, I suspect, more than because she's mortified —scurries past me out the door. She stops only to beckon K-2P to follow. "Come on."

The robot glides after her. "Yeah, I prefer to go where I'm respected and appreciated."

Once they're out, I shut the door behind me and take the seat opposite Reese. I don't talk right away. I let her roast a little. She's been acting all haughty and proper with me so far, but I'm happy to discover her naughtier side extends past office private dances.

Intrigued is the right word.

"Just so we're clear," I say after a while. "I don't have a small... *brain.*"

Reese looks like she's trying to suppress a groan of mortification.

"In fact," I continue. "No one's ever complained about my... *brain.*"

Now she actually groans. "Can we just not?"

I flash her a smirk. "What, discuss my *brain*?"

Her already-red cheeks veer toward purple now. "It's not appropriate."

"Oh. You can discuss my *brain* with a colleague, but if *I* discuss it with you, it's suddenly inappropriate?"

"Listen, I'm aware our introduction earlier has been *unconventional*. That I basically said hello, meet my boobs." She mimics grabbing the lapels of a jacket and pulling them open. I have to do my best not to let the memory of the very gesture get to my, well, *brain*. "But you've been sort of flirting with me all day, and that makes me uncomfortable."

I give her a serious look. I'm not a jerk; I don't want anyone to be uncomfortable around me. "If that's the case, I apologize. I thought you were flirting back."

She levels me with a hard stare. "I wasn't, and I'd like to keep our interactions from now on strictly professional."

I study her for a second, not sure if she's serious or in denial. "You haven't felt a spark between us?"

She takes a moment too long to reply. "No."

I raise my hands. "My apologies, then. I promise I won't tease you anymore. But if you change your mind, please proposition me any time." I add a wink.

"You're doing it again." She scowls. "Winks are not work-appropriate interactions."

"Sorry, sorry, I'm just not used to—" I stop before I come across like a total moron.

Too late. Reese rolls her eyes. "To women not falling at your feet enraptured with gratitude that you shed your light on them? Sorry, for me, looks or money count for zero." She taps a finger on her temple. "For me, it's all about the brain."

I guffaw at that. "All about the *brain*, huh?"

She throws her arms in the air, exasperated. "Not *that* brain. Actual gray matter."

"All right, Campbell." I extend my hand across the desk. "Friends?"

"I'd rather we stuck to colleagues."

I tilt my head. "*Friendly* colleagues?"

She lets out a huffy puff of air and shakes my hand. "Friendly colleagues it is."

Friendly is good. Definitely an improvement on the mixed signals I've gotten so far.

"I'll get out of your hair." I stand up. "Please don't be too crushed I'm leaving."

She gives me a fake-sweet smile. "I won't." She pointedly goes back to staring at her screen, which is opened on her desktop and not a work file if I'm right.

I make to leave but stop on the threshold. "Oh, and hey, Campbell?"

She glares at me.

"If you're ever in a jam, feel free to pick my *brain* whenever you like."

Reese glares at me, narrowing her eyes. "Seriously?"

I raise my hands. "Sorry, couldn't resist a last one. I'll be a good boy from now on, I promise." I knock on the frame of her door. "See you tomorrow, Campbell."

11

REESE

Tuesday morning, I find myself in the unusual position of dreading going to work for the second day in a row. At least today I'm not squeezed into chafing clothes.

I wave at the security guard as I swipe my badge and head down to the basement. I'm not as early as yesterday, so a few people other than Maria are already in.

"Hey," I give her a quick hello, surprised not to find K-2P by her side.

"Morning, boss."

"Where's your minion?"

Maria jerks her chin toward my office. "He's in there with your new roommate." She wiggles her eyebrows suggestively. "Apparently, they hit it off."

I do my best not to groan, and mouth-whisper, "Thomas is already in there?"

"Yep, dropped in about twenty minutes ago." Maria fake-fans herself. "Looking as palatable as a mini chocolate ice cream cone on a hot summer's day."

There's nothing *mini* about that man. Not his stature, not his charm, not his ego... and not his *brain*, if he's to be believed.

I shake my head and gingerly walk into my office. When I stick my head in, I immediately notice the new small desk pushed in the corner and the large man sitting at it with his back turned to me.

He's wearing another expensive-looking suit that stretches over his broad shoulders like a glove—probably tailor-made.

K-2P is standing near him next to the desk, emitting a series of angry beeps. Thomas laughs in response, the sound alarmingly pleasant.

I clear my throat. "Good morning, everyone."

Thomas jolts in the chair and spins around to face me. He smiles and my heart nearly stops. It's the same warm, easygoing smile I saw him toss around yesterday as I introduced him to the people around the lab. But the grin he flashes me now is accompanied by a hunger in his eyes that wasn't there for the others. An eagerness that seems reserved for me.

I swallow.

"Morning," he says, standing.

I frown. "Hi."

"I hope you don't mind that I made myself at home." He gestures to the small working station.

I cross the office to my desk, dropping my messenger bag on the floor. "The entire place is *literally* yours, so make yourself at home however much you want."

He tilts his head. "Not a morning person?"

"More not a babysitting-billionaires person."

Thomas laughs at my lame jab as if I've said something funny and charming.

I sit down, my face heating when I notice the way he's looking at me. As an excuse to look away, I open a drawer at random. I rummage inside for a pen with shaking hands. This man makes me irrationally nervous. I'm a level-headed person. But not around *him*, apparently.

Out of the corner of my eye, I track Thomas as he approaches my station and stops in front of me.

I find a pen, slide it onto my desk, then slam the drawer shut and peek up at him. Thomas is hovering next to my desk, his imposing figure too close for comfort, staring at me like he's undressing me with his eyes.

Sorry, buddy, you're not getting a repeat show of yesterday.

"Are you okay?" he asks.

"Fine." Not really, given the uncomfortable tingling in my stomach.

K-2P wheels closer, breaking the tension. "Good morning to you, too," he says, peeved. "It's always nice to be cherished by one's maker."

I suppress a smirk. "Morning K-2P, apple of my eye, my pride and joy, light of my life..."

The droid lets out a slow beep. "Better."

I bow my head ironically, not sure the robot will get the sarcasm, Thomas's gaze still burning heavily on the side of my face.

I ignore the still-hovering billionaire at my side and concentrate on the robot in front of me. "So," I say, straightening up. "Anything to report?"

K-2P doesn't answer. Instead, his head rotates 180 degrees, almost in slow motion, to stare at Thomas. "Mr. Mercer—"

"Please call me Thomas," the too-tall billionaire replies with a gentle smile.

It's strangely disarming.

"Thomas... Reese just said this entire place is yours, does that mean you can do whatever you want around here?"

"Err... quite the opposite, I think." Thomas squats down to be eye to eye with K2-P—or eye to sensors. And why do I find the gesture incredibly sweet? "Since I'm the one who sets the rules, I have to follow them to the letter. Lead by example, you know?" His eyes dart to me and, in a wishful tone, he adds, "Even when it's hard."

My heart melts a little, then the words "anti-fraternization policy" flash in my mind in a bright neon color.

Prince Charming down there doesn't even have to try. Whatever he does or says makes my knees go weak. If I keep swooning this hard, I wouldn't put it past woodland creatures to barge into the office and start singing a song as they clean—and this space is already crowded enough.

"And how concerned are you with optics?" K-2P tries a different angle.

Thomas frowns. "What do you mean?"

"He's just trying to trick you into taking him home with you over the weekend," I explain.

The robot sputters his lights in my direction. "This is outrageous! I am a highly sophisticated autonomous being with free will. I do not need your help in the matter of finding myself a home, thank you very much!"

"Is there any particular reason he can't leave the lab?" Thomas stands up, stifling a smile. "Is his battery not durable enough?"

"My battery can last a week when fully charged."

"He's an *uncommon* presence in here," I explain. "He's my project. My IP. Nothing to do with Mercer Robotics. I keep him here because it's where I spend most of my time and so that he can spend time with different people as well—evolve. But I wouldn't particularly like to advertise his presence, and marching him in and out of the lab every weekend would attract too much attention."

Thomas frowns and sits in front of me, finally relieving me of having to crane my neck to make eye contact. "Why?"

"Optics, as he kindly explained."

Thomas gives me a strange look, mercifully shifting his inquisitive, gold-flecked gaze to the droid.

K-2P continues on his quest for liberation from the lab. "You're the owner, the boss, you don't care about optics, do you?"

"Technically, my father is all those things."

K-2P emits the most pitiful of beeps. "Does that mean I still have to spend my weekends segregated here, alone, in the dark?"

"I don't see why you should."

K-2P spins around beeping happily, lights blinking. "So, I can come home with you?"

Thomas seems taken aback. "Don't you want to go home with Reese?"

The droid gives me his shoulders. "She didn't care about my well-being enough to risk her precious reputation; I don't think she deserves my company."

Thomas looks at me, baffled.

I just shrug in a *you made your bed now sleep in it* way and smirk.

He shakes his head and turns to the droid. "Then, yes, I guess we'll be roommates."

"Wheeeeeeeeee." K-2P speeds back and forth around the office, blipping.

Thomas stands up, looking at me in a way that not only could melt underwear but vaporize it. "He's extraordinary, you know?"

I swallow past the thundering of my heart. "Thanks."

"How did you make him?" Thomas takes a seat in front of me.

"Well, the hardware is pretty basic. Vintage, even, but I'm a big *Star Wars* fan and couldn't resist building my own droid."

"Please," K-2P interjects. "I'm far more handsome than those TV droids."

"Of course." I roll my eyes. "Anyway, his motion drive is basically off the shelf, same as those vacuuming robots you can program, but with a few improvements so that he doesn't have to bump into things to change direction and can also have intent when he's moving."

"You *did not* just compare me to a vacuuming robot."

Thomas laughs. "And the sassy personality? Does that come from you?"

"His mind," I make air quotes, "is a complex development on a language model I developed, and, yes, basically the only proprietary thing alongside a few tinkers on how he coordinates. The rest is all off-the-rack: sensors, speech functionalities, AI voices. He could speak in any accent, with any AI voice, in any language, even."

"But you've kept him with a general American accent and a mechanical voice."

I lock eyes with Thomas. "Apparently not mechanical enough if you mistook him for me yesterday."

The dimpled smile I get in return is devastating. "I had wondered if I was about to walk in on someone wearing a Phasma helmet."

Something tightens deep in my core. Thomas Mercer can't have those eyes, that smile, that face—okay, Maria, that butt, too—and *also* be a *Star Wars* fan. I'm just not equipped to cope.

I'm saved from answering by K-2P spatting. "At least he didn't compare me to C-3PO."

"Well, great." I drum my fingers on the desk. "Now that your superiority has been established, can we all get to work?"

Thomas claps his hands enthusiastically. "What's the plan for today?"

I raise an eyebrow at him. "Did you already read all the material I sent you yesterday?"

Thomas's face falls. "Well, no."

"Then I suggest you start there, and ask me any questions should you need to."

"Aye, aye." The smile is quickly back on his handsome face.

Oh my gosh, he must be one of those insufferable, perennially cheerful people.

He stands up and returns to his station, to power up his laptop.

I try hard to ignore the fact that he is in the same room as me, but the tingle in my stomach is a constant reminder. Also, I can hear him breathing and occasionally, I glimpse him shifting in his chair out of the corner of my eye, but I do my best to pretend he isn't there.

At least until he asks, "What's a Fourier transform?"

I flare my nostrils. "Can't you just google it?"

"I tried but the formula that came out isn't exactly a clarification."

"In simple terms, it's a mathematical operation that converts amplitude as a function of time to amplitude as a function of frequency for non-periodic signals." I let out a huff of air. "But you don't need to go that technical, just get a general idea of the products."

"Well, your research report is all about the technical problems you're trying to solve."

He might have a point.

"Okay." I stand up and go to the book rack in the office corner. "Maybe a general brochure would be a better starting point. I had one just over here..." I stretch on my tiptoes to get the brochure from the top shelf where I've stacked it atop technical manuals.

My fingertips are just skimming the plastic spiral binding, but I can't quite reach it. Before I even realize he's moved, Thomas is behind me, his breath hot on my neck. His chest almost pressing against my back but not quite as he stretches over me. I know I'm the one who asked for clear boundaries, but right now, I'd happily cross them. It takes all my self-control not to lean backward, close that final inch, and ease into him, giving way to his gravitational pull.

When I whirl around, our eyes lock in an electrifying moment that lasts an eternity before he takes another step back and hands me the brochure.

I hand it right back. "This should be easier to understand; it's made for clients."

His eyes never leave mine as he takes the binder. Then his gaze lowers to the document, and my heart hammers in my ears as I watch him flip the pages.

"Thanks," he says finally in that gravelly voice of his.

"No problem," I manage, before I plod back to my desk. *Flee* back would be a more appropriate term.

I tap furiously on my keyboard and try my best to focus on anything but Thomas "So Flipping Tall" Mercer.

But then he says, "I'll have this finished by the end of the day. Then maybe tomorrow you can introduce me to the remaining teams?"

"Tomorrow, sure."

Because he'll be here tomorrow, and the day after, and the one after that...

Yay, me.

With a deep breath, I turn back to my work, trying to black out Thomas's presence. With him busy reading, a peaceful silence finally settles over the room. Grateful for the quiet, I even concentrate and finish a few tasks. From time to time, I sense Thomas's gaze fixed on me, but thankfully he doesn't make conversation again. Still, I'm hyperaware of his every movement. When he's still. When he's typing. When he's whispering conspiratorially with K-2P.

After a few hours of this routine, Maria steps inside with a bright and inviting smile.

"Hey Reese," she says cheerfully. "A few of us are going to the Mexican place around the corner. Garrett proposed it but he was too scared to come in here and ask you along."

"Why?"

Maria's eyes dart to Thomas. "He was petrified of Mr. Alpha over there after their tussle-diddly-dee of yesterday..."

"We can't have that," Thomas chimes in, standing up. "I'm not that scary once you get to know me."

Maria gives him an intense, coquettish once-over. "Oh, I never thought of you as *scary*, big boss."

I can't believe she'd so openly flirt with him.

He flashes her a toothy grin that lights up the entire room and feels like sunbathing on a hot summer's day—warm, intense, and slightly dangerous if enjoyed for too long. "So you wouldn't mind if I joined you, too?"

I shoot him an incredulous look, but he just grins back at me.

"Not at all. The more the merrier."

In an almost too-fluid motion, Thomas dons a cashmere coat that drapes over him with an effortless elegance. The dark, thick fabric, accentuating his broad frame, hints at a luxury that's both understated and undeniable. As he turns, the coat's smooth satin lining catches the light, sending my way a faint, yet distinct whiff—part woodsy, part spice. Mouthwateringly dangerous. Divine doesn't quite capture it. The man's scent is intoxicating.

Apparently unaffected, Maria takes his arm and gently leads him out of the office and across the lab toward the elevator, chatting about the restaurant as they go.

I have no choice but to grab my puffer jacket and follow. I catch up as they step into the elevator and join them. In begrudging silence, I listen as Maria tells Thomas how the restaurant's burritos are to die for, but that they have some superb tacos, too.

The others are waiting for us in the lobby. There are about fifteen of us. Garrett turns pale when he spots Thomas and does his best to hide within the group. But the others don't seem too fazed our prospective CEO has joined us. Well, they don't know yet he's going to become CEO, but they do know Thomas is the heir apparent to the entire kingdom.

After a short walk down the street, we arrive at the small Mexican restaurant tucked away in a side alleyway near our office building.

Immediately upon walking through its doors, I am embraced by an array of colors and aromas. Traditional Mexican decor with vibrant tints pops off every wall and intricate patterns sneak along the restaurant's floors and ceilings. The smell of freshly cooked tacos wafts out from within, making my mouth water in anticipation.

We make our way inside to a table near a window with bright yellow curtains framing our view of the street. I've barely finished perusing the menu when a server arrives to take our preferences.

Once our orders are placed, conversation flows freely. We talk about work projects, current events, and other less serious topics—anything but what happened between Garrett and Thomas yesterday. They are studiously seated at opposite ends of the table while I ended up sitting right across from Prince Charming, making unexpected eye contact a frequent repercussion. My stomach drops out every time our eyes meet, and it seems I'm not the only victim of his boastful charisma.

The other ladies present are all but salivating over him. Over his broad shoulders, magnetic eyes, and chiseled jawline. Even Lizzie, who's not interested in men, as far as I know, seems enchanted, giggling at his every word and blushing when their eyes meet for even a fraction of a second. So much so that I wonder if I should've placed a side order for smelling salts with all the swooning going around. Not that I can talk. I should probably start bringing the salts to work for myself, anyway.

The guys also seem to like Thomas and are eager to talk about sports with him. All except Garrett, who sulks in his corner. While no one speaks directly about what happened between them yesterday, everyone can sense the tension radiating from Garrett's end of the table.

Thomas attempts to ease the tension between them and male-bond over their shared love of basketball—Garrett is wearing a Knicks sweatshirt, but nothing works. Thomas is met with cold-shoulder replies or monosyllabic grunts in response as Garrett mostly remains silent and aloof toward him for the duration of the meal.

The future CEO handles it with grace, never losing his enthusiasm or charm as he continues to make witty comments, crack jokes, or ask questions that draw out responses from everyone else at the table.

The server arrives with our food shortly after, and the conversation stalls for the first few bites while everyone is busy chewing until Thomas holds the stage again.

As he speaks, I'm captivated by his golden hazel eyes and cute dimples that show when he grins in amusement at something someone says. He laughs easily and often, which only adds to the warmth of his presence. His voice is strong and resonant against the soft chatter of the restaurant background noise and it carries across our table easily as he talks animatedly with Maria about the most recent episode of her favorite show while I discuss a recent article I read in a research journal with Lizzie.

As I'm talking, Thomas reaches across the table and plucks an olive from my plate. He pops it into his mouth with a twinkle in his eye that makes me blush so hard I forget what I was saying mid-sentence. The gesture is too intimate, simple but unsettling.

I have to drag my eyes away from his full lips where my olive just went to heaven and go back to my conversation.

But the entire meal continues to be littered by stolen glances, the occasional, unintentional brush of our knees under the table, and the random waft of his cologne I'm able to pick up even among all the food spices. Like in my office, the scent lands straight in my lower belly with the harrowing side effect of reminding me I'm a woman who hasn't been touched by a man in a long, *long* time. *Too* long, perhaps.

Being in Thomas's proximity, I experience a strange mix of contentment and unease. Torn between two conflicting desires: to play and to run away. Thankfully, the choice is not mine. The anti-fraternization policy makes it clear that "to play" is not an option.

By the time desserts arrive, everyone seems relaxed in each other's company despite Garrett's cool demeanor toward Thomas still lingering in the air like a stale fog. Thomas's magnetic charm has created a strange camaraderie in the group I never quite pulled off as department head.

Although I'm still not convinced he should have such a prominent role in our division, I have to admit that this man has something special. He can charm anyone with his wit and charisma but still maintain a genuine sense of humility while never coming across as overly boastful or arrogant.

When it's time for the check, Thomas doesn't let anyone pay. With the casualness of someone who's buying a cup of coffee—as opposed to paying for a fifteen-person meal—he takes a black credit card out of his wallet and slips it into the leather bill folder.

I'm not even sure the card is company issued. And I'm no pauper, but the invite-only black card that comes with hundreds of thousands of dollars of minimum spend sure is a wake-up call to the fact that Thomas might act like a regular guy, but he's anything but. He might not be a real prince, but he's probably richer than royalty.

Everyone thanks Thomas, including a semi-muttered thank you from Garrett, and we head back down the street to our building where everyone disperses—Garrett being the quickest to dart away. But before he does, he turns around and gives me a knowing look as if trying to convey a silent warning.

Thomas and I linger behind the others in the lobby.

Hands shoved in his pockets, he rolls on the balls of his feet. "Lunch went well, no?"

Too well. I'm still in turmoil over conflicting instincts, so instead of acknowledging the good hour of team building, I give him a snippy reply.

"Yeah, yeah, you're quite the charmer."

Tilt of the head. "You don't look too charmed."

"I find your bubbly personality irking."

"I find your constant scowls cute."

"Knock off the charm, it doesn't work on me."

Cute frown. "Not even a little?"

I'm charmed all right. But I can't admit that. "Nope. Anyway, if you want to be 'one of the guys' I suggest you dress more casually from now on. You already *are* a suit, you don't need to remind us constantly. This is a technology company, not a financial one. And we're more laid-back in the lab." I pull at my sweatshirt as a demonstration.

He raises his hands in mock surrender. "I get it: no suits necessary in the robotics lab." He stares at me for a moment too long before his lips curl into a smirk. "But just so I'm clear, what kind of casual wear are we talking about? Jeans? Button-down shirt?"

"You're smart, figure it out."

Thomas tilts his head. "Oh, I plan to." He crosses his arms over his chest, almost belligerently. "You're very hard to please, Campbell, but I'll do my best to meet your impossible standards."

I remain stuck on the *hard-to-please* part of his reply. The way the words *hard* and *please* roll off his tongue is sensual enough to do all the work for him, which makes my treacherous brain conjure up an image of how it'd feel to be pressed against a wall by him while he whispers sweet nothings in my ear. A shiver runs down my spine. Turns out I'd be super easy to please if he was the one doing the pleasing.

Despite what Maria says about handsome men, I've no doubt Thomas Mercer would be stellar in bed and would have no problem pleasuring any woman. Because life is unfair.

With a final smirk, he heads off toward the elevators.

My heart races and my cheeks flame as I watch him walk away with an air of confidence. Why, *why* of all the spoon-fed rich kids out there did I have to be saddled with a gorgeous, provocative charmer who, except for his expensive wardrobe, doesn't act even a little self-indulgent. And who annoyingly looks just as good going as he did coming. Watching the curve of his ass move against his tailored pants doesn't help sort myself out.

For a moment I stand there completely still, unable to walk or to process the conflicting emotions raging inside of me. Finally, gathering enough strength to cross the lobby, I head for a side hall and take the stairs to the basement. It's a precaution since I'm not sure just how unprofessional I'd turn if I were locked inside an elevator with Thomas "Sexy Butt" Mercer right now.

12

REESE

The next morning I'm already in the office when Thomas arrives. The moment my eyes land on him, I sorely regret telling him not to wear a suit. Dressed casually, he looks even more attractive than yesterday.

He's sporting a pair of tight-fitting jeans and a light-gray V-neck sweater, and I have to work hard to keep my jaw from dropping. The way the jeans hug his toned legs in all the right places is criminal.

The sweater is no better; it clings tightly to his torso in an obscenely soft way. His broad shoulders are accentuated by the snug fit, while the muscles of his toned arms are defined under the thin fabric.

His light-brown hair is combed back into an effortless style that appears both natural and perfectly styled at once.

And his face. Oh, gosh, it's a take-me-to-bed-and-do-whatever-you-please-with-me face. Subtle stubble frames his jaw with an aura of seduction like he's had morning sex and didn't have time to shave before coming to work. Which is probably the case. I'm still resisting the urge to google his relationship status but I remain convinced he isn't single. Best option, he's a natural flirt and doesn't even realize the effect he has on women. Worst case, he's a player who knows exactly what he's doing. Either way, he's untouchable for so many reasons.

The thought prompts me to clench my thighs under the desk. Thomas Mercer is all perfect angles and exquisite power and the casual clothes don't detract one bit from his halo of dominance.

My heart races as I avert my eyes before he catches me gawking. But I can sense his gaze on me—an electric spark traveling through the room—daring me to look up again and meet his eye.

I resist the impulse, doing my best to control my inappropriate reactions. What would I give to be totally indifferent to this man? But it's no use; suit or no suit, Thomas Mercer is simply too gorgeous for me not to take notice.

He continues on confidently into the office with a quick, casual hello. He's no doubt aware of how attractive he is, but he still manages not to come across as cocky.

As he gets to his desk with his back turned to me, I dare another peek. My chest tightens as my gaze lingers on his perfect derriere until he sits in his chair. I almost groan in disappointment at being deprived of the view.

Trying to compose myself, I quickly look away again and busy myself with shuffling papers on my desk, doing my best to avoid looking at his corner. But I still listen to him exchange morning banter with K-2P. Thomas "Nice Ass" Mercer even charmed the darn sour robot in less than twenty-four hours.

After what feels like forever, Thomas finally comes over and greets me with a smile that makes me forget how to breathe.

"Morning, Campbell," he says, his voice deep and velvety.

He's so attractive that it's almost mesmerizing to look at him—like staring into an open fire on a frosty night.

I fill my lungs with air and release it gradually. "Good morning, Thomas." I inhale again.

My cheeks flame up but at least my voice sounds normal and doesn't come out in a high-pitched squeak.

Thomas turns slightly, presenting me with his new wardrobe. He waits for me to acknowledge his casual clothes. When I don't, he flashes me a coy smirk as if he's fully conscious of the influence he has over me. Probably because he has it on every woman.

"Did you need something?" I ask.

His smirk widens, and the darn dimples appear while his eyes snatch mine. I couldn't look away if I tried.

"I've finished with the brochure and I'm ready for the next part of my training."

I all but melt under his gaze, and have to fight against the urge to reach out and squeeze one of those biceps. Test if they'd feel as hard as they look.

Nu-uh, I can't be near him today.

"Okay, then you should probably familiarize yourself better with each research project. Why don't you start with mobility? You and Maria seem to get along."

"Sure." His eyes flash, as if to say, *Pawning me off won't stop you from liking me.*

No, it won't. But at least I'll have a few hours of peace. Between yesterday's lunch and the first day's introductions, he's already met almost everyone in the lab, so a second tour of the lab would be superfluous. It's now phase two of his robotics training.

K-2P wheels closer to my desk. "Can I tag along?"

I stand up and gesture to the door. "Be my guest."

The robot looks at me. "Are you okay, boss?"

"Yes, why wouldn't I be okay?"

"Your face is unnaturally red."

I flush an even deeper shade of crimson. "Oh." I touch my

cheeks and feel the heat radiating off of them. "It's warm in here. It's nothing." I herd the droid out of the office. "Now, shoo."

Out of the corner of my eye, I catch Thomas lifting his eyebrows while that irresistible twinkle sparkles in his eyes.

I don't dare to look directly at him as we step into the main lab and head toward Maria's station. Still, I'm not blind to the satisfied, knowing smirk plastered on his stupid, handsome face.

Maria looks up and her face lights up when she sees Thomas. She stands, slightly leaning forward, like a sunflower turning toward the light.

After giving him a not-so-subtle once-over, she bats her eyelashes at him.

"Nice jeans." Her gaze lingers a moment too long on him—not that I'm one to talk. I was ogling him the same way a moment ago in my office. But seeing Maria mirroring my awestruck eyeballing irritates me, turning me almost territorial.

"The biz-caj look suits you," the head of mobility concludes.

Thomas scratches the back of his head in a self-deprecating, I'm-sexy-and-I-know-it gesture.

"Thanks."

"And to what do I owe the pleasure of the visit?" Her words drip with an over-the-top flirtatious undertone.

I step in. "I thought Thomas could shadow you today, and get a deeper understanding of the research on our mobile platforms with integral controllers and 7-axis robot arms."

Maria flips her hair nonchalantly, letting out a throaty laugh. "Of course. I'd love the company."

The head of mobility goes on and gives him a rundown of her various projects in that rehearsed, I've-given-this-presentation-a-million-times-before tone. Thomas pays close attention to every detail she explains, nodding along or asking questions about certain points of interest.

Eventually, after all the broad info has been discussed, Maria turns to him with a warm smile that once again doesn't sit well with me.

"You'll fit in just fine," she says with a slight giggle at the end of her sentence.

"That's good to hear," he replies, his voice a low, sexy rumble.

I'm clearly superfluous here with nothing to contribute.

With a curt, "I'll leave you two to it." I turn on my heels and leave, quickly heading toward the safety of my office. A Mercer-free space.

Except, the subtle hint of Thomas's expensive aftershave still lingers in the air and makes it impossible for me to concentrate on anything else.

* * *

That night as I get home, I bask in the certainty that I'm finally 100 per cent free of Thomas Mercer and his infuriatingly charming presence. But as I kick off my shoes and start rummaging through my bag, searching for my phone charger, I notice a blue Post-it note stuck alongside the interior lining. A few lines are written on it in neat handwriting.

Did you approve of my "biz-caj" attire today?

No signature. Not that I need it.

My face grows hot, and I smile.

Then groan. Of course he had to leave me a reminder of him.

What kind of game is he playing? Didn't we agree not to flirt? Is he flirting? Do I want him to flirt? Unfortunately, the answer is yes. No matter what I told him. Why is this man so difficult to overlook? A strange mix of feelings overcomes me.

Part of me is annoyed by his presumptuousness, while the other part feels a little flattered. Then I give up trying to assess my feelings and give in to a curiosity that's been plaguing me since he stepped into my office mid-striptease. I google him.

Page Six and various other gossip websites don't report a girlfriend. His socials are all public and, as I scroll a few pages of pictures, he always appears alone or with buddies. No recurring women.

So definitely single?

Thomas is many things, but he doesn't strike me as a shady dude. The opposite, perhaps, someone who's too direct. He wouldn't be sending a "friendly colleague" secret notes if he had a girlfriend.

I sigh and flop on the sofa, resigning myself to the fact that, in his vicinity or not, I'll be spending way too much time thinking about Thomas Mercer for the foreseeable future.

The next day, I'm slightly more prepared for Thomas's "business-casual" handsomeness and exert better control over the heat levels of my face.

I don't acknowledge the note. I catch Thomas looking at me funny more than once, fighting not to smile as if he knows that I've read the note and am pointedly refusing to discuss it. We enter a strange contest of pretending where neither of us wants to give the other the satisfaction of mentioning our secret first.

But if our gazes keep locking and smoldering into each other at this rate, I might have to request a fire extinguisher be brought into the office. I'm a match ready to be lighted, and he's a strip of striker.

The silent battle is at least short-lived as, today, I ship him off to shadow Lizzie, allowing me to push through another day with a few salvaged, unfried brain cells.

At home, I won't lie, when I go to fish my charger out of my bag, my pulse is out of control as I search around the bag with trepidation.

Thomas hid the note better this time and tucked it away in one of the side pockets.

No response? How rude, Campbell.

I chuckle.

That darn man.

On Friday, the silent war of furtive stares and suppressed smirks continues, all our stolen glances carrying the same coded message: *I won't mention the notes if you don't.*

We're both stony-faced. He's determined, and I'm stubborn. There's no way either of us is going to break first.

But his plan has a weakness. That he has to write and plant the notes. He can write them in private, sure. But to place them in my bag, Thomas needs access. I try to catch him in the act multiple times. I leave the office with various excuses, saying I'm going to get a coffee, go to the bathroom, go check on a colleague's work, then burst in a minute later, pretending I've forgotten something. But I never discover him anywhere near my bag.

And the silent battle continues.

But when Thomas gets up to leave for the day, I decide to take the risk and speak up. "Have a nice weekend," I say, my voice low.

He has this half-smile on his face and replies with a nod. "Sure, I'll see you on Monday."

The flirty tension between us is palpable, broken only by K-2P when the droid makes a noise of excitement, ecstatic that he's going home with Thomas.

Thomas turns to me with that insufferable, knowing smirk. "Anything I should know before taking this guy home?"

"Don't mess with his circuits and you should be fine."

"I'm fully charged," K-2P says. "Ready for our boys' weekend."

"I'm sure you'll both have an amazing time." I'm half-grinning and I know Thomas can tell how much I'm itching to call him out on the notes.

He looks at me for a moment, eyes too intense for anyone's good. "You too, Campbell. See you on Monday."

I look away, confused by the emphasis he puts on the words. When I look back up, he and K-2P have already gone out of the room.

I'm wistful for the entire metro ride home, simmering with so much pent-up frustration and confusion I can barely sit still. The first thing I do as I get home is to open my bag and search for a note. I'm not sure why I waited until I got home. Why I didn't search for it in the office, the moment Thomas got out. I guess it's become a sort of ritual. Also, these notes feel private. I don't want to read them at work.

But there's no note lining the side of the bag, or tucked away in any of the inside pockets. With a groan of frustration, I go to the couch and capsize the entire contents of the bag on the cushions. No Post-it flies out with them. I check the now-empty bag and there it is, blue paper attached to the bottom.

Made you work for this one. Am I to believe you're becoming fond of my notes?

   Have a great weekend, Campbell.

I hug the small sheet of paper to my chest, smiling like an idiot.

Is this what being courted feels like? Or is Thomas like this with everyone? Is Maria getting notes, too?

Some inexplicable deep instinct tells me that no, she's not getting them.

The notes are innocuous enough; even so, they feel special. Am I special to him?

Do I want to be special?

The honest, terrifying answer is yes!

It hits me with staggering clarity.

I lie back on the couch and let out a delighted, yet despondent sigh. If only the weekend were over already.

13

THOMAS

Late on Saturday morning, I'm still in bed, unwinding after a night out with my old Harvard buddies most of whom now are investment bankers, hedge fund whizzes, or tech entrepreneurs. We went to a few bars and a club, the best New York has to offer. And it should've been a great night. Everywhere we went, women flocked to us, competing for our attention. In the past, I would've been delighted, but not last night. There was only space for one woman in my head. I kept picturing Reese, trying to imagine how she'd comment on the music, the surrounding people, the drinks, the atmosphere.

What music does she like? What was she listening to when I walked in on her stripping? I never asked.

Last night, I also itched to learn how she'd respond to my touch if she were there with me. I missed her sharp wit and sarcastic comebacks.

I missed her.

Her brown eyes. Her smiles and most of all, her scowls. Her pink-tipped locks that I'm dying to slip through my fingers. Not to mention I've been plagued by vivid images of our first encounter, buttocks swaying, bra-cupped boobs, and toned stomach.

I pass a hand over my face, trying to wipe the images away. But it's no use.

That woman is a riddle. After our rocky start, I can tell she's warming up to me and that she, too, felt the spark between us. But also that she's trying to deny the attraction with all she's got and escape the pull. Why?

I roll to the side of the bed and find K-2P hovering next to it, red lights blinking behind his eyes.

"*Oye, tio.*" I jolt in bed. "*Menudo susto me has dado.*"

The red lights blink at me. "What?"

"Sorry, whenever I'm angry or scared the Cuban side of my brain takes over. I said you scared me witless."

"Are you part Cuban?"

"Yeah, my mom."

"So cool." The robot whirls excitedly. "You speak fluent Spanish?"

"Yes, I'm bilingual."

"Will you teach me?"

I pull up on the bed and frown at him. "Don't you just need a Spanish add-in uploaded to your frame to learn a new language?"

"I'd rather learn the traditional way."

"Okay, then. I'll teach you. *Te enseñaré.*"

"Weeeeeee." He blinks his lights with a chirp. "Anything I can do in return?"

"Actually, yes. Could you answer a few questions?"

"I can answer most questions."

"I'm not talking academics; I meant personal questions."

"Uuuuuuh," K-2P hoots. "Are we about to gossip?"

I smile because how can I not? She even made her droid irresistible. "Yeah, you could say so."

"Fire away." If K-2P had knuckles to crack, he'd be cracking them now.

"What do you know about Reese?"

The droid hums as he gathers his info. "She's from the town of Ashland, New Hampshire, and she studied mechanical engineering at MIT on a full scholarship. Reese also has a master's in mechatronics and a PhD in applied robotics."

"What about her family, are they close?"

"No. She's never met her father. He bailed when her mother got pregnant. And her mother isn't exactly a nurturing figure—"

"Not nurturing how?"

"Self-centered, more worried about her boyfriends than her daughter. She calls only when she needs money or something else. Reese has no siblings."

"Friends?"

"Not many, probably none. Only Maria, perhaps? But they don't hang out outside work. Reese thinks it's inappropriate to get too personal with anyone in our department since she's their boss."

Mmm. Is that why she's keeping me at arm's length? Because we work together?

"And why doesn't she have friends outside of work?"

"In school, she always moved ahead faster, graduated sooner than everybody else and that didn't exactly make her Miss Popularity."

I smirk. "Are you quoting her words now?"

"Affirmative." The robot finishes with a satisfied beep.

"Anything else?" I ask him, needing more information.

Another pause followed by another beep as K-2P collects his circuits. "Nope. She takes great pride in her work and is highly dedicated."

K-2P isn't getting the hint so, aware of the shady ethics of drilling the robot for personal information about his maker, I ask outright, "What about past boyfriends?"

"Two of notice. One was a systems engineering professor who turned out to have a secret family on the side. The other was a brainy engineer who couldn't cope with Reese's career advancing faster than his and her making more money." K-2P pauses for a moment to allow me to take in all that he has told me, before finishing with one last piece of vital information: "She hasn't been in any sort of relationship since that last one."

K-2P's answer leaves a sour taste in my mouth. I know what it feels like to be rejected for being who you are, and how unfair that is. So how do I show Reese I'd accept her fully? That her superior intelligence wouldn't be a problem for me. I might have more money, but I'll never have a mind as bright as hers.

My brows crease inward as I process this new insight into my mystery woman. Reese has been hurt before. Maybe that's why she's so determined to negate the spark between us. Or more simply she doesn't want to get entangled in a workplace romance after having sacrificed so much for her career.

But if she's willing to ignore the spark, I'm not. She's the first woman who's made me feel any sort of excitement since a few years back when my ex, Charlotte, wrenched my heart out of my chest, threw it to the ground, and walked all over it with her stiletto heels. I know what it's like to be hurt by someone you love. The pain has a way of seeping into our lives, leaving us broken and battered. I know the depths of that suffering, yet I am also driven by a desire to keep going, to heal, and eventually to find joy again.

Or at least, enough time has passed that I've sufficiently healed to want to try again.

"How long ago did that relationship end?"

"Roughly two years, when she got promoted to head of R&D at Mercer Robotics."

So, the wound is fresher than mine, but not so fresh that she can't be receptive to making a new connection.

Two years is a long time to be alone. I should know, I've only had insignificant trysts in the past four years—my fault probably as my heart has never been in it. But this time it feels different. Reese is different from any other woman I've met. She's someone worth fighting for.

"Do you think she might like me?" I ask, guessing what K-2P's answer will be, but still wanting to hear it.

The droid turns and focuses his lenses on me. "You're not her type."

From the way she looks at me sometimes, I wouldn't be so sure. "How am I not her type?"

Condescending beep. "Can you tell me what a Jacobian Matrix is?"

The word matrix only makes me think of the Keanu Reeves movie. "I guess a full-scale virtual reality construct of the world has nothing to do with it?"

K-2P lets out a beep all too similar to a scoff. "You're not her type." And as if to signal the conversation is over, he wheels backward and turns to exit the bedroom.

I take a deep breath before getting out of bed to follow him.

"What is a Jacobian Matrix?"

I'm not sure robots should be capable of condescension, but that's what K-2P dishes out to me. "The Jacobian Matrix represents the differential relationship between the joint displacements and the resulting end-effector motion of a robot's arm. Does any of that mean anything to you?"

"No, but I can learn..."

"Unless you want to go back to college and earn a degree in mechanical engineering with a specialization in robotics, I don't think so."

I shuffle into the kitchen, busying myself with making coffee. "Okay, how about an opposites attract approach, then? She's dated engineers in the past, and it has never worked out. Maybe I'll be the perfect match for her, no?"

One of K-2P's white lights blinks to life in his dome and he points it at me third-degree style.

"Do you want to just sleep with her or are you interested in more?"

"What are you, her father?"

"You could consider me more like her son."

"Don't worry." I raise my arms defensively. "My intentions are honorable. I can't promise you we will fall in love and live happily ever after, but I can tell you I'm not scared of exploring a potentially serious relationship."

As I say the words aloud, I surprise even myself.

"Well, okay then," the droid says. "You get the benefit of the doubt, but don't hurt her." He wheels to leave the kitchen but not without giving me a threatening beep first.

I slump against the counter and watch the droid roll away until he disappears somewhere in my apartment.

As I stare at the view of a cloudy Manhattan out my window, I wonder since when it has become surprising to want to explore a meaningful relationship. A newfound yearning that's more unexpected than I'm ready to admit.

Probably since Charlotte walked out on me and left me to go be with a "real" man. That stung. Got me jaded about love for a year or four.

With K-2P gone, the kitchen is completely silent, so quiet in fact that the silence is deafening. It's the same eerie stillness that has filled my empty apartment for four years now. The loneliness is almost palpable—a suffocating, invisible fog that's seeping into my lungs, threatening to choke me. In these last few years, my life has started to feel sort of pointless. Working, hitting the town with friends, pulling women, it has all blended into a vapid shell of a life.

I have to give it to the old man, maybe Dad was right when he insisted that I needed a shake. Because for the first time in forever, I'm looking forward to something, and it's Monday morning at work.

But first, I have to survive the next two days. I could call one of my single friends, but all they're interested in is sports and picking up women. The Knicks don't play until later tonight, and I had enough interactions with women I was not interested in last night.

I take my coffee cup and perch on the round dining table, looking out of the window. From this vantage point, I can see endless miles of open sky filled with possibility—a chance for something new and exciting.

I wash my coffee cup in the sink, change into sweats, and head to my building's gym. The usual crowd is there, engrossed in their workouts and oblivious to my presence. I warm up with a light jog and then progress to the lifting machines. As I move through my reps, some of the restless energy from earlier melts away.

After an hour of working out, I know how to spend the afternoon.

I shower and change into nicer clothes before I leave the house.

K-2P stops me at the door. "Leaving?"

"I have to go see my brother, are you going to be okay here on your own?"

"Sure, can I watch TV?"

"Err, yeah, I guess." I turn on the satellite and give him the remote. "We're going to watch the game together later tonight, okay?"

"Sure. My system has calculated a 64.7 per cent probability that the Knicks are going to win."

I lift my arm in a high-five. "Way to go, buddy."

K-2P lifts a mechanic arm and taps his clawed hand on mine.

Then he tries to pick a channel on the TV. He fiddles with the remote, letting out a frustrated beep-beep.

"Are you okay?"

"The buttons are too small for my fingers, but I can download the control app on my frame. Wi-Fi password?"

Not sure if I'm letting the future Skynet take control of the world by connecting him to the internet, I give K-2P the password and exit the house.

* * *

At my brother's penthouse apartment, I'm not the only guest. A beautiful woman is sitting on the opposite side of Gabriel's humongous sectional sofa, cuddling his cat, Latte, and sporting a smudge of chocolate at the corner of her mouth.

I plonk down next to her with a heavy sigh. "Hi, everyone."

"Thomas," Blake, Gabriel's girlfriend, greets me. She's used to me being the brother always in a good mood. Gabriel is the family grump. "What's up with you?"

I contemplate the ceiling before answering. "I've met the woman of my dreams."

Blake frowns. "And that's a bad thing?"

"Yes, since she wants nothing to do with me."

"Honey?" Gabriel turns to Blake. "Did you change the name on the door to The Lonely Hearts Club or something?"

"No."

"Then why are everybody and their mother coming over to complain about their love lives?"

I turn to the woman next to me. "You're here for woes of the heart, too?"

"Well, not exactly, but in a way..."

I nod understandingly and turn to Gabriel and Blake. "You're the happy couple in a grown-up relationship. The least you could do is listen to close family's and..." I glance at the woman, prompting her to clarify her status.

"Best friends," she offers.

"...and best friends' relationship troubles."

"They had sex three times already today," the woman says, supporting my claim.

Gabriel, who I know to be very private with his life, shuffles uncomfortably on the couch and scowls at Blake.

"You told her that?" he accuses.

She waves him off. "Women talk, get over it."

"Only three times, Gabriello?" I tease, using the nickname I know irks him to no end. "You're getting old."

"Quit it, Thomas, before I kick you out of my apartment."

I cup my mouth as if not to be heard by the others and turn to the best friend. "He's joking. I'm his favorite brother." Also, the only one he has. I offer the stranger my hand. "Thomas, by the way."

She shakes it. "Marissa."

"Ah, I've heard about you."

"Likewise," she replies.

I smile in acknowledgment and turn to the other two. "Anyway, I need advice."

"Wait a minute, I was here first," Marissa protests.

"I'm sure your situation can't be worse than mine."

Marissa shares her predicament, admitting the clinic she was having a solo IVF treatment at accidentally made her pregnant with her ex's baby. A non-issue, since she's clearly still in love with the dude and he wants to go all in with her and become the official baby daddy. I call Marissa out on her non-existent problem, and it takes her about two minutes to admit she doesn't have an actual reason not to get back with the doctor except that she's scared. I also manage to swindle her into giving me the cat in the process.

Once Marissa cracks a grin, I wink at her. "See? You're smiling finally. Everything will be all right. But what about me, what do I do guys?"

"How do you know this woman is not interested in you?" Blake asks.

"She told me flat-out on day one not to flirt with her."

"How did you meet her?" Gabriel asks.

"She's supposed to tutor me on robotics, as per Daddy's instructions. He's decided I should replace Proctor once he retires."

"Emmet Proctor?" Gabriel's eyes bulge. "Dad is giving you the robotics division?"

I shrug. "I had the same reaction. Sending a business major to lead a bunch of hardcore engineers is like sending a sheep to lead a pack of wolves."

"And why the pivot?" my brother asks.

"Apparently I have to step up if I want to deserve taking his place one day."

Gabriel low whistles. "You work together with this woman?"

"If you asked her, she'd tell you she's just babysitting me until I become her unworthy boss."

Both women chuckle and hoot at that.

"Hey," I scowl, "what side are you on?"

"That of the woman." Blake smirks evilly, and Marissa nods her approval. "Always."

"So let me get this straight, Dad gives you a new position to make you more responsible and instead, you flirt with his employees?" My brother massages his temples.

"Pretty much."

"Doesn't Mercer Industries have an anti-fraternization policy?" Gabriel insists.

"Anti-fraternization?" My mouth falls open. "That seems a bit extreme. I'm not sure we can tell our employees who to date."

My brother scoffs. "Ah, says the guy who clearly never had to deal with the breakdown of a workplace relationship between employees and the dysfunction that causes. Maybe Dad was right that you need to open your eyes."

"I didn't come here for a lecture. I came for advice."

Blake clears her throat. "What I think your brother was suggesting, albeit with his adorable grumpy tones, is that if such a policy exists, it could be why Reese is keeping her distance."

Ah!

"Here." Gabriel reads from his phone. "Mercer Industries expressively prohibits any romantic or sexual relationships between a supervisor and a subordinate (direct or proximate). This includes, but is not limited to, dating, romantic involvement, and sexual activity."

"Let me see that." Gabriel hands me the phone and I keep reading. "Exceptions: In scenarios where an existing romantic or intimate relationship is present prior to joining Mercer Industries, or when such a relationship develops between two employees who are not in a direct reporting line to each other. It's imperative for these employees to inform their supervisor or the Human Resources department."

"Those exceptions don't apply to you," Marissa notes. "You're going to be her boss."

"*Going to.* Technically I'm not her boss yet. We wouldn't be breaking any rules. And when I eventually became her boss, our relationship could fall into the already existing category."

"That's a stretch at best." Gabriel keeps being his usual optimistic self.

"Listen guys, I won't be her boss for another fifteen months. Anything could happen in that time; we could go on a date and decide we don't like each other. It could all taper off in no time."

"I don't know," Blake says. "You don't have a taper-off-in-no-time face right now."

"And how can you read my face so well?"

"You share a feature or two with this guy over here." She pats Gabriel's thigh.

"And what is my face telling you?"

"That's the Mercer endgame face, I'm afraid."

"Then I'm not going to let a stupid policy dictate who I can date." I throw my arms in the air, almost dislodging the cat, and turn to the women. "I should keep pursuing this, right?"

"Pursue how?" Marissa asks.

"Were you coming on to her?" Blake follows. "You're going to be her boss; you can't put her in that position."

"As Reese already pointed out, but the circumstances of our first meeting were slightly... unusual."

"Unusual how?" Marissa asks.

"I walked in on her doing a striptease in her office."

"Didn't you knock?" Blake asks appalled.

"I did, but she had headphones on, didn't hear me, and her droid told me to come in..."

Gabriel chuckles. "If you stumbled upon her having a dance in her office with headphones on, you're toast, man. Trust me, I speak from experience."

He gives Blake such a loving look it's revolting. I meet Marissa's gaze and she seems to agree. She crosses her eyes as if to say, *Gah, these two.*

I try to refocus the attention on me. "It doesn't matter how the meet-cute went. But long story short, I felt an immediate spark between us and was ready to ask her on a first date on the spot. But she's doing her best to keep me at arm's length and pretend the spark doesn't exist."

Blake frowns. "Are you sure you're not the only one who felt this alleged spark?"

"Oh, no, she felt it all right. She's just hell-bent on ignoring it."

"Because of the policy?" Marissa asks.

"Could be. But her droid also told me she got hurt in the past. And, yeah, that I'm going to become her boss doesn't simplify things."

"Mmm." Gabriel grabs his chin. "This is the first time I've heard you being enthusiastic about a woman since..." He stops.

I scratch the back of my head. "Since Charlotte? We can speak the name out loud."

"Oh," Blake says. "Is that the woman you had to grab him and take him to the mountain cabin to forget?"

"The very one," Gabriel confirms.

"You make it sound like I was about to slice my veins," I protest. "I wasn't that upset."

Gabriel mock-coughs into his fist. "If you call not showering for days, refusing to get out of the house, and nearly stopping eating not being *that* upset, then I was wrong to intervene."

I flutter my hands in the air, this time disturbing the cat so much he goes back to Marissa. "Regardless of how heartbroken I was or wasn't, Charlotte is in the past. It's Reese I'd like to focus on."

"I'm sorry," Marissa says. "But if she's told you she's not interested, there's not much you can do. She has to make the next move or you'll come across as an office creep who gives unwarranted attention to women who don't want it."

"I haven't been flirting since she shut me down."

Blake gives me a penetrating stare. "Not at all?"

"I left her a few Post-it notes, but nothing creepy, I swear."

"And how did she respond?" Marissa.

"She didn't."

"Did she even get them?" Blake.

"Yeah, I'm sure."

"How can you be sure?" Gabriel.

"We've been engaged in a silent staring battle not to mention them all week."

"So, she's flirting back?" Blake again. "Sort of?"

"Yeah, in a way."

Gabriel gives me a long stare. "If you're really interested, play the long game, brother."

"Meaning?"

"Let her get to know you. If something is meant to happen, it will. But she has to make the first move." Gabriel lets the message sink in before he continues. "Keep your boundaries."

"And if I do that, it's going to be okay with the policy?"

"No, you're still going to make a total fustercluck of things." Gabriel sighs. "So make sure she's really worth it before you do anything rash."

I accept my brother is right. I usually go after what I want hard and fast, but with Reese, I can't. The whole office power unbalance dynamic is against me. I can't push her. She has to come to me.

"Can I keep sending her the notes?"

Marissa scratches the cat behind the ears. "Are you 100 per cent sure they're not creepy?"

"Yes."

The two women exchange a stare and shrug.

"Then unless she asks you to stop, I don't see why not," Blake decrees.

I crack my knuckles. "Okay, then I have to up my poetry game."

And fast, seeing how I'm on the clock. I only have three months to make Reese fall for me, and I don't have a second to waste.

14

REESE

I am not checking out my reflection in the dark computer screen to see if any of the mascara I put on this morning has smudged. I'm not. If anything, I'm checking the blackened screen for any blemishes before I turn it on. Nothing is more disturbing than greasy fingerprints.

And it's a total coincidence that I put on my most flattering leggings with a bit of butt support to come to work. They just happened to be on the top of the pile this morning when I dressed. As was the cute fluffy rainbow sweatshirt I'm wearing on top. It's just a fluke that my clothes are prettier and less baggy this morning.

I'm also not waiting with a knot of anxiety in my belly for a certain tall, handsome, charming billionaire to walk his way into my office.

I'm *so* not.

A shadow walks past the opaque glass door, causing my heart to positively stop in my chest.

"Morning, boss." Maria pokes her head in.

"M-morning," I stutter back, still half-shocked with broken

expectations. And I might have to bring a portable CPR device to work if my heart is going to stop every time someone pokes their head through my door.

Maria's eyes narrow on me as she saunters in. She reaches my desk and plants her palms on the flat surface, leaning forward to get a better look at my face. "Are you wearing *makeup*?"

She stresses the word makeup as if I were Cruella de Vil wearing Dalmatian *puppies*. "It's just a little mascara." I wave her off.

"Hmph." She stands tall and crosses her arms over her chest with a satisfied pout.

"What?" I scowl.

"Oh, nothing. I just find it funny that you're wearing your hair down, have makeup on your face, and look"—she circles a hand toward my general chest area—"like you made an effort."

"Please, these were just the first clothes I found in my closet this morning."

Maria throws her head back and laughs.

My scowl deepens. "What are you laughing at?"

"My gosh, boss, you're such a terrible liar."

"I'm not lying."

Maria circles the desk and sits on it on my side. Then she reaches for my collar and pulls something off. "The price tag still attached to the cute sweats begs to differ."

I stare at the cardboard label, equally appalled Maria caught me in a lie and relieved it wasn't Thomas.

"What?" I squirm under Maria's amused gaze. "I bought the sweater on Saturday and dropped it on top of the pile. That's the only reason I'm wearing it."

Maria's grin widens. "It's okay, boss, if Thomas Mercer was looking at me the way he looks at you, I'd dress for work in much more scandalous clothes."

I roll my eyes, but the warmth on my cheeks tells a different story. Maria always knows how to push my buttons. "Can we please focus? This is still a workplace. Did you want to discuss anything work-related?"

Maria taps a finger on her chin. "Are the succession plan for the company and his delicious buttocks considered work-related?"

"No."

"Then, no." Maria hops off the desk and heads for the door. "I'll leave you alone so you can have a private Monday morning meet and greet."

My cheeks flame even hotter as Maria sashays out of the room. Private meet and greet? How does she come up with this stuff?

I drop my head in my hands; it's only been a week. How am I going to survive eleven more?

"Not a morning person?" A deep voice makes me jolt upright.

As I lift my head, I see Thomas standing there, looking as attractive as ever in jeans and another fitted sweater.

"Good morning, Reese," he says with a smile.

"Hi," I choke out, cursing myself for sounding so breathless.

"I hope I'm not interrupting anything," he adds, tilting his head.

"No, no, of course not," I reply quickly. "I'm just in severe need of caffeine."

Thomas's smile widens. "Good thing I came prepared, then." He lifts his arms slightly and drops one of the two paper cups he's holding on my desk.

I was so dazed looking at his face that I hadn't even noticed the coffee cups in his hands.

"Thanks," I croak, taking my cup and lifting it in a mock cheer.

I take a sip, expecting a plain Americano, maybe with some added milk and sugar, but my eyes widen as a perfect blend of creamy, nutty sweetness hits my palate.

"How did you know I drink honey almond milk flat whites?"

Thomas tilts his head to the side. "I might've had a little tip-off."

K-2P wheels to the corner of the office where Thomas's desk is located, muttering, "From me, the droid you once cared about." The robot drops into his charging station, adding, "My weekend was fantastic, thanks for asking."

I roll my eyes. "I take it you two had a blast."

Thomas studies me in a way that makes my throat go dry. "It was *interesting...*"

What does he mean by that? I glare at K-2P. What did the little snitch tell Thomas about me? He knows way too much. I should've never sent them home together. I'm about to downright ask when Thomas precedes me, saying, "So, who am I shadowing today?"

I let out a little exhale of relief that at least he doesn't expect us to spend the day together in this confined space. "I was thinking Ari."

"Oh, the one in charge of making robots for dummies, got it." He drops his messenger bag by his desk and walks back to the door, pausing on the threshold. "Cute sweats, by the way."

And then he's gone, taking all the air in my lungs with him.

I'm about to turn to K-2P to grill him, but the robot is already scurrying after his new best friend.

Okay, then. To be fair, I'd betray my maker and go after the hot billionaire if I were him, too.

* * *

The morning proceeds mostly smoothly until a Google Alert lands in my inbox a few hours later with an announcement from our biggest competitor, Bios Torc Solutions, stating the company has started a hand-guided programming research and cooperation program with Caltech.

Darn, being first to market in this space is essential. We need to secure a patent before they do. So far, we've been the only US-based company who's looking into this, but with BTS entering the game, the competition ought to light a fire under us.

I print out the press release and bring the papers to Ari like I would on any other normal day. That she and Thomas are working together is no factor in my eagerness to discuss the news with our industrial robots team leader.

I approach Ari's workstation where Thomas is trying to instruct the robot on what to do without using code, and the robot is responding in the usual way of getting lost after the first initial hits.

I clear my throat to let them know I'm here. "Hey."

"Reese, hi." Ari turns to me with a friendly smile.

Thomas's smile is everything *but* friendly. I'd call it belligerently charming.

"This just landed in my inbox." I hand the press release to Ari.

She takes one look and low whistles.

"Bad news?" Thomas asks.

The team leader answers him while still shuffling through the pages. "If you consider someone else potentially beating us to the punch of hand-programmed robots and us having wasted two years of research, then, yes, it's bad news." Then she looks up at me. "Do we know who their expert on the modeling of kinematics and dynamics parameters and errors is?"

"No, but I can fish for some intel."

"Yeah, let me know; those Californian hippies don't joke around. If they made the announcement, it means they're close."

"What's the main issue with this project?" Thomas asks. "Why doesn't it work?"

Ari slightly flares her nostrils. "If we knew what was wrong with it, we'd already have fixed it."

Thomas doesn't seem affected by the slightly snippy reply. "What I meant was, what are you observing, which results are not coming back as expected?"

"It's not precise. I teach it what to do by showing, guiding the robot. The end effectors and sensors measure and record the positions and should be able to replicate them." Ari shakes her head. "It works on the smaller co-bots—"

"Co-bots?" Thomas asks.

"Collaborative bots: robots that are supposed to work alongside humans. But this big guy"—Ari pats the robotic arm—"whenever the operator attempts to impose an impedance control that is appreciably dissimilar to the inherent hardware dynamics, the results are unstable."

I try to explain the problem in more human terms. "We're adding redundant degrees of freedom to compensate for the inertia." I stare at the big metallic arm. "Based on our calculations, the redundancy we're applying should be enough to get a precise result, but it's not."

Thomas studies me and then the big robot. "You mean redundancy works on the smaller robotic arms but not this one."

"Exactly."

K-2P, who's been listening strangely quietly to the entire exchange, chooses this moment to offer his wisdom. "Not all machines can have a superior AI like mine."

I brush his dome. "Yeah, you're the smartest robot I know."

K-2P rears away from me, probably still offended at my lack of devotion, and circles behind me to place himself by Thomas's side. Still, as he goes, he snickers, "Are those your butt-lifting leggings?"

Inevitably, Thomas's gaze drops to my rear end, and when his eyes lift again to meet mine, I want to crawl under the nearest desk and never come back out again.

Thomas's gorgeous eyes twinkle and his lips twitch, but he abstains from making any comment.

Trying to maintain a morsel of dignity, I turn to Ari instead.

"We need to come up with a solution before BTS beats us to the finish line."

Ari nods in agreement. "I'll call a team meeting, see if anyone can brainstorm potential solutions or a fresh approach."

I dare a side-peek at Thomas. His eyes are still calibrated on me. I look away, hoping my cheeks don't look as red as they feel hot. "I'll leave you to it, then."

I give them a curt nod before turning to leave. As I walk toward my office, I try to keep a normal pace, not to make it look like I'm properly fleeing the premises. But the almost certainty that Thomas is looking at my retreating, artificially uplifted behind still puts a spring in my steps.

Thomas goes to lunch with Ari's team, and I'm happy I'm not invited. *So happy.* In fact, I don't see him again until the end of the workday.

He shuffles into the office, looking slightly disheveled after an entire day on the floor.

"Tired?" I ask.

Whether or not he is, he flashes me a smile. One so warm it lights up the entire room. "Ari is intense." He points a finger to his head. "Lots of information to process."

Before I can stop myself, I flirt with him. "*Brain* not what it used to be?" And the stress I put on the word brain leaves no interpretation to the double entendre.

Thomas stares at me, intensely silent for a few heartbeats, eyes smoldering. I should back down, look away, but I can't. I couldn't take my eyes off him if someone pointed a gun at my head and told me to choose: stare at him or die. I'd go a lucky woman.

Without a word, Thomas bends to collect his messenger bag from the floor. When he returns upright, his eyes snatch mine once again. "*Brain*'s working just fine." His dimples make an appearance as he smiles. "Could always use a little exercise."

I swallow to resist offering to become his new personal trainer.

He knocks on the doorframe. "Night, Campbell. See you tomorrow."

Once he's gone, I sag back in my chair, crossing my arms on the desk and dropping my head on top. I stay that way until a beep alerts me to K-2P's presence next to me.

"Why are you so distressed?" he asks.

"I might have a crush."

The little droid emits a low beep that sounds like an awww. "And what's the problem? The basic human need to copulate shouldn't be something to be ashamed of."

"I don't want to copulate with Thomas," I chide. And before K-2P can call me out, I add, "And you can't repeat any part of this conversation to him. This is a private talk between you and me."

"Pity, because he seems really eager to copulate with you. Couldn't stop asking questions about you all weekend."

"What questions?"

K-2P gives me his version of a shrug. "Sorry, those were private conversations. I can't repeat any part of them back to you."

Impertinent, insufferable humanoid piece of metal. "I could extract your memory processors and read for myself."

K-2P plugs into his charging station. "I'd scrub them before you could access my frame."

"Shouldn't you be loyal to me?"

"Not when you're being dull."

"How am I being dull?"

"By not giving Thomas a chance; he's a wonderful human."

With that scathing nugget of wisdom, K-2P shuts down, and I know better than to try to get him to turn back on. I don't need dating advice from a machine.

15

REESE

Still, for the entire metro ride home, I dwell over K-2P's assessment of Thomas. My droid has always been distrustful of my previous boyfriends and with good reason. I'm surprised he'd champion Thomas.

But maybe K-2P is a better judge of human character than I am. Is Thomas really one of the good ones? From what I've seen so far, sure. Maybe he doesn't take things seriously enough, but that wouldn't be a drawback in a relationship. I'd be earnest enough for the both of us, and having someone taper my doom and gloom attitude would be a welcome novelty.

I'm aware of being too much of a buttoned-up worrier. So, yeah, someone with an easygoing personality could help me get out of my shell. But that's not the issue, is it?

No, the problem is that Thomas is going to become my boss soon. Already, as a very young woman in a male-dominated field, I have to work twice as hard to get any credit. But I *have* worked twice as hard. Trice as hard. All my life. And over the years, I've built a reputation for myself.

Now everyone gives me the recognition I deserve. The people in my department are happy to follow my lead—at least the ones who are left. A few of the oldies handed in their resignations when I was appointed head of research and development, refusing to report to a woman under thirty.

But those who stayed, the new hires I brought in, and the other department heads respect me now. But were I to openly date the CEO, assuming Nolan Mercer was willing to make an exception to the anti-fraternization policy for his son, that would all change in a heartbeat. I'd become the gold digger trying to sleep her way to the top. None of my accomplishments would be my own anymore.

Already, things get vicious when I have to compete for budget allocations with the other directors; imagine if I were sleeping with the man making those kinds of decisions. No, Nolan Mercer would never allow that. He'd probably suggest I transfer somewhere else, but I don't want to. And anyway, Thomas is heir to the kingdom. I could be accused of getting favoritism in any role or division at Mercer Industries. Plus, being director of R&D in robotics is my literal dream job. I can't risk it for a relationship that might fail like all my previous ones. What would I be left with? A broken heart and a crappy job?

But even if Mercer Sr. didn't force me to change role, a company is a vicious gossip mill. It'd grind my reputation to smithereens. And I've worked too hard to throw it all away on a handsome face and a pair of pretty eyes—smoldering as they might be.

Right.

I get home and sit on the couch to eat a depressing tub of plain yogurt.

No matter that keeping my distance from Thomas is the smart choice, it doesn't change the fact that I'm attracted to him and that the next eleven weeks are going to be pure torture.

As I sit there, feeling sorry for myself and licking the spoon after the last mouthful of yogurt, a thought suddenly barrels into my head. I drop the empty tub and the spoon on the coffee table and surge toward the entrance hall where I abandoned my bag on the floor.

I rummage inside, searching like a crazed person looking for an antidote to a poison they just ingested. Only the thing poisoning my heart is the impossibility of having anything with Thomas, and I'm not sure what I find in my bag will cure me of that disease.

The handwritten blue note could very well inject fresh toxins into my system.

Still, I sit on the carpet, sagging against the wall and hugging the note to my chest before even reading it.

I wait for my heart to stop beating so fast it seems to want out of my chest before I finally lower the note and drink in every word.

I would comment on your leggings today, but since we're strictly friends, I'll abstain.

The man is a tease, and he's worn me out, prompting me to do something I'd promised myself I wouldn't do. I search my desk for a Post-it block and a pen and craft a reply:

This is a special waiver; you can comment on my leggings.

The next morning, as soon as Thomas exits the office to shadow yet another team leader, I get up from behind my desk and tiptoe to the door. I poke my head out to make sure no one's headed this way and close it. The blinds have been down since my striptease last week, so I'm free to sneak to Thomas's desk and hide the note in his bag.

He won't read it until tonight. And I'll have to wait until tomorrow evening to read his reply. The wait is going to be excruciating. And the game I'm playing is extremely dangerous. But I can't help myself. For the first time in my life, I'm acting recklessly, I'm willingly playing with fire. But, gosh, getting burned never felt so tempting.

When I arrive home that night, I find another note in my bag. It says:

Why is your hair pink at the tips?

I grab a pen and write my reply on a separate note:

Because pink is fun.

The next morning when I arrive at the office, I know Thomas has found my note from the day before from the way his eyes linger on me a little longer than usual, smoldering away. I pretend not to notice and go about my day like an innocent little engineer who's not secretly flirting with her future boss.

But that night as I arrive home, my fingers are itching to read his note, and I'm delighted when I see it's on the longer side.

Thought I had to lure you out with a direct question, but I see that's no longer necessary. Thank you for the special waiver allowing me to comment on your legwear. I wanted to say that while your butt looked truly spectacular in those leggings, it didn't need any extra support. PS. I still want to know why pink. PPS. Are we still being friendly?

He doesn't know I already answered his question, so I tease him a little.

Keep up, Mercer, you already have the answer. And that's all you had to say about my leggings? Yes! Still being friendly. Friends can compliment each other's appearances. Like you can say I have a nice butt, and I can say you have pretty eyes without crossing a line.

Thursday night's note is brief but searing:

My idea of fun and yours are pretty different.

I tease some more:

What's your idea of fun? Do you need a special waiver to elaborate? Have a nice weekend, Mercer.

He'll read this tomorrow, on Friday night.

And as the moment arrives, I take out my own Friday night note filled with trepidation:

Just pretty? I thought my eyes were smoldering. And the things I have to say about your butt wouldn't just cross the line, they'd obliterate it. So my hands are tied here. Have a good weekend, Campbell...

I grab a notepad and recompose our two separate threads of conversation. I stick his notes to the sheet of paper and write the answers I gave below. Once I'm finished, I re-read the first one.

Why is your hair pink at the tips?

Because pink is fun.

My idea of fun and yours are pretty different.

What's your idea of fun? Do you need a special waiver to elaborate? Have a nice weekend, Mercer.

And then the second.

This is a special waiver; you can comment on my leggings.

Thought I had to lure you out with a direct question, but I see that's no longer necessary. Thank you for the special waiver allowing me to comment on your legwear. I wanted to say that while your butt looked truly spectacular in those leggings, it didn't need any extra support. PS. I still want to know why pink. PPS. Are we still being friendly?

Keep up, Mercer, you already have the answer. And that's all you had to say about my leggings? Yes! Still being friendly. Friends can compliment each other's appearances. Like you can say I have a nice butt, and I can say you have pretty eyes without crossing a line.

Just pretty? I thought my eyes were smoldering. And the things I have to say about your butt wouldn't just cross the line, they'd obliterate it. So my hands are tied here. Have a good weekend, Campbell…

Yeah, I'm afraid that line is already wobbling dangerously. Good thing next week I'll be mostly gone to a conference in Rome. I leave on Wednesday, 1 November, so I'll be at the office only Monday and Tuesday, which is great as I won't miss Halloween. We don't have an official company party, but 31 October is still a fun day at work. Everyone dresses up and, at the end, we vote on the best costume. The winner earns bragging rights for the entire year, a ring of power replica that gets the champion a boon from each of us, and an ugly-ass trophy with the words "Top Nerd" etched on the base that they get to display at their workstation until the next vote.

Last year, I earned second place dressed up like a ghostbuster. This year, I'm planning for something slightly more feminine. I was thinking of going as Rey from *Star Wars*.

I wonder what Thomas will dress up as.

16

THOMAS

Friday evening I'm alone at home. Alone if you don't consider the droid currently exploring the depths of my apartment—as if something significant might've changed from last weekend—and softly beeping in the background.

Tonight, I didn't even try to go out with my usual crowd of friends. I'm just not in the right head space. What would've been the point? Go to bars I've already been to a million times? See the same faces I see every time? Talk about the same inconsequential stuff? Being hit on by women who don't have eyes of the clearest amber brown, a tumble of dark locks that end in pink tips, and a brain so amazingly sharp no one can keep up?

Been there, done that. I'm over it.

As I sit on the couch in front of the dark TV screen, I flip Reese's last note through my fingers over and over again. I stare at the barely legible words crafted in the worst handwriting I've ever seen. Cursive letters curl in on themselves in jagged, too-compressed lines that are barely interpretable—both literally and figuratively. She's told me not to flirt and then she's giving me waivers to do it?

What's your idea of fun? Do you need a special waiver to elaborate? Have a nice weekend, Mercer.

How do I reply? Waiver or not, I can't give her any of the answers I'm itching to pen. I compose a million opening lines in my head and scratch each one as potentially inappropriate, crass, or downright obscene.

When I can't bear it any longer, I stand up, wish K-2P a good night, and go to my bedroom. I stick the note on the door of my closet together with the others, so they're the first thing I see in the morning when I get dressed. No matter the demanding challenges of upping my robotics savviness, going to work has never felt less of a chore.

It's the weekends that suck.

Once in bed, I take forever to get to sleep, and even when I do, it's a disturbed rest. So much so that I sleepwalk through all of Saturday. Partly because I'm tired, and partly because I don't know what to do with myself.

When Sunday morning comes, I'm even grateful for having to go to my parents' for brunch. At least I'll kill a couple of hours there.

But when I arrive at my parents' penthouse, I'm utterly flabbergasted when I find Gabriel already there, holding Blake's hand as they sit on the couch. The couch that is usually reserved for me.

This is unprecedented. My brother has never, *ever* brought a woman to a family event. And I can count the ones he introduced to my parents on the fingers of one hand. But Blake is different, she has been from the start.

"Thomas." Mom stands up to greet me with a crushing hug, then she pulls back, studying my face. "How's the new job? Is the new position stressing you out?"

I flash her a smile. "To the contrary, I feel revitalized."

"Happy to hear, son." My dad stands, too, and pats me on the shoulder, giving it a gentle squeeze. "Are you finding the R&D department stimulating?"

Gabriel coughs from the couch, getting up and pulling Blake along. "Bet he's plenty stimulated."

He's giving me shit about admitting I like the department head, so I discreetly flip him behind my father's back. In response, he scratches his eyebrow with his middle finger. Blake smiles while simultaneously rolling her eyes.

"It's challenging but rewarding," I tell my dad.

I'm not proud that my enthusiasm for the new job is not strictly professionally driven, but I couldn't have found a better incentive than wanting to impress Reese to up my game. Not that my average mind could ever make an impression on her. But I sure want to show her I care about her work, that she won't have to regret Emmet Proctor retiring, and that I can be a great CEO as well.

Mom steers us toward the dining room, and we sit at our usual positions except this time, Blake and Gabriel share the long side of the table opposite mine.

Dad brings around a bottle of champagne and uncorks it with a loud pop. The cork flies to the chandelier, making the crystals tingle before landing in a corner while Dad pours the bubbly liquid into high-stemmed glasses and passes them around.

Blake tries to refuse hers. "I shouldn't drink; I have a ballet class to teach in a few hours."

"Just a sip," my mom encourages, and Blake reluctantly accepts the glass.

"A toast," Dad says once everyone has a glass, raising his. "Blake, welcome to the family. We thought we'd never see this one settled down and we couldn't be more honored to have you here with us today."

Blake blushes, and Gabriel gives her hand a reassuring squeeze above the table.

"To Blake," my mom chimes in. "May you have a long and happy relationship with our son."

"To Blake," I echo, lifting my glass. "May you survive being saddled with the family grump." I tilt my flute toward Gabriel.

Everyone laughs, while my brother, true to his reputation, scowls.

We all take a sip of champagne, but I notice how Blake discreetly spits hers right back into her glass. I raise my eyebrows and look up at my brother. He's watching me watching her, and his eyes simmer with a silent threat—*don't you dare say a word*. My jaw slacks open.

Blake is pregnant?

And then, just because I'm an ass, I decide to rock my brother's boat a little.

I wait for our maid to serve the salads and for everyone to have gotten a few forkfuls down before I say, "Blake, welcome to the family again. Do you plan on having a big one?"

"A big what?" she asks, an innocent little lamb taking the bait.

"A big family," I say, smirking. "Gabriel has always wanted many kids."

"Is it true, Gabriel?" My mom frowns. "Why is this the first I hear of this, sweetheart?"

Gabriel's nostrils flare. "Because he's just being a smartass."

In the meantime, Blake has lost the ability to speak and her cheeks match the shade of the tomatoes in our salad. I wink at her and go back to eating the food on my plate.

But now that I've poked the bear, Gabriel won't just let me sit quietly and enjoy my lunch.

"So, Thomas," Gabriel says, all fake politeness. "What's the best part of the new position? Met anyone interesting?"

"I was pleasantly surprised; R&D is totally not what I *knocked it up* to be."

"Why? Has robotics *seduced* you?"

"It sure is a field *gravid* with opportunities."

At this point, Blake grabs her glass of water and downs it in a few long gulps.

"What about your co-workers?" Gabriel goes for the throat. "Anyone in particular you *fraternized* with?"

Dad frowns. "Boys, what's going on?"

With matching innocent grins, we turn toward our dad, saying in unison, "Nothing, Dad."

He rolls his eyes, while my mom reaches over the table to squeeze Blake's hand. "At least now I'm not alone in having to deal with their shenanigans."

Blake chuckles in response. "I don't know how you managed with these two when they were little terrors."

My mom winks. "We have an air horn for emergencies."

The entire table laughs, and after that, the meal proceeds with no further covert taunting between me and my brother.

Gabriel, Blake, and I leave the house together and pause to say goodbye on the curb.

I drag them a safe distance from the doorman, who's a notorious gossip, and say, "Guess congratulations are in order?"

Blake flushes. "You can't tell anyone. We literally found out only yesterday. Before we tell people, we want to make sure everything is okay because a lot of pregnancies—"

"Relax," I interrupt the nervous rant. "Your secret is safe with me." I pull her into a hug and pat her shoulders in mock pity. "But I'm sorry you're going to be stuck with the family grump for all of eternity and a minion replica, too."

Blake's smile is radiant as she pulls back. "Oh, I can live with that."

I squeeze my brother's shoulder next. "Congratulations, old man."

He gives me a nod and a somewhat appreciative grunt in reply.

"How's it going with your super smart lady?" Blake asks next.

I can't help the smile that pulls at my lips. "She's started responding to my notes."

"You finally discussed them?"

Hands shoved in my pockets, I roll on the balls of my feet. "No, she's sending secret notes in response, but we never acknowledge them other than in writing."

"Oh, that's so romantic. Is she flirty in the responses?"

I keep smiling like an idiot. "Yeah, definitely."

Blake smiles, then scowls. "But you're keeping your messages strictly friendly, right? Remember, she has to make the first move."

I think of the million inappropriate responses I want to give to Reese's last message and sigh. "Yeah, I'm keeping it friendly. Totally PG-13." Then with a wink, I add, "Except for when she gives me waivers."

"She does?"

"Yep."

Blake's eyes flit to Gabriel and back to me, her face positively glowing with love and affection for my brother. "I'm sure she'll come around; the Mercer men have a way of being irresistible."

She ruffles my brother's hair and I'm shocked by the look of pure adoration on his face as he grabs her hand and kisses her knuckles.

That's what I want. That's what I'll fight to get.

* * *

Sunday night, as I'm sitting in front of the coffee table surrounded by crumpled Post-it notes, K-2P wheels into the room and asks, "Can I talk to you about my Halloween costume?"

I lift my gaze to the little robot. "You're dressing up?"

"Yeah, you have to as well. It's a longstanding tradition at the office to go in full costume on the thirty-first."

"Really?"

Condescending beep. "Of course, don't tell me you didn't know?"

"How was I supposed to know?"

"Fair enough. Anyway, my costume. I was thinking of keeping it simple and just getting cat ears, whiskers, and perhaps a tail. What do you think?"

"Seems like an excellent idea. You know what Reese is dressing up as?"

"She hasn't told me, but from her breaktime Google searches I have a pretty good idea."

I lift a finger. "Hold that thought, we're going to discuss it in a second. But first, there's something I need to finish."

I grab a fresh Post-it note, suddenly very inspired on what to write.

17

REESE

I'm spending my lunch break locked in a bathroom stall with contraband stationery, trying *and failing* to come up with a message to sneak into Thomas's messenger bag.

I should've written it at home when I had all weekend to think of something. But after obsessing over what to say for two days straight, I couldn't draft anything half-decent. So, I thought maybe coming to the office and getting a little visual inspiration would help—Thomas delivered, strutting into the lab looking as impossibly gorgeous as ever.

Ideally, I should tone things down from where we've left them on Friday. Both our messages were bordering on outright flirting. But I also figured that since this week we'll exchange only two notes, I can keep the flirtation levels up to at least a Thursday if not a full-fledged, end-of-the-week, going-to-make-you-obsess-all-weekend Friday scale.

But what do I write?

I stare at a pic of his last message on my phone.

Just pretty? I thought my eyes were smoldering. And the things I have to say about your butt wouldn't just cross the line, they'd obliterate it. So my hands are tied here. Have a great weekend, Campbell...

Should I make a bondage joke about his hands being tied?
Nah, too much.
Comment on the alleged smolderiness of his eyes?
The guy has an already big-enough ego as is.
I could tease him about something else entirely, but I can't come up with anything good. My brain is wiped out. Blank.
I lean my head backward against the stall door, grimacing in frustration. Why is it so hard to write a message that's witty and flirty but not *too* flirty? I bite my lip and tap the pen on the paper. Just as I'm about to give up, inspiration strikes. I grab the pen and quickly write:

I hope you had a great weekend despite the lack of smoldering eyes compliments. I survived without butt-related ones.

Not stellar, but good enough. Only the note needs a finishing line. I bite the back of the pen... mmm...

If you want, I can add a flattery drive to K-2P to fully stroke your ego over the weekends.

It's not the best, but I can't come up with anything better and I actually have to grab a bite to eat if I don't want to pass out mid-afternoon from low blood sugar, so this will have to do.
I slip the note into my agenda to be planted in Thomas's messenger bag later and exit the stall. While I'm washing my hands, Maria enters the restroom. She's late to her lunch break as

well, so we decide to grab a quick hot dog from a cart outside. Despite it being late October, the temperature outdoors is mild, so Maria and I sit on a sunny bench to eat.

"Nice nail art," I comment, noticing her elaborate black and white polish.

"Thanks, boss, it goes with my costume for tomorrow."

"Let me guess," I say. "Wednesday Addams?"

Maria looks at me in mock shock. "What gave it away?"

I stare at the nail with "resting witch face" written white on black, the one that looks like a high-collared white shirt under a black blazer, and the one with a spiderweb.

I take in the remaining nails on her right hand, one white and one black. "You'd only need black tresses on that one." I point to the white one, and then at the black one. "And white WA initials to be any more obvious."

She smirks. "I was planning on adding those features tonight." Then her smirk widens. "What do you think the hot shot is coming as?"

I shrug, not wanting to give away how much I've obsessed over the same question. "Probably something obnoxiously wholesome like Captain America."

"Uuu-huu," Maria hoots. "I wouldn't mind seeing the big boss in a skin-tight body suit. Bet he wouldn't even have to add muscle foam pads." A pause. "Or crotch ones."

I roll my eyes. "Maria!"

"No, you're right. The selling point would probably be in the rear end."

"You're impossible." I shake my head at her and take another bite of my hot dog.

"Fine, fine," she relents with a chuckle. "I'm just saying, it wouldn't be the worst sight."

I laugh. "I'll try not to picture it."

Maria grins. "Good luck with that."

We finish our hot dogs and head back to the office building where the rest of the day passes without further mentions of Thomas Mercer's anatomical perfection or any more Halloween costume speculations.

Thomas drops in for a quick goodbye after another tour with one of my team leaders and goes home, leaving my chest in its usual fluttery state.

That night in my apartment, I check my bag and get the familiar thrill when I spot the blue note at the bottom. I read it and throw my head back laughing.

> *I can't believe you didn't tell me about Halloween's special dress code. If your droid hadn't told me, I could've come to work as the only asshole in civilian clothes. Mean, Campbell.*

I don't compose a reply straight away. First, I want to see what his costume will be tomorrow.

18

REESE

The next morning I'm sipping the traditional pumpkin spice latte —every year I have them delivered for the entire office alongside breakfast treats—and chatting with Maria at her station while K-2P is distributing the anonymous forms to vote on the best costume.

But my brain is only half into the conversation. My gaze keeps shifting to the lab's entrance, waiting for Thomas to make his appearance.

Maria distracts me with a question. "Boss, do you think we can improve our linear time-invariant control algorithm?"

"And how do you propose to do that? We spent a year perfecting it, how can we get it any more perfect?"

"Change the matrix of the set system output in future time."

"How?"

"If we change the control increment as state quantity, we could get an optimized target function."

Now she has my full attention. "We could set constraints," I reason. "And then solve the matrix with quadratic programming."

Maria's eyes brighten and she drops her latte to jot notes on a pad. "So that after solving the equation for the control increment sequence in future time, the system could predict the future output based on current information. That's brilliant."

I'm alerted to a shift in the festive lab's mood by the room plunging into a sudden silence. Even Maria drops her pen and stares at the door, mouth gaping.

I turn to the lab's entrance where a tall, dark, cloaked figure is striding into the lab, heading straight for me. He's wearing an all-black costume composed of a padded long-sleeved shirt, high-waisted pants, and a hooded cloak billowing behind him. His face is concealed by a battered black combat helmet inlaid with silver. The battle gear of the Knights of Ren.

Thomas is Kylo Ren... and I'm Rey.

I wait for his approach, unable to swallow, my throat cotton dry.

As he gets closer, my heart beats faster. He stops in front of me and removes his helmet, revealing his handsome face. My eyes widen as I drink him in—the intense gaze, the chiseled jawline, and those full lips. He smirks at my reaction, most probably too aware of the effect he has on me.

"Rey, huh?" he says in a low voice, barely above a whisper. "What are the chances?"

I immediately glare at the droid shuffling through the lab. *Pretty darn high if a cyber mole is involved.*

"Kylo," I respond, trying to keep my voice steady.

"Nice costume," he says, his eyes scanning me from head to toe.

I blush at his words but quickly recover. "You don't look so bad yourself."

Then, rather anticlimactically, Thomas smiles and asks, "Is there a latte also for me?"

"I'll get it for you, hot shot," Maria hurries to say.

As she brushes past me, she whispers in my ear from the side of her mouth, "I've nothing against superheroes, but if he doesn't look darn sexy in that villain costume."

Even if I couldn't agree more, I still roll my eyes.

Then she goes to fetch a pumpkin spice latte and hands it to Thomas, teasing, "Is that a lightsaber in your pocket?"

For a split second, my gaze drops to his crotch before I realize Maria is talking about a pocket on the inside of his cloak. I'm a total pervert.

I quickly avert my eyes as a hot flush rises to my face.

Thomas just chuckles, taking a sip of his latte. "Sorry to disappoint, it's just my phone." He pulls the phone out from his cloak and holds it up for us to see.

"Pity, lightsabers are so much more fun," Maria deadpans.

I take that as my cue to leave. "I'll go check where K-2P is with those cards."

Thomas raises one perfect eyebrow at me, which I bet he doesn't even have to pluck. "What cards?"

"The ones to vote on the best costume."

"Do I get a vote, too?"

"Here, take mine." I hand him the card so that I won't have to circle back to him. I won't pretend I'm not a huge Reylo fan. Seeing Thomas dressed up as my biggest sexual fantasy is testing my self-control.

I reach K-2P and hiss, "You're a snitch."

The robot turns to me, and even if he doesn't possess facial features, he looks offended. "Why are you doubting my loyalty?"

"Did you tell Thomas to dress as Kylo Ren?"

"Why would I?"

"Because you knew I was coming as Rey, you meddling piece of metal."

"Ah! But did I know? Nope, because you never actually told me."

I drop my jaw, trying to remember if I ever discussed my costume with K-2P. I don't remember having an actual conversation with him about it. So, I close my mouth and just glare at the droid.

"That's what I thought." It's his last comment before he wheels away. But I can still smell his metallic fingerprints all over this. I might not have told him directly, but he knows me. He must've picked it up somehow, if not from full-scale espionage.

I drop my hands, fed up with smartassed robots and fineassed bosses and make a round of the lab to talk with all my team leaders to see if anyone needs my input on anything before I leave tomorrow.

The lab's festive mood continues throughout my rounds. People are walking around in their costumes, taking pictures, and getting into character. I'm impressed with some of the get-ups. Ari, who looks like a life-sized Lego character, and our head of programming Salim, who's a giant Rubik's cube.

But despite all the distractions, my gaze keeps flitting back to Thomas in his Kylo Ren outfit. No matter that for the entire day, I try to put as much space between us as possible. Even at a distance, he looks so good in that black cloak, it's totally unfair. He even has the height to pull it off.

Regardless of how gorgeous a villain Thomas is, the first prize for best costume goes to our robot controllers specialist, Tabitha. She came in as Mystique from *X-Men* in a skin-tight blue wet suit, her face and hands painted blue. It can't have been comfortable, but at least the effort has been worth something. I voted for her, too. After I give away the grand prize, it looks like everyone in the lab is ready to call it a day. Me too. I also still have to pack for tomorrow's trip.

But when Thomas pops into our shared office to get his things and gives me a simple goodbye, I'm deeply disappointed.

Doesn't he know we won't see each other until next week? Wait, *does* he know? I don't think I mentioned the conference to him other than in the parting note I hid in his messenger bag earlier, which is the closest I've allowed myself to get to him today. But other than that, I haven't talked to him about the trip to Rome. As I'm racking my brain, scanning the entirety of our past conversations—sometimes I wish I were an AI and that all I had to do was insert a keyword like "conference" to access all my past interactions on the topic—Maria enters the room, mock-fanning herself.

"Well, well, well. Aren't we looking flushed?" the head of mobility teases with a grin.

I shake my head, exasperated.

"Aw, come on. Don't you think the force is trying to send you a message?"

I shoot her a warning look. "Don't even get started."

"Fine, fine. I come in peace."

"Meaning?"

"Just wanted to test the temperature after our villain left and ask you for any last words before you're off to Italy."

"Actually, yes, can you babysit Thomas while I'm away? Tomorrow is his last day of shadowing and he's supposed to follow Garrett—"

"Uh, and you conveniently chose to flee the country for that."

I won't lie and say that I didn't cowardly wiggle out of seeing how spectacularly awkwardly that goes. I smile a sweet smile. "Perks of being the boss."

Maria's smile is even more viciously sweet as she mock curtsies. "In that case, it'll be my pleasure to look after the hot shot. Have fun in Italy and eat a lot of gelato."

Maria leaves, and, for the first time since my secret correspondence with Thomas started, I don't have the self-control to wait until I'm at home to read Thomas's note, the one where he'll be replying to my offer of installing a flattery drive dedicated to him in K-2P.

I rip the blue Post-it right off the bottom of my bag and smile like an idiot as I read:

If creating the drive will force you to research all my best qualities, sure, why not?

*   PS. Did you think Ben Solo deserved better?*

19

THOMAS

Tuesday night, at home, I find Reese's note in my messenger bag, but I don't open it right away. First, I change out of the Kylo Ren costume, shower, and pull on a pair of sweatpants and a clean white T-shirt.

But even after I'm showered and changed, I don't read the note. Instead, I take it with me to the couch where I sit, flipping the folded sheet of paper between my fingers.

Today went well, I think. I was Kylo Ren, and she was Rey... K-2P's spying was spot on. And she seemed to like my costume, but then she spent the rest of the day pointedly avoiding me. What is it with her? I know she likes me. Her notes prove it, or she wouldn't bother responding to them. And the way she looks at me sometimes, like she wants to pounce on me. Her eyes tracing over my body, admiring every inch of me.

But then she goes all rigid and pulls away, keeping her distance like she fears what could happen if we got too close.

Why?

I understand that me possibly becoming her boss is less than ideal, but not unsolvable—even with that darn anti-fraternization policy in place. I've been at Mercer Robotics only a few weeks and no official announcement has been made about me taking over as CEO. Only the board knows—I could still switch departments. Another CEO is going to retire from one of our other divisions eventually. Or better even, I could start at a lower level, shadowing the current CEO of another division for a few years before they retire. That would allow me to learn the ropes in less of a pressure cooker environment. Shadowing the man I'll have to replace for years seems a better approach than this "throw you into the fray" method my dad has forced on me.

But if I tell Reese all this, would she just laugh in my face? Am I deluded for thinking the only obstacles to a potential relationship between us are our jobs?

From what K-2P told me, I'm not smart enough to be her type, but I'm not sure genius scumbags are what's really best for her. Plus, even if I don't have an engineering degree and can't debate impedance control—see? I'm already picking up the jargon—with her, it's not like I'm an idiot.

Could she ever be interested in exploring something with me? I honestly don't know. She's giving me mixed signals. Maybe I should come out and ask her outright.

I stare at the note in my hands; she's responding to the message where I called her mean for not telling me about the Halloween costume tradition. Like every new message she sends, this could help me decipher the mystery that she is.

I unfold the note and read.

Glad K-2P was there to save the day, and you could've always claimed you were dressed as Christian Gray or something, so I don't feel sorry.

That makes me chuckle. Christian Gray, huh? Someone's been

fantasizing about naughty billionaires. See? She's flirting. But the note is not over. I read the rest.

> *Since we won't see each other until Monday, I'm going to leave you with a Star Wars pun to carry you through the rest of the week.*
> *What kind of car does a Jedi drive?*
> *A ToYoda.*

Wait, what? Why won't we see each other until Monday? I'm not going anywhere. So where is *she* going?

If K-2P were here, I could ask him. But during the week, he still sleeps in the lab.

So?

I stand up and start pacing the living room. I grab my phone from the coffee table and call my executive assistant.

She picks up on the fourth ring. "Boss?"

"Ellen, good evening, I need you to find out where Reese Campbell will be this week."

A beat of silence. "Now?"

"Yes, now."

"It's nine at night."

"Ellen, you're the only executive assistant I know who didn't have to work a minute of overtime in her entire career. Please help me out."

She sighs. "Fair enough, boss. I'll call you back as soon as I know something."

"Thanks."

We hang up, and I keep pacing the living room and forget about eating dinner altogether until Ellen calls me back an hour later.

"Yeah?" I pick up before the first ring is even done.

"Whoa." Ellen sounds startled at my immediate response. "Someone's been waiting by the phone."

"Did you find out where she's going?"

"Yes, boss, she's attending an international conference on computational intelligence and virtual environments in Rome. The conference is from Thursday through Saturday, but she's flying out to Rome early tomorrow morning. And on Friday, she's giving a presentation on human-computer interaction technologies for measurement systems and related applications."

"Just to be clear, we're talking Rome, Italy, and not Rome, Georgia, or some other place in the United States?"

"Yep, boss, Roma, Italia."

A break in a beautiful European city could be the detached-from-the-office breather we so desperately need to figure out if there could ever be an us. I know, technically, it'd still be a work trip, but attending a conference won't be the same as being in the office with a thousand eyes on us. And it's Rome, for goodness' sake. I will never get a better opportunity to get Reese to lower her walls. If the pasta, wine, and gelato don't do it, nothing will.

"Ellen, please get me the details of her itinerary and book me on the same trip. Do I need an invitation to attend the conference?"

"I'm pretty confident I can get you a badge, boss."

"Great, Ellen, and you can take the rest of the week off since I'll be gone."

As soon as I hang up, I rush into the bedroom and start packing a bag. Nothing says "That's Amore" like a surprise trip to Rome.

20

REESE

The 4.30 a.m. wake-up call is brutal but worth it. Tonight, I'll be eating gelato strolling the streets of Rome, and enjoying *la dolce vita*. The thought of being away from work and relaxing for a few days makes me excited. I mean, I'll still be working, theoretically, but weirdly enough, considering I'm a grumpy introvert, public speaking has never been a source of anxiety for me. Not when the topic I have to speak about is one I know inside out like human-computer interaction frameworks.

I dress in comfy travel clothes, wearing my "Ben Solo deserved better" sweatshirt under my jacket as a tribute to Thomas's note of last night. Yep, he nailed it. I am one of the millions of fans who think Ben shouldn't have died at the end, and that he and Rey should've gotten their happily ever after.

But, happily ever afters are no longer a certainty in movies.

And if Rey and Ben couldn't make it in a fictional world, Thomas and I surely can't make it in the real one. We're doomed. I can't date my future boss, period. I should probably stop sending him notes as well. But I keep telling myself there's no harm in them. He'll be gone in two and a half months, off to a different department. Our weird dynamic has a clear expiration date, there's nothing wrong in wanting to enjoy playing while it lasts. Or so I'm trying to convince myself because last night, all I could think about was Thomas in his villain costume and the very naughty things I wanted him to do to me.

Good thing I won't have other visuals of the man to fuel my vivid imagination for the next five days. A break from Thomas Mercer and his sexy everything—face, smile, ass, dimples—is just what I need.

I grab my suitcase, ready to go even if I skipped breakfast. I plan on having it later at the airport. Since I'm taking an intercontinental flight, I have to get to JFK hours in advance, so I'll have plenty of time to eat. And I don't even have to call a cab.

A company car should be waiting for me outside my building to take me to the airport where I'll be flying to Rome in business class. One perk of working for a large conglomerate like Mercer Industries is that they give their executives the luxury of traveling in style.

As I step out of the building, a sleek black Mercedes is already parked off the curb—as expected.

What's not expected is the tall, sexy man leaning against the side of the car sporting a self-satisfied smirk. Thomas is dressed in casual clothes, jeans, and a jacket. He hasn't shaved, and the scruff on his square jaw is unleashing the weirdest impulses in me. For one, I want to rub my cheek against it, feel the bristle on my skin, and then I'm dying to kiss that wicked grin right off his smug face.

"Morning, Campbell." He beams at me.

I swallow the shock. "W-what are you doing here?"

"We have a flight to catch. I thought carpooling would be a more environmentally friendly means of transportation."

My mind races as I try to make sense of this. "Oh, you're going somewhere?"

"*We*," he says, pointedly looking at me, "have the *same* flight to catch."

"You're coming to Rome? Why?"

"As future CEO of Mercer Robotics, I must keep up to date with the latest technological developments."

I cross my arms over my chest. "Oh, really? Because even Proctor never came to these events. CIVEMSA is one of the most technical conferences there is, not a business major in a ten-mile radius, I promise."

The smug smile he flashes me next is equally infuriating and irresistible. "All part of my training, I can assure you." He steps aside and opens the car door for me. "Shall we go, before we become late?"

My heart races as I give my suitcase to the driver and climb into the car.

I can't believe this is actually happening. We're going to be spending the next few days together in one of the most romantic cities in the world. So much for my much-needed break. Being in Rome together will be a test of my resolve and my ability to keep my distance from him. And I don't know if I'll be able to resist Thomas's charm for that long.

At the same time, I can't deny that a part of me is excited at the prospect of exploring the city with him. And maybe, just for once, to make a mistake? A huge, dimpled, sexy mistake.

Just the thought gives me goosebumps.

As the car pulls away from my building and onto the empty streets, Thomas turns to me with a mischievous glint in his eye. "So, Campbell, ready for a Roman holiday?"

I try to keep my features impassive to set the right tone for the trip. "This is a business trip."

"Absolutely," Thomas says with such a straight face he makes me doubt if he might really be tagging along to learn more about computational intelligence.

As the car merges onto the interstate, I steal quick glances at him from the corner of my eye. He's checking emails on his phone, his lips pursed in concentration. I clear my throat, suddenly nervous about breaking the silence.

"So, did you pack everything for your 'training'?" I ask, hoping to start a casual conversation.

Thomas looks up and meets my gaze, amusement dancing in his eyes. "Got all I need right here." He stares at me pointedly.

I roll my eyes at his teasing tone. "You're impossible," I mutter under my breath.

He chuckles softly before leaning closer to me. "But you like it," he whispers, his breath hot against my ear. I inhale sharply at the sensation, pretty sure I'm about to give a demonstration of spontaneous combustion when he adds, "In a friendly professional way, of course."

I glare. There's nothing friendly or professional about him joining me on this trip. This is a full-on ambush of my self-control.

On the rest of the drive to the airport, I try to keep my mind focused on the presentation I'm giving the day after tomorrow, but it's hard. Thomas is right beside me, his scent a mix of musky cologne and something woodsy that makes me want to bury my nose in his jacket and breathe deeply. He says nothing for a while, and I keep stealing glances at him when he isn't looking—precision-pointing technology becoming the furthest thing from my mind. It's remarkable how attractive he is, with those sharp cheekbones and piercing hazel-green eyes flecked with gold. And that scruff. It's torture.

"Are you nervous about the presentation?" Thomas finally asks, interrupting my thoughts.

My heart jumps in my chest. "No. Not really. I know what I'm talking about."

"Really?" His smiles will be the death of me. "Because you seem a little *preoccupied*."

Yeah, but visual analysis technologies have nothing to do with it.

"I'm fine," I retort, trying to sound confident.

"Okay, okay, no need to get defensive." Thomas raises his hands in a gesture of surrender. "I'm just saying, if you need someone to practice your presentation with, I'm here."

I scoff at the offer. "Right, because you have nothing better to do than listen to me talk about gesture-based interfaces for hours on end."

"Well, that, or pretend to be interested in the Roman ruins all by myself," he says with a grin.

My lips twitch against my will as I imagine Thomas Mercer wandering around Rome with a tourist map and a fanny pack. "Fine," I concede. "You can sit in on my rehearsal tonight."

"Excellent," he says before settling back into his seat and returning to his emails.

We keep silent for the last few miles, each of us focused on our own thoughts. But it's not an uncomfortable silence. More effervescent. It's filled with tension that simmers around like smoke from a fire that hasn't even been lit yet—like everything we're not saying is just bubbling under the surface, waiting to be unleashed.

We arrive at the airport with plenty of time to spare. Once we've recovered our suitcases from the trunk of the car, I head straight for the check-in line, but Thomas grabs my suitcase and steers me in a different direction. "Wrong way, Campbell."

I frown. "How is this the wrong way? It says check-in right there."

"My assistant already checked us in last night, we only have to drop off our baggage, and then we can enjoy the first-class lounge."

"I'm not flying first class," I protest.

Thomas gives me a stare that could melt glaciers. He's worse than global warming. "Now you are; I've upgraded you."

I swallow hard as a flush of embarrassment sweeps through me. "Thomas, I can't accept that. It's too much."

"Nonsense," he says with a smile. "Think of it as a perk of being the soon-to-be CEO's travel companion on a business trip."

I hesitate for a moment before relenting. It's not like I can afford first class anyway, and if Thomas is offering, who am I to turn it down? We make our way to the baggage drop-off and breeze through security thanks to our priority boarding passes.

As we step into the luxurious first-class lounge, my eyes widen at the sight of plush armchairs, complimentary drinks and snacks, and even a private shower area. This is a level of luxury I've never experienced.

Thomas, on the other hand, is right at home in this environment. He comes and stands next to me. "Had breakfast already?"

"No," I say, my mouth watering. I'm not sure if it's from the lush buffet or the sexy billionaire by my side.

I pile a plate with cinnamon rolls and almost die of delight when I take a bite of one and it's still warm. "These are the stuff of dreams," I mumble between chews.

Thomas chuckles. "Glad the service is up to your standards."

"Do you always travel in style like this?"

Thomas's gaze drops to the floor as he scratches the back of his head, embarrassed almost. "This is actually a slight downgrade for me."

"A downgrade?" My mouth gapes. "What's above this?"

He looks up again. "I usually fly private... with the family jet."

The world tilts. With Thomas, it's so easy to forget how much money he has. But now he just said private jet like a regular person would say *bike*. "Sometimes I forget you're so rich! How do you stay so"—I circle a hand in his general direction—"normal?"

His lips quirk. "I hope I'm at least a bit extraordinary."

He's *all* extraordinary. "I meant so down to earth? You never use your money as leverage."

"Guess my mom taught us right." Thomas shrugs. "She didn't come from money like my dad. And she always made it a point that we didn't make our billions a source of discomfort for anyone. Money is not an indication of any person's worth."

"Well, she did a stellar job," I say, slightly out of breath.

Our eyes lock. Everything around us fades away, leaving just the two of us standing there, lost in each other's gazes. The glint in his eyes makes me nervous. He's up to something, I can tell. Swirling in his hazel irises I see a heat and a determination that make me a little lightheaded. As if I were standing at the edge of a cliff about to take a step into the void. But before I can even process what's happening, Thomas clears his throat and sets his empty plate aside.

"Anything to drink?" he asks, gesturing toward the lounge bar. "I can order you a cappuccino."

My response comes out in a croak. "A cappuccino would be wonderful, thank you."

Here I am, thinking about charged gazing into each other's eyes and falling off cliffs, and he's thinking about coffee.

We spend the next hour lounging in the first-class area, chatting and enjoying the luxurious amenities. By the time our flight is called, I feel more relaxed than I have in weeks.

On the plane, I don't even try to play it cool. I've never flown first class in my life, so I push every button in my seat, stretch it until it becomes a single bed, and pull it back up. Then I explore the contents of the complimentary beauty case: ear plugs, a sleeping mask, a moisturizing spray, and socks.

I stare at the socks, puzzled. "Why are they giving us socks?"

"They're single use, so you can pad around the plane without shoes if you need to stretch your legs."

"Oh, wow, good to know."

Thomas and I are seated next to each other, but the seats are so large that it's not uncomfortable—neither physically nor emotionally.

Still, as the plane takes off, my heart pounds in my chest. I'm not sure if it's from the altitude or the anticipation of the destination—and I'm talking figuratively here.

21

THOMAS

"Dear passengers," an announcement over the speaker system of the plane jolts me awake.

I look to my left and find Reese smiling at me. "Morning," she mouths, even if the sky out the plane window is already dark. With the flight taking over eight hours and Rome being six hours ahead, we're due to land at night.

I didn't mean to fall asleep, I wanted to enjoy every second of this trip with her. But the comfortable seats and the soft hum of the airplane's engines made it impossible not to nap. I stretch my arms and legs, still groggy.

The journey map on my screen has been turned off. Did Reese do it once I fell asleep? That'd be so thoughtful. "Where are we?" I ask.

Reese shushes me, pointing at the speakers on the plane's ceiling, meaning she wants to listen to the public announcement.

I do the same.

"...we regret to inform you that because of a technical issue, we ran out of fuel sooner than expected and had to schedule a layover in Nice to refill our tanks. We apologize for the inconvenience this may cause to your travel plans."

I watch Reese; she's gripping the armrests of her seat with white knuckles.

"Relax," I soothe. "We're in no danger."

"Sorry if hearing the plane is having technical malfunctions and is running out of fuel doesn't put me at ease." She scoffs. "You know how many things could go wrong?"

"No, but I have a sense you're about to tell me."

She nods. "The pilot could decide to climb to an altitude above eleven kilometers. That's dangerous."

"Why would he do that?"

"The thin air reduces the plane's fuel consumption."

"Okay. But it doesn't feel like we're climbing. I'm sure the pilots have everything under control."

"Not if the gauges don't work. If the fuel one is misbehaving, others could, too. And if the sensors don't work, all we have standing between us and certain death are the nerves of steel of the captain. And even then, if he's getting the wrong readings on airspeed, he'd have to guess the flight angle and thrust to maintain a steady airflow across the wings. But his guess is as good as yours, and he could plunge us to the ground or rise too much and make the plane stall and then crash... just to name a few."

"These are the moments I'm glad I understand so little about turbine engines."

"It's more of a fluid dynamics issue. You can't mess with the Bernoulli Principle."

"Still blissful in my ignorance about the whole concept."

That makes her crack a small smile. But to appease her anxiety, I stop a passing flight attendant.

After being reassured that the lack of fuel has been caused by a shortage with the refurbishing cistern at JFK and not a sensor malfunction, Reese visibly relaxes.

The laid-back attitude, however, positively evaporates when, after sitting for an hour on the tarmac at Nice, we're informed that the plane hasn't been cleared for takeoff, and we'll have to catch a connecting flight to Rome the following morning.

But, on the plus side, the airline is going to accommodate us in hotel rooms for the night.

By the time we get to the "hotel"—more of a dingy airport motel with flimsy walls and questionable stains on the carpet—the mood has definitely dampened.

So much for the luxury travel experience I wanted to give Reese. Before arriving at the hotel, we had to queue to retrieve our luggage at baggage claim, then wait to be put on a bus and be shuttled here, and now we're stuck in an endless line with all the other plane passengers to get assigned to our rooms. Somehow, we ended up almost last in the check-in line—the hotel apparently doesn't differentiate between first-class and economy ticket holders.

When our turn arrives, I gesture for Reese to go ahead.

"Thanks," she says and proceeds to the check-in.

I wait next to her as she gives her data to the receptionist, a nice young lady called Amélie, according to her name tag. Amélie inputs everything on her computer and, finally, with a smile, announces, "You're in room 708. Is one key okay or would you like two?"

Reese scoffs. "Why would I need two keys?"

Amélie's smile falters, and her gaze shifts to me uncertainly. "In case you both want a key?"

Reese follows the receptionist's gaze and chuckles nervously. "Oh, no, we're not sharing a room."

"I'm sorry, what?"

"We"—Reese flips a finger between us for emphasis—"are not sharing a room."

"But you were under the same booking," Amélie protests.

"It's a business trip, we work for the same company but we're not, you know..."

Amélie nods. "Let me check real quick what I can do for you." She types furiously on her keyboard, then lifts a worried gaze to us. "I want to apologize for the mistake, but it looks like we're out of rooms."

Reese, who's kept smiling up to now, frowns. "What do you mean out of rooms?"

"We only have one room available for you to share, all other rooms have already been assigned or have been reserved for the remaining passengers of your flight."

"That's unacceptable," Reese complains, then turning to me, she adds, "Say something."

I try to summon some inner indignation, even if, to be honest, having to share a room with Reese seems like a gift from the heavens. "Is there another hotel we could stay in?"

Amélie shakes her head before she even replies. "I'm sorry, sir, but the Marathon des Alpes-Maritimes Nice-Cannes will run tomorrow; most hotels in town are fully booked."

Reese is positively puffing smoke out of her ears and nostrils. "What about *out* of town?"

Amélie goes back to typing. "Maybe you could find some place to stay, an hour, an hour and a half away, but I would advise against that option."

"Why?"

"The airline has placed you on an early connecting flight tomorrow morning. If you go out of the city, you'd have to leave at four in the morning to get back to the airport in time. Plus, with all the traffic restrictions and diversions downtown and along the coast because of the marathon, circulation will be a nightmare. I'm not even sure you'll be able to get back here from there."

"We'll take the room," I interject.

"What?" Reese snaps. "Are you crazy?"

"We'll take the room, thanks." I ignore the protests and make to steer Reese away, whispering in her ear, "I can sleep on the floor, no big deal."

Her eyes drop to the stained carpet, and when she looks back up at me, doubt is written all over her pretty features. She fights against me to stay put at the reception desk, asking, "Is the room at least a double?"

"Yes, Miss." Amélie is finally happy to deliver a piece of good news and Reese seems to accept her destiny. "Your room is on the seventh floor; elevators are that way."

The receptionist points us to the back of the hall and the very smart, very pissed woman next to me finally lets me lead her that way.

As the slowest elevator in the world makes its climb to the seventh floor, Reese maintains a frowny, grumpy attitude, keeping as far away from me as she can, arms protectively crossed over her chest.

"Come on," I tease. "I promise I don't snore if that's what's worrying you."

She glares at me. "It's not that. I don't have any pajamas."

I raise my eyebrows questioningly. "You didn't pack your PJs?" Then, I know I shouldn't, but I can't resist a little dig. "Or are you telling me you prefer to sleep naked?"

Her cheeks flush crimson. "I don't sleep naked, and, of course I packed my PJs, they're just not appropriate for a room-sharing situation."

Oh. My attention levels spike. "Why not?"

She points down at her baggy clothes. "I know I dress pretty casually, but I like fancy sleepwear."

"And by fancy you mean?"

"Silk..."

An image of her in underwear the first time we met pops into my head, and I can't resist smirking.

"Don't make that face," she chides.

"I wasn't making any face," I lie. I probably had the expression of a pervert ready to pounce on her. "And I also have nothing against silky sleepwear."

"It's not that I try to be sexy," Reese blabbers, clearly nervous. "I just like the sensation of the silk on my skin." She touches her belly as a demonstration. "How cool and soft if feels against—"

Before she can continue, I close the distance between us and press my hand over her mouth to stop her from talking.

Her eyes widen in surprise, and I have to muster all my self-control to talk in a steady voice as I say, "You're describing freedom to a man in prison. Please stop."

We stare at each other, and I've no idea what's going through her head. But I know I'm afraid that if I remove my hand from her mouth, I'll lose a battle I've been fighting with myself for the past few weeks and kiss her.

22

REESE

Kiss me.

Kiss me. Kiss me. Kiss me.

It's all I can think while my back is pressed against the hard metal wall of the elevator and with Thomas standing so close to me. His beautiful eyes sizzling with intensity.

I want him to remove his hand from my lips and replace it with his mouth. Worse even, I want him to press me all the way into the wall and kiss me senseless. I know I shouldn't want this. That it's wrong. But I can't deny the pull anymore, the attraction is there, and it isn't going anywhere, no matter how hard I've been fighting it or trying to deny its existence.

Thomas seems to battle the same instincts. His breath is coming out ragged and heavy. And the way he's looking at me...

Kiss me.

When he, oh so slowly, removes his hand from my mouth, I hold my breath, thinking he's finally going to do it. I can't help the little gasp that escapes my lips as his gaze drops to my now-uncovered mouth.

Now. He'll kiss me now.

But then his gaze drops further down to the floor, and, with an imperceptible shake of his head, Thomas takes a step back just as the doors of the elevator slide open.

I flee more than exit the elevator car, heading down the hall in the wrong direction until I realize the arrows leading to our room number are pointing in the opposite way. I retrace my steps and scoot past Thomas, not daring to meet his eye. With trembling hands, I try to insert the room key in the proper slot and fail. Okay, steady breaths. Thomas didn't get a second key, so I'm the only one who can let us into our room. But this stupid key just won't fit in the narrow slit.

"Need a hand there?" Thomas's deep voice vibrates against my ribcage from behind.

He's standing a couple of steps back, and, even if we aren't touching, the heat of his body on my back is an open flame. Even more so when he reaches out and covers my hand with his big one, steadying my arm enough to slit the key in and pop the door lock open.

I push my way in, desperate to put some much-needed distance between us. But it looks like that won't happen because, of course, the room only has one bed.

I groan in disbelief. "She said the room was a double!"

Thomas slides in after me and takes in the single bed—not even a king size, barely a queen—more likely a full. "She probably meant double as a room for two not one with two beds. Few European hotels have separate beds."

"Sorry." I wheel on him. "I don't jet to Europe that often. So, what are we going to do?" I demand, because if we can't even share a five-minute elevator ride without keeping our hands to ourselves, there's no way I'm sleeping in the same bed as this impossibly sexy man who didn't kiss me just now.

Thomas shrugs. "I told you, I can sleep on the floor."

I stare at the yucky carpet, which I doubt has ever been properly cleaned. "You're not sleeping on the floor."

"Then I'll sleep above the covers, no big deal." He throws me a look I can't interpret, all intense and frowny. "I'm sorry about the elevator, I'll keep my hands to myself, I promise."

The only thing he should be sorry about is that he didn't kiss me. Why didn't he kiss me?

I'm pretty sure I was sending strong kiss-me vibes.

I nod.

He smiles. "Ready to pull out all that silk?"

I glare. "I'm sleeping in my dirty travel clothes."

My travel leggings are comfy and underneath the sweatshirt, I'm wearing a plain white T-shirt, so it won't be too bad.

Thomas smiles. "The hardships you put me through."

I try to keep a stern, this-is-still-a-strictly-professional-relationship face, but my stomach chooses this moment to loudly grumble and make me lose all credibility.

"Hungry?" he asks.

Thomas goes to check the minibar, which of course is empty, and looks up at me. "I doubt this fine establishment has room service, but I'll go scavenge for something to eat, okay?"

While he's gone, I relax on the bed and have a mini breakdown.

I can't believe I'm stuck in a hotel room sharing a tiny bed with Thomas Mercer. The man I've been fighting my attraction to and future CEO of Mercer Robotics. And now, here we are, about to sleep in the same bed. Well, he'll be sleeping above the covers, but still. It's too much.

I flop down on the mattress and let out a deep sigh. I've been trying to squash down my feelings for him for days, but every time he's near, they come bubbling to the surface. There's an electric current running between us that I can't escape.

Now all I can think about is kissing him, touching him, being with him. And why he didn't do all those things to me in the elevator. Has he lost interest?

What is wrong with me? Whether he's interested or not, it's irrelevant. I can't let anything happen between us. We work together, we're here on a *business* trip. I need to maintain a professional relationship with Thomas. My. Future. Boss.

But as he comes back into the room with some grab-and-go sandwiches, a heap of tiny bags of chips, and some candy bars he scavenged from the vending machines downstairs, my resolve weakens.

"Not exactly gourmet food, but it'll do," he says as he hands me a bag of chips and a bottle of water.

I smile, I can't help myself. "How's this for a downgrade from your usual travel standards?"

Thomas shrugs. "Not at all."

I frown. "You mean you often sleep in dingy motels with dubious hygiene standards?"

"No." He levels me with a golden-speckled stare. "Yet, I've never had a view quite like this."

The view of the airport out the window is foggy and mildly depressing. But he's not looking out the window, is he? No, he's looking straight at me. And he's so close, so tall. Oh, gosh. I avert my eyes before I do something very stupid.

Thomas sits on the bed next to me to eat, and I want him so badly it hurts. The tension between us is palpable. I struggle not to meet his eyes; I'm afraid of what will happen if I do. I'd probably get lost forever in their hazel-green-golden depths, if I'm not already.

I need to break this tension because I can't bear it. So I say the first silly thing that pops into my head. "Which program do Jedi use to open PDF files?"

I finally meet his stare as I finish the question.

After I saw him dressed as Kylo Ren, I googled a couple of *Star Wars* puns. I'd intended to use them in our notes like I did in my goodbye yesterday, but now I'm glad I have a conversation filler.

Thomas blinks at me with a helpless expression, his lips curling at the corners.

"Adobe Wan Kenobi," I say.

He throws back his head and laughs, and the sound is a corkscrew in my belly.

"What did Obi-Wan tell Luke Skywalker when he had trouble eating Chinese food?" Thomas fires back, not missing a beat.

Has he been researching *Star Wars* puns to share with me, too? This one wasn't on the website I used.

My turn to stare at him blankly.

"Use the forks, Luke."

I laugh, and after that, the tension relaxes throughout our impromptu dinner of vending machine food.

Thomas lets me use the bathroom first, and when I come back out, he's already changed into a clean white T-shirt and gym shorts. He's hardly indecent, but even the inch of toned thighs covered in a flurry of blond hair visible above his knees seems somewhat scandalous.

"Bathroom's all yours," I squeak.

As I wait for him to come back out, I hide under the covers, pulling them up to my chin, which is ridiculous considering I'm fully dressed.

When Thomas emerges from the bathroom, he chuckles at my childish behavior. "Are you afraid of the monsters under the bed?" he teases. "I can check."

More of the monster that will sleep above the covers.

"I'm not a kid," I retort, scooting over so he has enough room next to me. "I'm just cold."

"Sure," he says, giving me a knowing smirk. "Cold in a hotel room with the heater on full blast. Got it."

I glare. He smiles.

"What do you say?" he asks as he climbs up onto the bed next to me, above the covers, just like he promised. "Lights out?"

"Sure. I set the alarm for tomorrow morning but maybe you should set one, too, just to be safe."

He does so and then flicks off the overhead light, plunging the room into almost total darkness.

"Goodnight Reese," he whispers into the night.

"Goodnight," I reply, tucking in close to the edge of the bed away from him and staring straight up at the black ceiling.

I lie there in silence for what feels like an eternity, not able to sleep or relax. Initially, I can tell Thomas is awake, too, but eventually, his breathing becomes deeper and more regular. He has fallen asleep, but I can't.

I don't know how long passes before he talks. "No, no, I know... fine... *claro*."

At first, I think I imagined the sound of his voice, but then he continues. "...won't forget... so close now... *un mate*..."

His gibberish words make me realize that he's talking in his sleep. And what's with the Spanish?

Cautiously, I grab my phone and unlock the screen to have some light. Yep, Thomas's head is lolling on the pillow, mouth ajar. He's totally cute and 100 per cent asleep.

"Thomas?"

"Yeah."

"Do you talk in your sleep?"

"*Si*." He snorts and turns on his other side so that he's facing me.

"Why in Spanish?"

"*Mi mamá*."

His mom?

I lower the light away from his face so as not to wake him.

I hesitate, biting my lower lip. "If I ask you a question, will you tell me the truth?"

He hums in response. I consider the ethical implications of what I'm about to do and decide to screw morality. I need to know, so I ask him, "Why didn't you kiss me... before... in the elevator?"

The lines on his face relax and he speaks, "I can't."

"You can't kiss me?"

He lets out a confirmatory hmm. "*No puedo.*"

"Why not?"

He shifts again, now onto his back. He's still sleeping and yet speaking as if he were awake. "My brother says so."

I frown. His brother? I've never met Gabriel Mercer, but now I hate him with a vengeance. Or maybe Thomas just isn't making any sense. Why wouldn't his brother want us to kiss? I'm half tempted to put the phone away and to go back to *not* sleeping... but I'm also very much curious to find out more.

"Your brother says you can't kiss me, why?"

Thomas mumbles something I don't understand, then says in a clearer voice, "I'm the boss, you have to make the first move." More gibberish sleep talk follows in a garbled mix of Spanish and English of which I understand only the words harassment and *justicia*.

His mouth moves, but no sound comes out. I point the phone's light back toward him and lean over to see his face better. His eyebrows are pulled together as if he's deep in thought or having a bad dream. Then finally, after what feels like an eternity of silence he speaks again. "It's all about the candy, you know. Have to cook it just right. If not, then go back and try again." His voice is dreamy yet focused on something I can't understand at all.

Looks like if I don't prod him, he'll keep spinning nonsense.

So, I poke. "But did you want to kiss me?"

Thomas's lips curl up in a smile as he answers. "He said I'd fly away if we do."

That makes even less sense, but the next thing I know, Thomas is scooting closer and hugging my waist. Even with the covers between us, I can feel the heat of his body and the rise and fall of his chest as he breathes. Cuddling the future boss is risky, inappropriate, and wrong... still, I lean into him, scooting down so that he can lay his head on my chest.

"I want to kiss you," he says, his voice a low whisper that makes my skin tingle, "but I can't. You have to kiss me."

I stare down in a panic, worried he woke up, but his eyes are still firmly closed, his breathing too smooth and regular for him to be awake.

I swallow. The thought of kissing Thomas has taken over my mind completely. Now that I know for sure that he wants to kiss me, all I have to do is to acknowledge that I want the same. That or pounce on him on the first occasion. But I have never in my life made the first move with anyone. I'm simply incapable. The idea terrifies me. It doesn't matter that he just said he wants it as much as I do. I can't just grab the back of his neck, pull him toward me, and kiss him.

I'm scared. Scared of rejection, scared of judgment and criticism, and I'm more insecure than ever before.

What if I'm not attractive enough? What if the way I kiss isn't good enough and Thomas doesn't like it? All the men I've had in my life either used me as their side piece, unbeknownst to me, or dropped me in the blink of an eye when I no longer fit into their pre-conceived ideas of me. Not to mention my father who never even bothered to meet me.

What if Thomas is just chasing after a shiny new thing and once he gets it, he also tires of me? Then I'll be stuck working *for* a man who rejected me, or I'll have to find a new job. I don't want a new job. I love the lab and the team I've built at Mercer Robotics.

All these doubts rush through my mind. The fear of being inadequate makes me uncomfortable. In my job, I'm confident, capable, and competent. I know data, I can prove theories, and I can hold my own against anyone. But in my personal life, I'm just the opposite. Insecure, inexperienced, clumsy. Growing up with an absent father and a mother who always chose her men over me sure didn't help in making me emotionally confident.

But maybe for Thomas, I could overcome all those fears if what I was risking was only my heart. I did it before, and even if neither of my past relationships ended well, I survived. But having a relationship with Thomas, if that's even what he wants, and this isn't all just a game for him, would fire up so many complications. An eventual break-up would wreak havoc on the only aspect of my life where I'm in charge: my career.

I can't let it happen. I fear what may come out of crossing that line with him. And yet... here I am, happy to cuddle with Thomas in bed in the least professional of ways.

I try to push the idea of kissing Thomas out of my head, but his proximity makes it impossible. The way his soft hair falls against my skin, the way his breath tickles my collarbone, the way his arms hold me close... it's overwhelming. And nice. And cozy. And doesn't feel wrong at all.

It's okay. I can let myself enjoy this little tidbit of closeness, I reason with myself. Just for a moment. Just for tonight. It doesn't have to mean anything.

I take a deep breath and hug Thomas tighter, snuggling closer still. His soft breaths grow deeper and slower, the sound like the tide of a gentle sea soothing me into sleep. I drift into nothingness, my thoughts still lingering on what would have happened if I'd been brave enough to make the first move.

23

THOMAS

I wake up on a pillow of softness that smells like honey and wildflowers. The scent is so intoxicating that at first, I'm not sure if I've awoken to reality or a dream. But then the steady thud of Reese's heartbeat reaches my ears, and it becomes clear this isn't anything but real life. My eyes open to the still almost completely dark room; the alarm hasn't sounded yet and the sun won't come up for another few hours.

Even in the semi-darkness, it doesn't take long for me to catch up to the fact that I'm in bed with Reese. Even if I went to sleep above the covers, the bedsheets now provide but a flimsy barrier between us. My head is resting on her chest, her arms cradling me, my hand spread on her belly, and our legs intertwined like coiled ends of a rope, wound up so tightly we've become one.

I want to stay like this forever, but I know it's not possible. *Not right.* Reese is sleeping, hugging me was a reflex. I try to pull back, but as I make to move, she snuggles even closer to me, her soft breaths brushing against my neck. Even in her sleep, she's so damn adorable.

The questionability of staying put doesn't stop me from

admiring her, or from absorbing the warmth of her body against mine, or thinking how, right now, I need to figure out how to handle my feelings for her.

I can't force Reese to kiss me, even though every fiber of my being wants her to. But I also can't keep pretending like nothing is happening between us. I mean, come on, we're cuddling in bed! She's hanging on to me like her life depends on it.

But if I tell her how I feel, what if she puts up more walls? Or worse, what if she goes back to being uncomfortable around me and our working relationship becomes awkward? That'd be the last thing I'd wish to happen. I don't want to pressure her into anything she's not ready for. It's clear she's hesitant about exploring whatever this chemistry between us is, and I have to respect that.

As much as it kills me to hold back my feelings for her, I know it's what's best for us right now. But that doesn't mean I can't show her in other ways how much I care. By being the best colleague. The best of friends. Show her I'm serious boyfriend material. That I'm patient, funny, kind, reliable, and genuine. Maybe then, when she's ready, she'll see me in a different light.

The alarm on my phone goes off, and I reach with an arm over my nightstand to silence it. But it's enough to wake Reese.

I watch as she stirs, slowly coming to. She looks down at me with puffy eyes and a sleepy smile.

"Good morning," she whispers.

"Morning," I reply.

We remain still for a few moments, just looking at each other and enjoying the silence. But then Reese's alarm goes off, too. She blushes, probably realizing how inappropriate our position is, and sits up abruptly, shaking me off rather unceremoniously to silence the phone.

"We need to get ready," she says, all business now.

I nod in agreement and we both start getting dressed. And I can tell we're out of her comfort zone again. Reese is bucking around the room like a startled deer, giving me the side-eye as she awkwardly pulls her "Ben Solo deserved better" sweatshirt over her head and tries to smooth down her hair, which is now the cutest rumpled bird nest haloing her face.

A thought strikes me. Was that sweatshirt a code answer to my question in the last secret note I sent her? She didn't expect to see me yesterday on her trip, but was wearing the sweatshirt a way to feel closer to me as she departed?

I'm itching to ask, but so far, the unspoken code about our secret notes has been to not speak about them, so I can't mention them directly. But I can still flush her out.

"Hey," I say. "Nice sweatshirt. You a Reylo fan?"

Reese stops fussing with her hair and looks at me with wide, Bambi eyes, blushing furiously.

I wink at her.

She swallows and blurts, "I have to brush my teeth." Then she backtracks into the bathroom and shoves the door in my face.

Definitely a Reylo fan.

24

REESE

I shut myself into the tiny bathroom and lean my back against the wooden door. I need a cold shower. A bucket of ice thrown over my head.

How am I going to survive three more nights on this trip?

Hopefully by sleeping in my own room in my own bed—alone, no cuddling.

The imprint of Thomas's body is still searing a blistering path down my front. It's like my skin is burning wherever we were touching and the adjoining areas are tingling with frustration. I really need that cold shower, but I need a change of clothes first.

I put this sweatshirt on at random just trying to add separation layers to Thomas's proximity. But today, we'll be cabbing straight to the conference center from Fiumicino Airport, and I can't very well show up in a Star Wars sweatshirt. I have to change into a suit.

I dart back out of the bathroom to grab the one I packed and, of course, pick the exact moment Thomas is pulling his cotton-white T-shirt over his back.

Transfixed, I stare as the muscles in his shoulders and lower back ripple under his skin.

I gasp, and Thomas turns to me, showing off even more perfect muscles.

I can't stop myself, my eyes travel over his sculpted pecs, down to his perfect six-pack, and to the V of muscles disappearing under the band of his gym shorts, which are hanging obscenely low on his hips. I drink it all in until Thomas clears his throat.

He's caught me staring because I'm being *that* obvious. My eyes snap back to his, and his eyebrows raise in amusement. My mouth goes dry and I have to force myself to look away from his handsome face and perfect body before I start drooling like a fool.

"Um, excuse me," I stammer as I rush past him toward my suitcase. "I need to grab a change of clothes."

Thomas chuckles behind me, and heat rises to my face while my heart races. I dig through my suitcase, snatching up a blouse and a black pencil skirt, anything to distract me from the way Thomas's upper body will be permanently imprinted in my memory—besides being already imprinted on my chest.

This is getting ridiculous. I can't keep lusting after him like this. It's distracting and unprofessional.

I grab the suit jacket last, trying to steady my breathing as I do so. When I turn back to face him, Thomas has already finished getting dressed and is sitting on the edge of his bed, putting on his shoes.

I eye him, skeptically for once and not appreciatively. "Is that how you're dressing for the conference?"

He blinks at me. "Aren't we stopping by the hotel in Rome before we go?"

I shake my head. "No time. Suit up."

And with that, I lock myself in the bathroom again. I shower quickly, give my hair an approximate blow-dry, and change into my suit. In front of the mirror, I arrange my hair in a professional low chignon, hiding the pink tips. I put basic makeup on and nod at myself in the mirror. I look professional enough, now all I have to do is to *act* professional and I'll be fine.

When I exit the bathroom, Thomas is still in his sweatpants. "What are you doing?"

Before answering, he takes me in. His eyes travel from my face down to my black skirt, lingering on my legs, but he doesn't comment. "I'd like to freshen up before I change into a suit."

Oh, right, I've been hogging all the bathroom time. Despite it being my fault, I chide him. "Be quick, we only have fifteen minutes before the shuttle to the airport gets here."

Thomas grins at me and stands up from the bed, grabbing his toiletries and a garment bag before heading into the bathroom. "I'll be quick, don't worry."

His shoulder brushes with mine, and my empty stomach flip flops on itself. I watch him disappear behind the door, trying to squash the now familiar flutter in my stomach.

Get a hold of yourself, I scold myself internally.

This isn't the time or the place to let my attraction to him get in the way.

While I wait for Thomas to finish his shower, and to distract myself from the thought that he's standing naked in the next room, I pack the last of my things and put on a pair of flats that I'll swap for heels at the conference center. I wait, sitting on the bed, biting on a nail and fighting not to nip the edge off, all the while wishing I could see through walls.

When Thomas finally emerges from the bathroom, I wish I'd let him keep his sweat-wear. Because the man standing in front of me now is like a walking, talking, breathing Armani ad come to life. His still-damp hair is swept back from his forehead, and his sharp jawline is neatly shaved. His crisp white dress shirt fits him like a glove, emphasizing the muscles in his chest. The dark-navy suit he's wearing is tailored to fit him impeccably, while a classy light-blue tie hangs around his neck slightly askew—a minor detail that makes him real, human, flesh and bones, and frustrated dreams.

A sudden urge to run my fingers through that neatly combed hair overpowers me. I want to tousle it while pulling him down to me by his tie to kiss him.

I swallow hard as he smirks at me, noticing me staring.

Thomas tilts his head. "Better?"

I don't know what possesses me, but I stand up and walk up to him to straighten his tie. As I stop a mere step away from him, the heat coming off his body hits me like a low drum in my belly, his spicy scent an attack on my senses. I try to ignore the way my heart is pounding in my chest as I adjust the knot of his tie, but it's no use. My fingers shake with an unbidden desire.

As I finish straightening his tie, I look up into his deep hazel eyes. The smirk is gone from his face. Thomas is looking down at me with an inscrutable expression. A lock of light-brown hair has escaped the comb-back and falls over his forehead, making him irresistible.

I pat his chest and try to speak like a normal person, but my words come out in a coarse whisper. "You're perfect now."

I take a step backward. He pushes the lock of hair back and turns away from me, going to zipper up the last of his stuff into his bag. Still giving me his shoulders, he says, "We should get going if we don't want to miss the shuttle."

I nod, trying to compose myself, and shake off the urge to push him against the wall and kiss him like there's no tomorrow.

We grab our suitcases and head out of the hotel room, walking side by side down the hallway. The tension between us tangible again.

We stop in front of the elevator, and while we wait for it to arrive, I can't bear to look at him.

A few more stiflingly awkward seconds, and Thomas leans down to whisper in my ear, "Campbell?"

My breath hitches in my throat. "Yes?"

"How do Ewoks communicate over long distances?"

The rigidity eases off my shoulders, and I look up at him, shaking my head, already smiling.

"With Ewokie Talkies." Thomas delivers the punchline, and we both chuckle.

The elevator doors slide open and we step inside. Maybe the trip will be fine after all. We'll be fine.

25

THOMAS

The shuttle to the airport is waiting for us outside the hotel. We board it and settle in our seats in comfortable silence for once. Reese is staring out the window, but that doesn't stop me from glancing over at her and noticing how beautiful she looks in her professional attire.

Last time I saw her in a suit she was already halfway to taking it off. I chase the memories I shouldn't have away and concentrate on the present.

Her makeup is minimalistic yet stunning. Her hair is styled in a sleek chignon, the pink tips hidden, and I itch to pull out just a strand. To tell her she doesn't have to change who she is just because we're going to a conference. Not that I'm complaining about seeing her in a skirt. But I know these clothes are not her. That she's just dressing for a part she thinks she has to play.

Reese catches me staring in the bus window and smiles, making my heart skip a beat.

I look away like an inexperienced teenager who can't handle riding on the school bus next to his crush.

Once we get to the airport, we're too busy with traveling practicalities for me to dwell on my unrequited feelings—security checks, a quick breakfast in a boulangerie, and boarding the plane.

The flight to Rome is so short we've barely reached cruise height when the plane starts descending again. The cab ride from Fiumicino to the conference center is a little bumpy but, uneven roads aside, it goes smoothly. At least until Reese grabs a pair of black pumps from her bag and swaps shoes. The gesture of her sliding on the heels is so darn sexy that I have to grab the car door armrest so tightly my knuckles go white.

Seeing her in a tight skirt for the first time doesn't help.

Good thing we'll be in a wide, public space soon and not alone, confined in the back of a cab, or in a tiny bed, or in an elevator car together. I could use the extra breathing room. My self-control is already hanging by a thread as is.

Reese catches my intent gaze on her feet and blushes. I clear my throat and look away, trying to focus on the surroundings instead. Rome is breathtakingly beautiful with its narrow, winding streets and centuries-old buildings. It's hard not to appreciate all the history surrounding us, but I still get distracted every other minute —the view inside the taxi is as stunning as the one outside.

When we finally reach the conference center, the main hall is bustling with people coming from all over the world and speaking a multitude of languages. Reese and I check in at the registration desk. Our fingers brush as we reach for our badges at the same time, and it's another electric jolt.

I do my best to ignore it. "So, Campbell, where are we off to first?"

"There's a super cool presentation on immersive hand instructions in AR for asynchronous remote collaboration on spatio-temporal manual tasks that I don't want to miss."

I chuckle and shake my head.

"What?" she asks self-consciously.

"That you can even remember that title amazes me. Sometimes I forget you're a genius."

"I'm not a genius." She waves me off and studies the conference center map to find the presentation room, beckoning me along. "This is my bread and butter. Will be yours, too, soon."

"Maybe." I shove my hands in my pockets. Time to test the ground a little.

Reese stops short. "What do you mean, *maybe*?"

Okay, let's show a few cards. "I have a lot of reasons to stay at Mercer Robotics, but... I may have an even better one to pick a different division to lead."

Her jaw drops. She takes a few seconds to realize that her mouth is dangling open and closes it.

Then Reese swallows visibly, eyes wide and twinkling. A gentle flush creeps up her cheeks, and she lowers her gaze, shuffling her feet. "Do you think your father would let you switch?" She looks at me now. And my heart pumps in my chest because, oh, *she's interested*. "He seems a man used to getting what he wants," Reese continues. "And you've already been presented to the board."

"To the board, yes. But no public announcements have been made. We'll have to see."

There's a teasing glint in her eyes as she asks, "Gosh, are we robotics nerds that bad you don't want to be saddled with us?"

I hold her gaze. "Quite the opposite."

Reese looks away, shy once again. "K-2P will be crushed."

I shrug. "We can still have sleepovers."

I meant with the robot, but what happened last night is still fresh in both our memories; my skin tingles at the thought of sleeping holding her in my arms while Reese's cheeks color even more.

"K-2P will be happy to know that." Reese glosses over what we're both thinking.

"I hope so."

My father is sure not going to like the switch, but if I make my case right... He let Gabriel go, why shouldn't he let me find my path as well?

Maybe because in the past thirty years, I've never expressed an interest in anything other than falling in line and looking pretty for the cameras.

Well, things change. Fingers crossed it'll be for the better.

Reese and I meander through the corridors of the conference center and, after a few turns, we reach the right room. We find two seats next to each other toward the back and settle in. While we wait for the panel discussion on augmented reality and immersive spatio-temporal whatnots to start, Reese takes out a notepad and a pen, ever the straight-As prodigy.

As the lights dim and the first speaker takes the stage, a late-comer arrives, taking the free seat on Reese's other side and prompting her to lean slightly into me. Her arm brushes against mine, sending a spark up my limb. I try to ignore the heat spreading through my body as I focus on the speaker's words. But it's no use. Every time Reese moves, her scent fills my nostrils and I have to resist the urge to lean over and inhale deeply.

I glance over at her and see that she's biting down on her lip, deep in concentration. It doesn't help that she keeps crossing and uncrossing her legs, giving me glimpses of her toned calves. I shift uncomfortably in my seat and drag my eyes away from her legs to her face. A lock of hair has come loose from the chignon and is falling over her eyes. I have a sudden urge to reach over and tuck it behind her ear.

But touching her hair isn't exactly appropriate behavior for a work conference. So, I clench my hands in my lap and sit straight like a good boy, listening to the presentation.

And once the first lecture is over, Reese drags me to as many as we can fit into the day's schedule. We even skip lunch, and only eat chocolate bars we get from a concession stand. At one point, she even sends me to a different session from hers, tasking me to record it on my phone so she can watch it later.

One might think a conference in Rome would be an excuse to let loose and enjoy a less stressful day than at the office. But Reese is all business, business, business. She soaks in the knowledge like a sponge, and I honestly can't tell how her mind can contain all that information.

If we ever have kids, I hope they take after her. Aaaand I might be getting slightly ahead of myself.

By the time the last session ends and we're free for the evening, I'm practically vibrating with anticipation. Because the day might've been all about business, but my plans for tonight are entirely recreational.

I've asked my assistant to switch hotels, ditching the practical, close-to-the-conference-hall inn for a more quaint hotel in the city center. Tomorrow, coming back here early will be a hassle, especially because traffic in Rome is awful. But tonight, taking a stroll through the city's whimsical streets will be magical.

As we slowly file out of the conference hall, Reese tucks her notepad under her arm and beams at me. "Great day, huh?"

"Yeah, it was... um... really informative." I nod, a little tongue-tied.

Sometimes I wonder if we're too different, if she's really too smart for me, or if I am too dumb for her. Because today has been a little overwhelming for me; I couldn't follow or understand half the things that were being presented.

When we finally get out of the building, Reese goes to join the line for taxi cabs. I gently grab her by the shoulders and steer her toward the black car service I've ordered. A tall man in a black livery is waiting for us by the side of the road, holding a screen with Mercer Robotics typed across.

Reese low whistles. "Am I getting the VIP treatment?"

"Perks of traveling with the heir to the kingdom."

Her smile falters, and I know I've said the wrong thing. I bump shoulders with her, changing the subject. "What do you say? Quick shower back at the hotel and then dinner out?"

She doesn't respond right away. We follow the driver to his black car and it's a full minute of riding before she says, "Aren't you tired? I was thinking of getting room service, or eating another one of these chocolate bars." She takes one out of her bag. "They're the best thing I've ever had."

I make a mock-outraged expression. "We're in Italy and you want to eat a snack? That is a crime against the best cuisine in the world, Campbell, and I can't, in good conscience, let you perpetrate it."

"I was just saying I'm a little tired to walk around the city searching for a restaurant. I also don't want to end up in a tourist trap."

"Don't worry, I know a place."

She rolls her eyes in a you're-impossible way. "Of course you know a place."

"So, is it a yes to dinner?"

She fights a smirk and fails. "Should I dress fancy?"

"Dress however you like, I don't care."

"But is it a fancy place?"

"The opposite of fancy." I smirk, bringing a hand to my chest. "I feel deeply stereotyped here. Just because I'm a billionaire, it doesn't mean I eat only in fancy places."

Reese waves at our driver. "Says the guy who couldn't wait for a regular taxi and ordered a black car."

I chuckle and lean back into the plush leather seats. "Touché, Campbell. But trust me, you'll love this place."

The car pulls up to our hotel and after the check-in and another static-filled ride in an elevator, we part ways in front of our respective room doors.

"Meet back out here in forty-five?" I ask.

Reese nods and gives me a small smile.

I watch her disappear into her room before turning to enter my own. Inside, I toss my suitcase onto the bed and make my way toward the lavish bathroom. I strip down, stepping into the shower where I let the hot water wash away the grime of our short flight and long day ready for a night of good food and even better company.

26

REESE

Don't think about Thomas Mercer being naked on the other side of that wall.

We might be in two separate rooms now, but they're still adjoining, and I can still hear everything that's happening in his room.

The shower is running, and Thomas is probably underneath the hot jet now. Wet skin sleek under the stream of water, muscles rippling as he brings his arms up and tilts his head back. And I can only dream what a work of art his butt must look like right now.

Arrgh. Listening to him shower, *twice* in a day, is just too much.

The water turns off, and I remember we're supposed to meet again in less than an hour. I should get ready, take my own shower, and not stare into space fantasizing about my boss being naked and wet, skin glistening, muscles rippling... and I'm doing it again. I can't stop.

I undress and shower at record speed, quickly toweling off. With my hair in a towel, I walk over to my suitcase, staring at it for a moment before deciding on an outfit. Jeans and a cozy sweater will do, I suppose, paired with my comfortable walking shoes for our after-dinner stroll, and a jacket. Even if it's November, the weather in Rome has been mild.

Applying makeup *twice* in a day is unthinkable for me. But I'm having dinner with Thomas in Rome, so I force myself to dust my cheeks with blusher and elongate my lashes with a thick coat of mascara. No lipstick. I go just for ChapStick, and that's more for lip comfort than an aesthetic choice.

Oh, so you don't want to make sure your lips look soft and totally kissable in case the boss decides to press you against an ancient building in a dark alley and have his wicked way with you?

No. Nope. The boss has made it clear he won't make the first move. And I'll never muster the guts to kiss him first, so nothing is going to happen.

At least while Thomas is the heir apparent to Emmet Proctor. I try to stifle the flame of hope that's been blossoming in my heart since he mentioned earlier that he'd be willing to switch divisions for me. That's what he meant, right? That if something between us were to happen, he'd ask his father to transfer him. The company policy would no longer apply then. And even if I got the side-eye for dating the future president of the group, he'd be in a complete separate facility, with an independent budget, and no direct power over me. It wouldn't be perfect, but it could work.

Still, it'd be better if things proceeded the other way around. First, he should move divisions, and then we'd be free to kiss day, night, and all the hours in between. Maybe I should make that clear tonight at dinner.

I know it's a big ask. I've met his father. Nolan Mercer won't just roll over and have all his succession plans derailed. Especially for something that's *nothing* at the moment. Thomas and I haven't kissed, we're not dating. If I were a parent and my son told me he wants to put his future on the line for a woman he's never even kissed, I'd probably laugh in his face.

But the way Thomas looks at me... it's like he knows something I don't. Like he's already made up his mind about us. And what else can I do? I can't help how I feel, and the chemistry between us is undeniable, uncontrollable, inevitable. Every time we're in the same room, it's like there's a force field pushing us together. And every time we touch accidentally, it feels like an electric shock.

Before I can talk myself out of it, I slip on my jeans and sweater and I'm pulling on the jacket when I hear a knock on the adjoining room door. My heart races as I realize once again how connected our separate rooms are. I quickly finish getting dressed and smooth down my sweater before taking a deep breath and unbolting the connecting door.

Thomas awaits on the other side clad in a light wool sweater and jeans, his light-brown hair neatly styled and his hazel eyes sparkling in the dim light. He looks like a million bucks, and we're two worlds apart. Yeah, we're both wearing jeans and a sweater but his clothes look like they each cost more than my monthly salary.

"Ready?" he asks, holding out his arm for me to take.

I nod and keep a few-feet distance as we make our way out of the hotel and down the winding streets of Rome. The air is thick with the scent of flowers and food. A thrill of excitement at being in such a beautiful city, but especially at exploring it with Thomas, prickles at my scalp.

"Italy is so beautiful," I say, looking around at the charming buildings and twinkling lights. And for a moment, I even forget to drool over my companion because the city at night is so enchanting. The cobblestone streets, the monuments, the fountains.

"I thought you might like it," Thomas replies with a small smile. "Staying at the hotel would've been a waste."

"You're right. Thank you for taking me out."

The restaurant turns out to be one of those hidden gems that only locals know about, tucked away in a quiet alleyway just behind a great square.

Through one of the restaurant windows, we see a portly woman in a white apron kneading a ball of pasta dough. Then at a speed that makes me think she's artificially accelerated, she rolls the dough in a thin spool, cuts it into strips, and then rolls each strip into smaller pieces of fresh pasta.

With my mouth already watering, I say, "Please tell me we're eating here."

Thomas smiles down at me and holds the restaurant door open for me. "Sure are."

The inside is bustling with sounds, smells, and colors. The aroma of herbs and spices fills the air, and the clattering of dishes and sizzling of pans can be heard from the open kitchen.

As the host leads us to our table, Thomas's hand is on my lower back, guiding me through the crowded restaurant. We sit down near a window, and a friendly server hands us leather-bound menus.

The menu is all in Italian, but Thomas takes care of translating for me, helping me choose what to order. I get a *carbonara,* and Thomas orders a *cacio e pepe.*

While we wait for the food to arrive, I drop my napkin on my legs, smoothing it down with unnecessary precision. Then I look up and decide to be brave for once in my life.

"I've been thinking about what you said earlier..."

Thomas's gaze focuses on me, intent. As if he knows exactly what I'm talking about and doesn't need to ask. "And?"

"And I can't date my future boss." My entire body flushes hot as I let the words out. I've never been this bold, this direct. But Thomas makes me feel safe and like I can be myself. "I've worked too hard to get to where I am, and my career is the only aspect of my life I have sorted out. And I know you technically haven't asked me on a date, but—"

Thomas reaches across the table and takes my hand. "Didn't I? I thought I made it clear from day one where I stood regarding us."

Maybe, but the insecure girl within me who wore braces until she was thirteen, who had her face covered in acne until she was twenty-four, and who never was a popular kid in high school or college or grad school needs to hear it spelled out.

That girl has never known unconditional love. Growing up, whenever my mother was around, she resented me, blaming me for her latest boyfriend of the hour leaving her or my father—a father who decided I was not worth anything before I was even born. And now Mom calls only when she needs money. My first serious boyfriend was an older professor with a secret family who probably was only interested in having sex with someone younger and gullible. And the man I dated after him dumped me because I started making more money than he did.

I survived all that, but even now, I'm not great with people, at understanding them or being liked or loved by them. Numbers have always been my refuge. No wonder my best friend is a robot. And it's hard to let myself believe that a man like Thomas, someone who could probably have any woman on the planet, would want *me*. So, yeah, I need him to reassure me.

"Can you tell me again?"

His thumb brushes over my knuckles. "I want to date you. You're the smartest, most beautiful woman I've ever met, and I want to explore the spark we have. I understand your concerns, but even if we haven't known each other for long, I'm sure we could be great together. But I respect your ambition. I promise I would never let our personal relationship interfere with your professional life."

My inner circuits get overloaded, sparks are whizzing everywhere, my wiring overheats, and I lose the ability to speak. "That is,

I mean, you are—" I grab a glass and down some water. "Sorry, I'm not very good at expressing my feelings." I chuckle nervously. "Give me a differential equation to solve any day, but please don't make me talk about..." I wave my hand in his general direction.

Thomas smirks. "It's okay, I'm not that good at math, so we can help each other out."

Our food arrives, and Thomas is forced to let go of my hand.

I take the first forkful of *strozzapreti alla carbonara* and almost forget entirely about our conversation as the delicious pasta melts on my tongue.

Thomas lets me have a few bites before he speaks again, "So I wouldn't be crazy if I asked my dad for a switch? I would have a good reason to do it?"

For once, I find it easy to express exactly how I feel, with no fear of rejection. "I don't know if it'd be worth it; your dad is probably going to raise an eyebrow at the request, and I can't tell you we will work out because I can't know... All I can tell you is that if you were to no longer be my future boss, nothing would stop us from giving it a shot. I mean, if that's what you want..."

Thomas's smile is almost feral. "It is what I want."

His tone is low and husky, raw with emotion. It makes a tingle spread right from my scalp down to my toes.

A silly smile spreads on my lips as the heat of his gaze lands on me. It's almost too intense to bear. But I revel in it, basking in the glow of Thomas's attention and affection.

"I want that, too," I say, surprising myself with the certainty in my voice. I reach out to brush my fingers over his and relish the warmth of his skin. "Well then, I guess we'll just have to wait and see what happens."

The rest of the meal passes in a haze of laughter and flirtation, our shared attraction growing stronger with each passing moment. As we walk out of the restaurant and back to the hotel, Thomas takes my hand, lacing our fingers together. The tingling that shoots up my arm is so strong I almost lose sensation in the entire arm.

Up on our floor, we stop in front of our respective doors. I know I said nothing can happen until our work situation is sorted, but the need to kiss him is so strong my body can hardly contain it.

I look into his hazel-green eyes, willing myself to do it.

Kiss him. Kiss him, you chicken. Just grab him by his expensive sweater and kiss him already.

I can't. I can't. I can't.

"I guess this is goodnight," he says.

No. No. No. No!

"Yes."

Thomas cups my cheek, his fingers lacing into the hair on the side of my head, and he drops a chaste kiss on my forehead. "Goodnight, Campbell."

"Goodnight," I squeak and flee to my room.

Inside, I pace in front of the door connecting my room to his. Frustration, dissatisfaction, and unrequited longing bubble inside me.

He's the sun, and I'm a planet trapped in his orbit. I can't get away and I can't go to him either. When I let myself go, I can get a little closer and bask in his heat. Those are my summers. But then my head cools and I circle away again, keeping my distance, alone and cold in an endless winter. Until I can't bear it anymore and drift closer again. Spinning, spinning, in a never-ending ellipsis that is churning my heart to shreds with each new revolution.

These maddening feelings swirl and boil around in my brain until I can't take it any longer. I kick the wall and throw myself over my bed, suffocating a defeated scream into the comforter.

I hate being smart. I hate being level-headed. I hate making the right choice. And most of all, I hate being a clucking chicken who can't make the first move.

27

REESE

After a fitful night of restless tossing and turning, I still wake up in a good mood because summer is coming and I'm eager to head down to the breakfast room, eager to see him. To burn some of my jittery energy—I want to avoid greeting Thomas like an over-caffeinated chipmunk—I take the stairs down to the dining area instead of the elevator.

Thomas is already there, nursing his coffee and looking as if he hasn't slept a wink either. I smile at the sight of him.

When our eyes meet across the room, his face lights up with a smile that makes my heart race.

He stands up, pulling a chair out for me. But before I can sit, he pulls me in a deep hug. His muscular arms wrap around me like a warm blanket, and I'm engulfed by an instant sense of peace and comfort. I allow myself a moment of indulgence to breathe in his scent—soap, man, and endless summers.

Another heartbeat and I reluctantly extricate myself from the embrace, sitting in the chair he's pulled out for me.

"Good morning, Campbell," he says with a nod, his voice deeper than usual.

"Morning," I squeak, wishing I had a programmable speech interface that could compensate for fluttery hearts.

Thomas seems oblivious to my agitation. "What's on the agenda today?"

I laugh nervously. "I have to give my presentation."

"Are you nervous?"

About the presentation? No. About him being in the audience? Yeah-ah!

"I've given this presentation before." I bite down on a croissant and shrug. "I should be fine."

"Good. I'm sure you'll do great." Thomas nods, taking a sip of his coffee.

As he drinks, I can't keep my eyes from wandering down to the way his lips glide over the rim of the cup. My mind races, wondering what those lips would feel like against mine.

Mentally slapping myself for the umpteenth time for not kissing him last night or the night before, I avert my eyes and concentrate on breakfast.

It's a lost cause. I could spend the entire day staring at the masterpiece his mouth is, but fortunately, duty calls. I need to keep reminding myself that this is still a work trip and not a romantic getaway in Italy. Until something changes, he's still going to become my boss and is therefore off-limits.

We finish breakfast and head back up to our rooms. I quickly change into my suit, tucking in my shirt and pulling the jacket neatly over it. When I step out into the hall again, Thomas is already there looking as dashing as ever in a light-gray suit with a crisp white shirt underneath.

As he looks me up and down with admiration in his eyes, my heart gets replaced by a bass drum beating at an incessant tempo in my chest. My palms get sweaty while my mouth goes dry.

He takes a few steps closer and reaches out to push away a

strand of hair from my face. His fingers linger on my cheek for a moment before he lowers his hand, leaving me wanting more.

"Ready?" he asks with a crooked smile that sets my heart ablaze. I nod, not trusting myself to form coherent words in this state.

After a slow taxi ride where I fidget the entire time given our proximity in the back of the car, we reach the conference center. I follow Thomas into the lobby, carrying my notes for the presentation. I don't have to speak for another two hours, but I want to make sure I have all the material ready.

When I'm sure I have everything in order, I check my watch. We still have plenty of time to kill. We could make a quick detour to a machine learning presentation on the automatic synthesis of admissible functions for variational learning before going to my hall. It shouldn't be far from where I have to give my speech, so we could do both.

When I lift my head to check the overhead signs and orient myself, I spot my ex-boyfriend across the room instead. I squint, hoping it's just the light playing tricks with my sight, but no, it's him: Professor Samuel Williams. My quantitative methods in systems engineering professor. Yep, the one I dated after grad school while I was getting my PhD and who also turned out to already have a wife and two kids he neglected to tell me about.

Nausea rises within me like a welling tide, threatening to overwhelm me as anger and embarrassment flush through my veins.

All my confidence in my presentation skills evaporates. On instinct, I grab the jacket of Thomas's suit and hide behind him. I mean, he's a tree trunk of a man, I should be safe.

Thomas tilts his head backward, peering at me over his shoulder. "Hey, everything all right back there?"

"Please get me out of here."

Thomas's back tenses under my hands; he must register the

agitation in my tone, but, luckily, he doesn't ask questions as we awkwardly side-shuffle to a corridor where I collapse on a plastic chair, hyperventilating.

Thomas kneels before me, hazel-green eyes boring into me, steadying me. "What's going on?"

I shake my head, fighting for every breath.

He places a hand on my shoulder, applying pressure in a comforting gesture. "Take a deep breath, Reese. In and out."

It's the way he says my name more than anything that steadies me. I follow his lead, inhaling deeply and exhaling slowly. It takes a few moments, but eventually, my breathing returns to normal.

"Better?" Thomas asks, his voice gentle.

I nod, wiping at the tears that have fallen without my consent. "Yeah. Sorry about that."

"Don't apologize." He reaches out to brush an errant tear from my cheek with his thumb—it sort of makes me want to keep crying. "Do you want to talk about it?"

I take another deep breath, steeling myself to speak.

"I saw someone." I pause, unsure of how much I want to reveal. "An ex."

Thomas's eyes widen. "Ah. I see..."

"I'm not still into him or anything," I explain. "But it's been years since I last saw him, and gosh I still hate him." A bitter laugh escapes my lips.

Thomas stands up from his kneeling position on the floor and sits in the chair next to me. "Why do you hate him?"

"He..." Before I know it, the entire story is spilling out of me. "We were together for two years and for that entire time, he had a wife and kids, a separate life I knew nothing about, that I didn't even suspect. I was so naïve. I drank up every one of his lies, never questioning why we couldn't spend a single holiday together or why he was gone most weekends."

Thomas stares straight ahead. "How did you find out?"

"His wife came to his city apartment while I was there."

He looks at me now, eyes intense. "What did you do?"

"Ah." I slap my thighs. "I panicked, of course. I pretended to be the cleaning lady and scrubbed the entire place before I left forever."

Thomas raises an eyebrow at me, his lips twitching.

The smile is contagious. "She even paid me fifty dollars for cleaning their toilets, isn't that precious?"

We stare at each other for another heartbeat and then burst out laughing.

As our laughter fades, I instinctively lean closer to him, bumping our shoulders. "I bet you've never had such a humiliating break-up."

"Hey." He gently lifts my chin. "He should be the one ashamed of himself. And my last girlfriend all but cheated on me before she dumped me."

I frown. "What do you mean?"

"That even if she hadn't technically cheated, she was already in love with another man when she left. A *real* man"—Thomas makes air quotes—"as she called him, not a man-child like me." He lowers his head.

I take his hand. "You're not a man-child!"

He tilts his gaze up to me, a grin on his face that doesn't match the sadness in his eyes. "That's not what you thought when you were sent the CEO's son to babysit, though, right?"

I squeeze the hand I'm still holding. "Maybe at first, but then I got to know you. Don't sell yourself short, Thomas, you are kind, intelligent, intuitive, charming, fun..."

He turns toward me fully, cupping my cheek. "You know what scares me the most about potentially dating you?"

I give him a tiny shake of the head.

"That one day you might realize I'm not smart enough for you, that my mind will never be bright enough for you."

I flash back to our first conversation about his "brain."

"I have no doubts your *brain* will be fully satisfactory," I joke. He smirks. Then, turning serious, I gently tap his temple. "But it's what's behind here that I really like." I lower my hand to tap his chest. "And here."

His eyes darken. Thomas grabs the finger I poked him with and kisses the tip. "Thank you for saying that; you've no idea how much that means to me."

I blush. "Anytime…"

Thomas stays quiet for a moment, watching me before he speaks. "Do you think it's a coincidence your ex is here?"

I shrug. "He's not a speaker, but I guess the only way to find out for sure is to see if he's in the audience at my presentation."

"Would that be an issue for you?"

"Probably. I still break out in hives of mortification whenever I see him."

"Then you keep your eyes on me the entire time, all right?" Thomas stands up and offers me his hand. "You're going to kill it, Campbell."

28

REESE

As I walk into the conference hall, I spot Samuel sitting in the first row, an amused sneer on his face. I ignore him and walk right past his seat to the podium, willing my heartbeat to slow down and my hands to stop sweating. Once I'm behind the lectern, I pull up my slides and clear my throat.

I shift to the initial slide and begin. "Good morning, I'm Doctor Reese Campbell, Head of Research and Development at Mercer Robotics, and today I'm here to speak about human-computer interaction technologies for measurement systems and their related applications. Nowadays—" My gaze drifts to where Samuel is seated, leering at me, and I falter. I take a long, slow breath and remember Thomas's words—*eyes on me.*

And that's exactly what I do. I shift my gaze to the right where Thomas is and stare into his beautiful eyes. The brown in them grounds me while the green makes me come alive. "Nowadays, we interact with machines every day. Modern technology is every-where: in appliances, lights, cars, and wearables like smartwatches that give us information at a glance that they gather from sensors and sophisticated electronic components, most of which are connected to the internet and powered by Artificial Intelligences. We use them to communicate, to monitor our health, to make our lives easier." I take a breath and smile, Thomas smiles back. "And this is mostly what collaborative robotics is about, making sure that our interactions with the machines that surround us and aid us on a daily basis are easy and fun and not a source of frustration..."

An hour later, I end on a high note. "Co-bots are the future of robotics and I firmly believe that through collaborative human-computer interactions, we can achieve great things. I will now take questions."

Samuel's hand is among the first to shoot up in the air. I do my best to ignore him for as long as possible until I can no longer. I nod in his direction, bracing myself. "Professor Williams, you had a question?"

"Dr. Campbell, how do you respond to the ethical concern that human skills will be eventually replaced or altered as a consequence of repeated interactions with co-bots within the existing manufacturing systems?"

It doesn't matter that I'm the one on stage and he's the one sitting in the audience, his slimy handsome face still has the power to make me feel like a student under exam.

My gaze drifts to Thomas once again, and he mouths a "You've got this" at me.

Samuel's head snaps toward Thomas at the same time, and the look of pure contempt on my ex's face gives me the strength to carry on.

I draw in a long breath and look the slimebag straight in the eyes as I give my answer. "Thank you for your question, Professor Williams. It is important to address the ethical concerns surrounding human-robot interactions as we continue to develop and implement these technologies. However, I want to emphasize that the goal of collaborative robotics is not to replace human skills but to complement them, allowing the human and mechanical ecosystems to coexist in a collaborative playing field where synergies are exploited to their maximum capacity. Some jobs might become obsolete, but they will be replaced by new, more rewarding opportunities." Satisfied, I look away and address the audience at large. "If there aren't any other questions, I'd like to thank you all for coming today and for your interest in collaborative robotics. Let's continue to work together and push the boundaries of what is possible with these innovative technologies."

As I step off the stage, a sense of relief washes over me. Without missing a beat, Thomas takes my hand and whisks me away. I follow him, not sparing Samuel a second glance or thought.

* * *

As I collapse in my bedroom that night, I'm exhausted. The adrenaline has left my system and I'm utterly drained. I'm in no state to go out for another romantic stroll through the city and have already changed into sweats. Still, it smarts that Thomas hasn't asked me out again.

In fact, we haven't made dinner plans at all. Maybe he took me literally when I said I couldn't date him until he was no longer on a path to becoming my future boss. And since last night felt like a first date of sorts, he doesn't want to put me in that position again. It wasn't a business dinner for sure.

A little distance is good. Thomas is respecting my wishes. It's good to be respected. Only now, I'd much rather be ravaged than respected. And what a waste of a night in Rome.

I lie on my bed staring at the ceiling, trying to push thoughts of Thomas out of my head and focus on something else. Anything else. I'm mostly unsuccessful, when a knock resounds on the door.

All tiredness forgotten, I eagerly stand up and find the object of my obsessive thoughts on the other side.

Thomas is holding two paper bags in his hand and a tray of drinks in the other.

"Hey, I thought that after today you could use a quiet dinner in." He lifts the paper bags as a demonstration. "But if you prefer to go out, I can drop these in my room and we can go."

I'm half tempted to grab him by the collar of his unbuttoned shirt, forget the food altogether, and eat his gorgeous face for dinner instead. But of course, I don't. I can't.

I simply nod and open the door wider. "Dinner in sounds amazing."

I take the bags from him and move onto the bed, peeking inside. "What did you get?"

"*Arancini* and *panzerotti*. They're not strictly typical food from Rome, but they're among the best specialties from the south of Italy."

I inhale the delicious scent wafting up from the bag. "They smell heavenly."

I spread the small paper trays over the bed, and we dig in with gusto. As we eat, Thomas tells me stories about his travels through the south of Italy. He speaks passionately about the food, the culture, and the people. I smile as I listen to him; his enthusiasm is infectious.

Once I've scarfed down my entire half of the food and maybe some, Thomas grabs something from the pocket of his jeans and throws me my new favorite chocolate bar. "Got you one of these for dessert."

I squeal like an excited child and tear open the wrapper. The rich, creamy white chocolate melts in my mouth, mixing with the perfect crunch of the wafer. I close my eyes and savor the delicious blend of flavors.

When I reopen them, Thomas has already cleared away the empty containers and is standing up.

My good mood drops at the thought of him leaving.

"Guess I should be going."

Stay, I yell in my head.

"Thanks for the incredible dinner, Thomas," I say instead. "It was amazing. Italian food is the absolute best." I lick the last traces of white chocolate from my fingers.

His gaze lingers on my fingers, and I self-consciously drop them from my mouth.

I stand as well, clumsily wiping my hands on my leggings to walk him to the door.

We pause on the threshold, and he pulls me in, dropping a soft kiss on my forehead. "Good night, Campbell, you rocked today."

I take a step back and the distance between us hits me like physical pain. "Good night," I whisper.

I watch him step aside to enter his room and when he's gone, I develop the same symptoms of an addict experiencing withdrawal. My hands shake, my heart is pounding in my chest, and I become slightly nauseous.

I retreat to the bathroom and splash my face with cold water, brush my teeth, and dab more cold water behind my neck and on my chest, but I'm still boiling.

I walk back into my room and sit on the bed, staring at the thick wooden door separating me from the thing I want most in the world. My thoughts are a jumbled mess, my heart is thumping so hard I can feel it in my throat. I can't stop thinking about the way Thomas's lips felt on my forehead, how close we were standing, and how his gaze lingered on my mouth.

On impulse, I stand up, unlock my side of the door, and give it a soft knock.

No response.

I knock more decidedly.

One. Two. Three. Four. Five seconds pass and then the door flies open.

Thomas is on the other side, in his white cotton T-shirt and gym shorts, too handsome to resist. He smiles, crosses his arms over his muscular chest, his biceps deliciously bulging, and leans against the doorframe. "Hey."

A simple greeting, but I swoon. I have to make a conscious effort just to keep upright.

"Forgot something?" Thomas asks, probably seeing how I'm just standing in front of him, stricken and mute.

I bite my lower lip. *Be brave, Reese. Be brave.*

"I know I said nothing could happen while our work situation isn't sorted out, but..." Thomas tilts his head and his smile widens as I blabber on. "But I also thought, we're in Rome. So, when in Rome, or what happens in Rome..." I put my hands forward. "And I know you won't kiss me first." He frowns now as if he has no idea how I know that's his position, which, fair enough, he has no way of knowing I got it out of him while he was sleeping. "But what if I *asked* you to kiss me?"

I stare into his eyes and all the amusement is gone. Thomas drops his arms, staring at me with predatory intent as he pushes off the doorframe and takes a step toward me. "Just so we're clear, are you asking?"

I swallow and stare him directly in the eyes. "Yes, no. I don't know."

Thomas's eyes flicker with intensity. Time stops for a second, then he takes hold of my waist and pulls me toward him, setting every nerve ending in my body alight. With a feverish intensity, I wrap my arms around his neck and finally sink my fingers into his hair as he drags me into his room to press me against the wall.

With one hand still on my hips, he places the other flat on the wall next to my face, dropping his forehead to mine.

"There's nothing I'd like to do more now than kiss you," he whispers, his voice broken, rugged. "But I haven't talked to my father yet, and I'm not sure what our situation is going to be."

I'm panting heavily, my heart full of both desire and fear. "Sorry, I don't want to mess this up," I say breathlessly.

Thomas leans forward to kiss the tip of my nose. "We won't," he says firmly. "I'll make sure of it."

He nuzzles my neck and drops his hand from the wall to take my hand in his, enveloping me with warmth.

"I meant it when I said I wanted this," he says into my hair.

We stand there for a moment longer, just holding each other.

I close my eyes and absorb his closeness, feeling everything from Thomas's breath on my neck to the subtle energy coursing through our fingers as they entwine.

I'm safe in his arms with an emotion that surpasses physical pleasure—a soul-deep connection that tells me we are meant for one another.

"S-so, we're definitely not kissing?" I ask, voice trembling.

"No." His reply comes as a strangled groan over my neck. He drops his forehead on mine again, whispering, "But I promise waiting will be worth it."

I believe him. One hundred per cent. Turns out being respected is so much better than being ravaged. Any man could've taken me to bed tonight and to hell with the consequences. But it takes a real man to say no. To wait despite the way his body vibrates against mine with need, the same longing we share. And, anyway, Thomas's way of respecting me still feels a little ravaging.

He drops another kiss on my forehead and then lifts his face away from mine, barely putting any distance between us, but it's enough for me to want to pull him closer again.

I don't. I just keep staring into his smoldering eyes.

He stares right back. "You'd better say goodnight to me now, baby."

The way he says baby lands straight in my core like an incandescent meteor, while the idea of having to say goodbye to him, to have to go back to my room alone, freezes my throat. Hot and cold. How about we find a warm middle?

"Can I sleep with you tonight?" I blurt out. "Just sleep."

Thomas smiles down at me and shakes his head.

"If you don't want to, I can go back to my room."

I make to scoot sideways, away from him, but he pins me in place with his hips.

Oh gosh.

"Of course I want to, Campbell."

"Then what is it?" I grip his arms because I need the support or I'm going to slump down this wall like a limp rag.

"It's that I'm still in prison, only now you've also left the door open and asked me not to escape."

"Am I the prison in this scenario?"

He shakes his head. "No, baby, you're freedom, you're the light at the end of the tunnel. But I'm still a prisoner tonight." He presses a soft kiss to my collarbone. "The most willing one."

That seems to have settled it for him, because next he grabs my hand and says, "Come on." He tugs me toward him. Then, unexpectedly, he scoops me up and carries me over to his bed.

Before he can drop me, I protest, "I need to change first."

Thomas does a one-eighty with me still in his arms and brings me back to my room. He gently drops me on the floor and sits on the bed.

I walk between his legs and pull his hair back, admiring his beautiful face. "Close your eyes."

29

THOMAS

I close my eyes and weirdly enough *not* seeing what's happening is more sensual than if I was watching her undress.

Reese stays put between my legs as she pulls the soft sweater she was wearing over her head. I can tell that's what she's doing from the sounds and movements she makes. I brush my hands up the back of her thighs over her leggings until the fabric comes loose, and she shimmies out of it. She must be down to her underwear now, and there's never been sweeter torture than not being able to see her in it.

Reese leans sideways. If I had to guess, to retrieve those silky PJs from under the pillow. Fabric swooshes. Then she's back to standing straight between my legs.

I explore with my hands. She's half bare and half covered in silk in what I suppose are PJ shorts and a loose tank top. I'm dying to know what color.

Speaking like a man who hasn't had a drink of water for days, I ask, "What color is the silk?"

Her fingers brush over my hair, making my scalp prickle, the goosebumps traveling down my spine.

"A deep green with an orange carrot pattern."

My eyes flutter open, my lips pulling apart into a smile. "You're lying."

I look down at her and a breath catches in my throat as I take in the simple pale pink silk, and all the smooth skin in between.

I pull her up and drop her onto the bed, tickling her sides. "Didn't anyone tell you it's bad to lie?"

She laughs and tries to wiggle free. "Please, stop. Please."

Her laughter is music to my ears. I keep tickling her until tears stream down her face.

When I finally stop, she's panting, her cheeks flushed with color. She looks up at me with wide eyes that are full of emotion.

I have to muster every drop of self-control I possess to pull away from her and roll over to my side of the bed.

"You'd better burrow under those covers if you want me to keep acting like a gentleman," I threaten.

Reese is still catching her breath. "Are gentlemen notorious for their merciless tickling?" she teases but still wiggles under the soft, white covers, leaving only a sliver of her tantalizing skin exposed. Collarbones shouldn't be that sexy, but I might die if I don't touch one of hers now. I trace a finger down her left one, and she shivers under the blankets.

I shake my head and crawl in beside her, pulling the blankets up to our chins.

"Are you cold?" she asks.

I turn my face on the pillow to watch her. Her hair is fanned out around her face, framing it in a brown-pink halo like Botticelli's Venus.

"No, this is just a precautionary measure."

She blushes and bites her lower lip.

"Don't do that," I say, tucking a strand of hair behind her ear.

"You have the most beautiful eyes," she says.

I grin. "Smoldering, I believe someone once said." I waggle my eyebrows.

"Jerk." She pushes me away but I grab her and tuck her into me.

Her warmth against me is divine. I bury my face in her hair to savor it better, reveling in the sweet scent of her shampoo. She reaches for the switch on the wall and plunges the room into almost complete darkness.

In the dark, she whispers, "I never thought *not* being kissed would be so romantic."

"I never thought I'd be the one to say no to kissing you."

"Have you wanted to do it for a long time?"

I pull her further into me, molding her back to my front. "I've wanted to kiss you since day one, Campbell."

She makes a small noise and turns in my arms to face me. Even if we can't see each other, I know she's looking at me. Reese tentatively traces her hand up my arm and cups my face, dropping a gentle kiss on my cheek. "Thank you for waiting."

I want to say thank you for existing, but that seems a little melodramatic. Instead, I flip her back into a spooning position and ask, "Which website did Chewbacca get arrested for creating?"

She shakes her head on the pillow.

"Wookieleaks."

Reese laughs, which makes me smile, and I'm still smiling when I fall asleep with her in my arms.

30

REESE

Waking up next to Thomas is not awkward even if I'm half-naked and he's... happy to see me? I scoot away from the warmth of his body before I auto-combust and do something stupid. After putting a little space between us, I drink in his beautiful sleeping face like a total creep who watches people sleeping.

I groan.

Eyes still closed, he reaches out for me and pulls me back in, careful to keep a respectful distance between us. "Don't freak out, Campbell, we're fine."

And somehow, I believe him. I snuggle back into his embrace until the alarm sounds and we're jerked back to reality.

Our time in Rome flies by all too quickly and before I know it, we're headed to the airport and back to the States.

As the plane takes off, I can feel Thomas's eyes on me. I turn to face him and find him smiling at me; the smile quickly turns into a mischievous smirk. He reaches for my hand and our fingers intertwine, the usual tingles shooting up my arm.

The entire time on the plane, I can't stop smiling like an idiot whenever our eyes meet. And when we land, I'm not even that tired

—mostly energized. Admittedly, traveling comfortably nestled in the first-class thrones might've helped.

We make our way through customs and baggage claim—which takes forever—and when we reach the arrivals hall where all the other passengers are being met by friends and family, a company driver is waiting for us with Mercer Robotics spelled out in black pixels on a white screen.

It's a jarring return to reality. One where Thomas, as of now, is still on a path to becoming my future boss and therefore undatable. Untouchable. Unkissable.

Subconsciously, I take a step away from him, putting some professional distance between us.

Since it's Sunday, at least we're not going straight to the office but back to our respective places. Thomas insists on driving to mine first.

We're quiet on the drive, lost in our own thoughts. When we reach my apartment, I want nothing more than to invite him in— and if we'd ridden here in a regular cab, I probably would have. But our driver works for the company, he could spread gossip, and so I purse my lips and keep quiet.

We end up having the most awkward parting on the curb. Thomas seems undecided on how to say goodbye, when it looks like he's going in for a hug, I push my arm forward and offer him my hand to shake.

Thomas smirks but still takes my proffered hand—but in a way that's not strictly professional. I don't know how a handshake can be turned sensual, but he manages it. It could be the way he touches me, the twinkle in his eyes, or the playful smile that tugs at his lips.

And when he winks at me and says, "See, you tomorrow at the office, Campbell," my heart does a somersault.

I watch him climb back into the car and wave at me through the window. As the car pulls away, a pang of sadness hits me. I turn around and head into my building, feeling despondent. In my apartment, I sag onto the couch and grab my purse, wanting to send him a text or at least stalk his Instagram a bit. Instead, hidden in the folds of my bag, I find a blue note.

The thrill is so intense because I wasn't expecting this one.

Rome wasn't built in a day, but I'll talk with my dad soon.
 Thomas, x
 PS. What do you call an invisible droid?
 C-through-PO.

The joke is so cringe that I laugh my head off. Then, I hug the Post-it to my chest as I smile at the ceiling. Monday morning can't come fast enough.

31

THOMAS

The moment I turn the corner from Reese's building, my phone rings in my pocket. Gabriel.

"Where are you?" He growls down the line the second I pick up. "You're thirty minutes late for brunch."

Brunch at my parents, shit. I'd completely forgotten about it.

"Ah, yeah, sorry, I don't think I'm going to make it."

I can almost picture Gabriel's raised eyebrow. "How come?"

"I just landed after an intercontinental flight, and traffic is bad. No chances of me getting to the Upper East Side in time."

"Intercontinental? Where did you jet to?"

"Rome."

"A little Roman holiday?"

"No, I was at a business conference."

"Ah." I hear shuffling noises as if Gabriel is moving away from the rest of the family, and then he speaks again. "Were you alone or with a certain pretty department head on your *business* trip?"

"I was with Mr. Mind Your Own Business, have you heard of him?"

"Oooh, someone's touchy today. So, what should I tell Mom and Dad?"

"That I just came back from a work trip and I won't be able to make it."

I end the call, relieved that I won't have to face Dad today. I want to pull out of Mercer Robotics, but my father won't enjoy having his plans thwarted, and that's definitely a conversation I'm not looking forward to having.

When I arrive at the office on Monday morning, Reese is already there.

"Morning," I say as I walk through the door.

She lifts her head and beams at me. "Morning."

My first instinct is to go to her and pull her into a hug. But I have to keep myself in check—also, K-2P gets in my way, whirring and spinning in what I assume is the droid version of wagging his tail.

I laugh and ruffle his metal exterior before heading over to my desk.

The droid follows me. "Did you miss me?"

"I did, but I was in good company." I shoot Reese a look from across the office. She isn't looking at me, but her cheeks slightly color all the same. "What about you? Did you have fun with Maria?"

K-2P beeps in affirmation. "Even if she made me watch *The Bachelor* with her."

I snort a laugh. "You not a fan of reality TV?"

"I don't understand why people watch that show, and the guy wasn't even that hot."

I honestly don't have a reply to that.

After a while, Reese stands up and walks by my desk, a gleam in her eye. "I need to do the rounds and let everyone know I'm back. Wanna come with me?"

I nod and follow behind her as she sets out across the lab. We make our way around, stopping at each station to talk to the various team leaders about their projects. Everyone is eager to share their progress with Reese—from coding robots that can detect motion, to developing new AI algorithms for facial recognition software.

Reese listens attentively to each of her team leaders, not missing a single detail. She offers her expertise where needed and gives praise where it's due. Her enthusiasm for each project is infectious—it's clear how much she loves what she does here at Mercer Robotics.

When we run into Garrett—the process technology team leader—his eyes light up when he sees Reese, and he immediately starts talking excitedly about his work. I notice the dude does his best to pretend I don't exist.

After some more small talk and a few jokes between them, Reese and I continue on our tour of the lab while Garrett returns to his workstation with a spring in his step. Clearly, the guy has a crush on her, and hates me, making it even more clear why we can't openly date while working in the same division. But that's going to end soon.

All the status advancement reviews go pretty well, except for the giant robotic arm in the middle of the lab which is still misbehaving.

When we come back into the office, Reese sits at her desk and drops her head in her hands.

"That giant thing not following instructions is bothering you, huh?" I take the chair opposite her.

She straightens up. "I just don't understand what we're doing wrong. We've tried everything, but we just don't seem able to switch from point-based teaching to path-based teaching."

I wish I could be of some help, but she might as well be speaking Parseltongue. "I'm sorry."

"It's nothing." She waves me off. "I'm sure we're going to crack it, eventually. I just wish we didn't have the added pressure of Bios Torc Solutions being on our heels," she says, talking about the Californian hippies—as Ari called them—trying to develop the same technology.

"I'm not worried," I say, and Reese frowns at me interrogatively. "If anyone can solve the issue, it's you."

Her eyes flicker up to meet mine. "Thanks for the vote of confidence," she says softly, breaking eye contact to look down at her hands. "But don't be so sure."

I am overcome with the urge to reach over and take her hands in mine. To kiss every single one of her knuckles.

But Maria interrupts my amorous impulses, barging into the office without knocking.

"Hey, big bosses, we're going to lunch, you want to..." She trails off. "Did I interrupt something? Were you two having a moment?"

"No, of course not." Reese stands up abruptly, looking the opposite of collected. "I'm coming..." She blushes furiously. "To lunch, I mean..."

I smirk at Reese's apparent agitation and stand up as well, ready to follow her out of the office.

Maria grins knowingly and steps aside to let me go first while linking arms with Reese.

I peek behind me; they're still rooted in place. "You coming or what?"

Maria raises a finger. "We'll be right there, hot shot. We only need a minute."

I shrug and go meet the rest of the group who are gearing up with coats and scarves to brave the chilly November day.

Whatever Maria has to say, it's probably better if I'm not there to hear it.

The woman scares the living hell out of me.

32

REESE

As soon as Thomas leaves the room, Maria turns to me with a Cheshire Cat grin on her face. "My. My. My. You could cut the sexual tension in this room with a knife. Did something happen in Rome?"

I roll my eyes. "No, nothing happened in Rome. It was a business trip," I say dismissively, but I can feel the heat coloring my cheeks.

Maria raises an eyebrow, clearly not convinced. "Uh-huh, sure. Well, if you ever want to vent about your repressed feelings for Thomas, you know where to find me."

I laugh and playfully shove her. "Shut up, Maria."

We walk out of the office and join the others, making our way to a nearby bistro for lunch.

I make a point of sitting at the opposite end of the table to Thomas.

I know it isn't fair to him, but I'm too embarrassed by the reactions being near him causes, especially when we're in public and within view of our co-workers.

When we finish our meal and head back to the office, I grab my laptop and am about to flee the room to go work someplace else, when Thomas steps in, blocking the door.

He takes one look at my flustered face and the laptop in my arms and it's as if he can read "escape plan" on my forehead.

Thomas suppresses a smile and steps slightly to the side to let me pass, but as I'm scurrying past him, he stops me, grabbing me gently by the arm and leaning in to whisper in my ear, his voice low and serious, "We'll figure it out."

I look up at him in surprise. I'm dying to ask when he's going to talk to his father about making the switch from Mercer Robotics. But he told me yesterday in the note that he's planning on doing it soon, and I don't want to seem pushy. Clingy. Needy. Desperate. Even if I feel all these things.

I wish feelings were as simple as an algorithm. I could change a few variables and tell my heart not to trash in my chest every time Thomas looks at me this way. But love is irrational, impractical, inconvenient. There's no logic. It's the opposite of an algorithm. No control. Only a plunge into the void and blind faith.

So, I simply nod and flee the office to go work in an empty conference room in a quest to avoid his proximity as much as I can for the rest of the day.

When I come back a few hours later, Thomas is nowhere to be seen, and I have no one to blame but myself for the pit of disappointment in my stomach. I wish K-2P goodnight and grab my things to head home.

As I eat microwavable fettuccine Alfredo on the couch alone, I'm melancholic about Italy. I stir the food in my bowl without much appetite. Now that I've tasted real pasta, the way it's supposed to be made, the knock-off version is no longer cutting it. I drop the half-finished meal in the sink and go grab my bag from where I've dropped it on the floor. The only thing that could cheer me up right now is one of Thomas's notes—at least while the author himself remains off-limits.

I find the blue Post-it lying at the bottom. But before I read it, I change into PJs and get ready for bed. I bring the small sheet of blue paper to bed with me and finally scan the handwritten note.

Is Maria onto us? Don't worry, I've made an appointment to speak with my father tomorrow morning.

PS. I left something for you in your desk, first drawer on the right.

The note brings me relief and unrest simultaneously. I'm glad that he's going to talk to his father right away like he promised, but now I'm also frothing at the mouth to know what he's left hidden in my desk.

Ah, well, I guess I'll have to wait until tomorrow to find out.

I scoot under the covers and switch off the light. Resting my head on the pillow, I close my eyes. Then open them, staring at the black ceiling. I turn on my right side and force my lids shut. I toss and roll over to my left side. Then I sprawl on the bed in starfish pose and exhale a puff of air, trying to calm my restless mind. But I can't shake off the need to find out what surprise Thomas has left for me.

Well, it's not like I'm going to get up in the middle of the night and go back to the office just to find out. It's not. I couldn't. Could I?

I turn the lights back on and check the time on my phone. It's barely a few minutes past nine—a slight jet leg had me go to bed early—but now I'm wide awake. I could go back to the office and be back in bed before eleven. And it'd be better than spending the entire night tossing and turning, wondering...

My mind made up, I throw the covers away from my body and hop off the bed. I grab a pair of black sweatpants and a hoodie that

I pull over my silk PJs. Sneakers and a coat are next, and then I'm already out of the apartment and sprinting down the road toward the dark subway station at the corner.

The train is the same as always, still full of people coming back from working late or heading out for a night of fun. But the journey feels longer than it ever did, making me sigh in relief when I finally arrive at the station closest to our offices.

The streets here are dark and desolate at this hour as Mercer Industries headquarters are located in an office district. I hurry the few blocks to the building and swipe my badge at the entrance doors, feeling much safer as I slip past them.

The hall is still and quiet as I cross the lobby, but as I reach the lower level, I find the lights in the lab still on. I expect to find Maria lost working on one of her algorithms, or Ari testing out a new prototype... but to my surprise, when I peep through the glass door windowpane, I discover K-2P standing next to Thomas while they both look intently at the giant robotic arm that has been giving me so many headaches lately.

They seem totally lost in their research while completely ignoring the time...

I cautiously open the lab door, not wanting to startle them.

Thomas still hears the noise and lifts his head.

"Hi," I say, already slightly out of breath as our eyes meet. I cross the lab to join them at Ari's station. "What are you still doing here? I thought you'd already gone home?"

"I was upstairs, bribing my father's assistant for a last-minute appointment." Thomas smiles, melting all my reproductive organs. "Then we got lost having a look at the big guy," he explains, patting the misbehaving robotic arm. "I know I don't understand anything about robots, but I was pretty good at statistics in college. So, I asked K-2P to run a diagnostic on all our failed trials and see if he could find a pattern."

My gaze drifts down to my small droid. "Did you find anything?"

He gives me a negative bleep.

"I'm sorry." Thomas shrugs. "I knew it was a long shot, so I didn't want to say anything about it."

"And you spent all evening here, working on this? Why?"

"I saw how worried you were about this project and wanted to pitch in."

Before my heart can burst into flames and explode in my chest, he adds, "Sorry I'm useless." He rotates his shoulders. "And now I'm also sore."

"Sore?"

"Yeah, this guy"—he pats the robotic arm again—"is a pain to move. We ran a few simulations and the recoil almost kicked me flat on my bum, I don't know how Ari operates it with those skimpy arms of hers."

"Oh my gosh." I slap a hand over my forehead. "Oh my gosh! This entire time we've been looking at this wrong. We've been going for a sensor-based, hand-guiding system, compensating only for the inertia of the robot but not the inertia of the operator. That's why it never calibrated right, but if we switched to a method based on torque control..." I look at Thomas and my entire world tilts.

33

THOMAS

"...We could use the dynamic and friction models of the robotic arm along with the motor current to predetermine the user intentions on where to move the end-effector instead of directly recording the external force with sensors..."

I raise my eyebrows and smile at Reese. I didn't understand a single thing she just said, but it looks like she's having a moment.

She paces in a small circle, holding her chin in her hand. "The new approach could be a game changer."

Abruptly, she stops and looks up at me. "You're a genius."

I'm about to say that I did nothing when she does something even more unexpected. She grabs my face and stamps a kiss full on my mouth. "You're a flipping genius."

She's smiling widely, and she's not letting go of my face, I note. Instead, her hands wrap behind my neck and her fingers sink into my hair, causing a shiver to run down my spine.

Our gazes hold, and I get lost in the warm brown of her irises.

I want to kiss her again, deeply, passionately. I want to feel her body pressed against mine and taste the sweetness of her lips. But I can't. Not here. Not until I've spoken to my father.

"Thank you," I say with a smile, making to pull away from her grip, but she doesn't let me go.

"What are you doing?" I whisper.

Her fingers keep caressing the hair at my nape as she replies, "I'm being brave."

A jolt of electricity runs through me as Reese leans in again, and this time the kiss has more intent. Her lips are soft and warm against mine, and the scent of her shampoo fills my nostrils. My arms wrap around her waist, pulling her closer to me. I'm almost afraid she'll disappear if I let go.

For a moment, everything else fades away—the lab, the robot arm, even K-2P emitting alarmed beeps next to us—and it's just Reese and me, caught up in each other.

Reese presses into me to get closer, and the momentum pushes us backward until my butt hits the workstation behind me. In a moment of slight insanity, I pull Reese up and flip us around so that now Reese is seated on the workbench, legs wrapped around me, eyes hooded with desire.

She pulls me down to kiss me again. I know I shouldn't let this continue. We should press pause and talk. Not to mention we are in the middle of our office, and anyone could walk in on us at any moment even if it's late at night.

But, gosh, I don't want this to stop.

I give myself a few more seconds of life in paradise before I break the kiss, and breathlessly pull away from her. "Reese," I say, almost pleadingly. "We need to stop."

She looks at me with dazed eyes, her pupils blown wide. "Why?" she asks, as if nothing else matters at this moment.

"I haven't spoken to my father yet."

"But you will, tomorrow, and I want you. I want you *now*."

The meaning of her words doesn't really sink in until she gently shoves me away and hops off the workstation, slipping her hoodie over her head. Underneath, she's wearing one of her maddeningly sexy silk pajama tops.

K-2P emits another series of distressed beeps.

Reese turns to the droid and, voice thick and hoarse, she commands, "K2-P, please go take a stroll at the vending machines."

The robot bleeps in dismay. "Yes, my optical sensors don't need to see this."

We watch him hightail it and we both laugh as he disappears out of the lab.

I drop my forehead to hers. "We don't have to do anything tonight, you know, there's no hurry..."

"No hurry?" she croaks. "I feel like I might die if you don't kiss me again."

I can't reason being this close to her, so I take a step back. But it's a mistake because she uses the extra space to get rid of the sweatpants. Now she's standing in front of me wearing only a flimsy top and silk shorts.

My eyes widen as I take in her body, completely caught off guard by her sudden boldness. But before I can even think of a response, she steps closer again, pushing me against a different workstation. Her body is pressed against mine, and I can feel every curve and contour of her as she presses against me and kisses me passionately.

I capitulate. My hands reach up to tangle in her hair as our lips meet again. The heat between us is intense, and I know right then that I'll never be the same after tonight. I'll never feel complete without Reese.

"Thomas," she whispers, pulling back and breaking me out of my trance. Reese gently caresses the side of my face as she gazes at me. "I think I might be in love with you."

I swallow hard as I watch her, a smile tugging at my lips. "Babe,

I think I might've been a little in love with you since the day I met you."

She pouts. "Just a little?"

"No, not just a little." I cup her cheeks and make sure that she hears me. "A lot in love with you, stupidly in love with you, in fact."

She searches my eyes. "I still can't believe that this is real, that you're real..."

"I'm real." I grab one of her hands and bring it over my heart. "This is real."

"Then give me what I want."

"Anything, baby, just tell me what it is you want."

"You, I want you."

34

REESE

Thomas's pupils double in size instantly, he scoops me up and carries me inside my office, the only private space in the lab, locking the door behind us.

He presses me against the wall and his lips descend on mine in a kiss that's desperate in its urgency.

My body responds eagerly, pressing up against his muscular frame with equal ferocity.

His hands are everywhere, roaming over my back, tangling in my hair, gripping my hips. The heat between us is almost unbearable. I moan into his mouth as he nips at my bottom lip before taking it between his own, sucking on it until I'm panting for breath.

Breaking the kiss, Thomas looks down at me with darkened eyes. "You have no idea how long I've wanted to do that," he breathes against my lips.

"I'm pretty sure I do."

"I've never wanted anyone like this."

I smile, breathless and giddy with desire. My knees go weak as he brushes his hand against the side of my face in the most tender caress. Then he kisses my mouth, feather-like soft, then my cheek, my earlobe. A gentle nip.

I moan again as he trails kisses down my neck and onto my collarbone. I've finally touched the sun and I'm burning and it's the best thing that ever happened to me.

"Tell me what you want," he whispers into my ear.

My entire body is trembling with desire. I want everything, but the only word I can manage to say is his name in a pleading whisper for more. "Thomas."

When he smiles, it's like the flutter of a thousand wings in my chest. His mouth caresses mine with gentle intensity while our kiss deepens again into something richer that awakens me on such a basic level all I can do is surrender to it entirely. My senses are filled with Thomas, from his scintillating touch to the sweet taste of him. The moment feels suspended in time as if neither one of us can take it slow or fast enough.

I'm vaguely aware of him reaching for the back of my pajama top, and then the flimsy fabric swooshes over my head and lands on the tile floor with a soft swish.

I return the favor and free Thomas of his cashmere sweater and the T-shirt underneath.

Now that I'm free to let my eyes roam over him, I take a moment to admire his broad chest, his shoulders, and his sculpted stomach.

I trace a finger down his pecs. "You're so beautiful."

The grin he flashes me in return is devastating. "As if you could talk, baby."

I watch him drink me in, and I've never felt more desirable in my entire life.

Thomas's mouth goes to my neck while his hands caress every inch of me before finding their way under my pajama bottoms.

A gentle push and the shorts are gone, joining the silk top on the floor.

Thomas scoops me up into his arms like I weigh nothing.

We are both breathing heavily as he lifts me up onto my desk. We kiss again and again until Thomas, visibly trembling pulls back.

His smile is soft and gentle, his eyes dark with desire. "Are you sure about this? Because I can't hold myself in check much longer…"

My only response is to unbutton his jeans. "Good, because I don't want you to hold back."

* * *

When Thomas is done *not* holding back, my office is a little worse for wear. A metal clip might be permanently stuck to my butt, and my desk may never be the same.

Still, I can't stop smiling. And even more weirdly, I don't feel awkward, not even when Thomas gets re-dressed and scuttles out of the lab to retrieve my lost sweats while I put my pajamas back on.

Once we're both decent again, I can't help myself. I go to him and hug him. I bury my face in the hard softness of his chest and breathe him in.

He gently strokes my hair. "Everything okay?"

"Never been better," I respond. "Can't say the same for my office."

I relish the low rumble of laughter that bubbles up from his chest. "Yeah, we'd better clean up before someone walks in here tomorrow morning and sounds the alarm."

Reluctantly, I let him go, and, together, we clear the mess. I collect a pen holder that tumbled to the floor, searching for the spilled pens, while Thomas gathers a stack of papers that have flown everywhere. Next, we clean up my photo frames that have miraculously remained intact. The same could not be said of the broken coffee mug Thomas retrieves from under my chair.

From his kneeling position on the floor, he looks at me with a cute frown. "Sorry about this." He puts the pieces together and smiles at the writing on the side of the mug: Yoda the best boss in the galaxy.

"Don't worry," I say. "Maria got me that; she'd be proud of the way it met its end."

Thomas throws the shards into the bin, and just like that, the office is back in shape. *Almost.* The desk is still slightly crooked, but there's nothing to be done. My desk may not be level ever again, and I'm okay with that. *Worth it.*

I catch Thomas's eye just as he looks away from the desk. We burst out laughing. Then he drops an arm on my shoulders and steers me out of the office.

K-2P is outside. He wheels past us sputtering. "If you're done sating your base human instincts, I'd like to plug in for the night."

"Good night." I lean in for a kiss to the dome but he wheezes past me, indignantly muttering, "You think you can kiss your droid with that mouth?"

I stare up at Thomas, beaming and blushing. "Fair enough."

He drops a kiss on top of my head. "Come, Campbell, I'm driving you home."

Because of the late hour and all the extracurricular activities, I almost fall asleep in the car. But as we stop in front of my building, I'm suddenly wide awake again.

"Do you want to come up?" I ask.

Thomas turns to me, hands still on the wheel, his expression positively ravenous. "I'd love nothing more, babe..."

"But?"

"But I have to see my dad early tomorrow morning and I'd

better show up with at least a few hours of sleep under my belt and in a clean suit."

"Yeah, you're right."

Still, I unbuckle my seatbelt and shave at least another half hour of sleep from under him. That's how long our goodnight kiss takes.

"See you tomorrow," I whisper, biting my swollen lips, and before I can change my mind, I hop out of the car and run the few steps up to my building.

When I get back into bed, many hours later than I'd initially planned, I fall asleep the moment my face hits the pillow.

35

THOMAS

The following morning, I strut into Mercer Industries' headquarters not nearly rested enough but still feeling on top of the world. Reese loves me. The smartest, most beautiful woman on the planet has chosen me. Is in love with me. I stroll past the entrance, parading myself like a king.

The extra spring in my gait, however, comes to a screeching halt the second I push past the turnstiles, and my father's personal assistant zeros in on me from across the lobby. Monica's heels clack loudly on the marble floors as she marches toward me and, not so gently, grabs me by the elbow to steer me toward the elevators. "Your father wants to see you in his office."

I check my watch. "Our appointment isn't for another half an hour."

"This cannot wait, Thomas."

Uh-oh. If Monica is using my first name, then something terrible must've happened.

The ride up to the fiftieth floor is silent and tension-ridden.

When I can no longer bear suspense, I mouth, "A heads-up would be nice."

Monica stares up at me and blushes, subtly shaking her head.

Okay, I should be in for an interesting meeting, then.

When we get to my father's office, the door is open.

Monica signals for me to go in then she bolts for the safety of her desk.

I knock on the open door to make my presence known and step into the office.

The head of Human Resources is sitting in a chair, back ramrod straight while my dad is standing, shoulders tense as he faces the wall-wide windows.

Keeping his back turned, he speaks. "Imagine my surprise this morning, son, when the head of security called me saying we had a *situation* that needed my attention."

I know better than to ask what the situation is; he's going to tell me.

Instead of speaking, my dad turns and with a remote in his hand, points at a flat screen mounted on a transportable cart.

As soon as he pushes play, the screen lights up on black and white footage of the robotics R&D lab.

Initially, K-2P and I are the only ones in the frame, then Reese joins us and I wince, knowing what comes next.

The footage is muted, but if there ever was no need for sound in a motion picture, this is it.

"Do we have to watch the whole thing?" I ask, gritting my teeth.

"Both Grant and I"—he gestures at the HR director—"the security guards on duty last night, and the head of security have already watched it. I thought a replay might bring you up to speed on the delicacy of my conundrum."

"If you really need a father-son teachable moment."

I have mixed feelings as I watch Reese on the screen as she removes her hoodie. On one side, damn, she's sexy, and she's mine.

On the other, I really don't appreciate how many people have seen this.

After Reese and I barrel into the office, my dad pushes the fast-forward button and keeps it pressed. For. A. Long. Time.

He raises an eyebrow. "At least you did the Mercer stamina justice."

The recording ends with Reese and I walking out of the lab.

Another push of a button and the screen goes dark.

My dad drops the remote on his desk with a loud clunk. He's still standing, and that doesn't bode well.

"While fraternization among employees who are not in a direct reporting line to each other isn't forbidden, you'll be Dr. Campbell's supervisor soon. Regardless, the usage of office facilities for dalliances is highly proscribed. A fireable offense."

Dread creeps down my spine like a stream of molten lava. "Dad—"

He raises a hand to silence me.

"Now, I can't very well fire you, nor Dr. Campbell it seems, at least if I don't want to leave this company open to several potential lawsuits—"

"Reese would never—"

"You don't know what she would or wouldn't do." He's not shouting, but the deadly calm in his voice is far worse. "When I assigned you to her division a month ago, I didn't imagine her foolhardy enough to become involved with my son. Or to have sex with him in her office.

"Now, Grant assures me that as long as you both sign a module saying the relations were consensual and no harassment has taken place, we should be covered from the brunt of potential legal repercussions.

"The head of security has already wiped the company drives of all recordings, the phones of the security guards on duty last night were checked for eventual second-hand footage, and they both came out clean. I'm confident we can keep the video from being leaked to the press. The tabloids would surely have a field day with such material."

My dad nods at the head of HR, and Grant stands up, handing me two sheets of paper. "Please sign one, and have Dr. Campbell sign the other."

"Thank you, Grant." My dad dismisses him. "Please close the door on the way out."

Once my dad and I are alone, there's a long beat of silence before he sighs and finally sits at his desk. "I expected better from you." He lets the words sink in, lets them hurt a little before he continues, "I get it, you're young and hot-blooded, Thomas, but she's an employee. And you have responsibilities, or you will have them soon once you sit in this chair. You can't keep on acting like an unruly teenager whose actions have no consequences."

I take the chair opposite him. "Dad, this is not what it looks like."

"No? Then what is it, Thomas?" His voice is hard, but there's a glimmer of sadness in his eyes. "Didn't you just get caught on camera having sex with an employee? How do you suppose anyone is going to respect you—or *her*—if news gets around? Already getting the heads of production and sales at Mercer Robotics to accept you as the new CEO was going to be hard, now it's going to be near damn impossible."

"Good."

His eyes narrow. "What do you mean *good*?"

"I don't want to be CEO of Mercer Robotics."

He leans back in his chair. "Let me guess, something to do with Dr. Campbell."

"She won't date me if I'm her boss."

"I have substantial video evidence to the contrary."

I wince again. "Last night was a lapse in judgment, I'll give you that, but it wasn't just sex. I'm in love with her, Dad. That's why I wanted to see you this morning because I can't be at Mercer Robotics. I want to move to a different division."

"You've just been announced to the board."

"Then unannounce me."

Dad massages his temples. "Have you any idea how immature that sounds? I can't present a succession plan to the board and then call them a month later and say I've changed my mind. That's no way of conducting business, it'd make me—*us*—look ridiculous."

I take a deep breath and steady my nerves. "Dad, I understand that, but a board of crusty old men is not my priority right now. I love Reese, and I can't lose her."

My dad leans back in his chair; I can practically see the cogs whirring furiously in his head. He thought he'd brought me here for a scolding and instead, I'm the one dishing out the medicine.

"Okay," he finally concedes. "But you can't leave right away."

"Why not?"

"I need to come up with a presentable alternative before you switch divisions."

"How long are we talking here? How much time do you need?"

"Give me six months."

36

REESE

When I walk into the lab the next morning, my belly flutters as I remember what happened here last night. I shake my head in an effort to chase the memories away, and head straight for Ari's station. I want to share with her the idea of switching to torque control.

But as I approach her desk, it's hard not to be reminded of how I kissed Thomas for the first time against her worktable, or how he flipped me onto the tooling bench next door.

My flashbacks aren't the only unusuality today. There also seems to be an odd amount of chatting around the lab. My normally quiet, introverted engineers are buzzing with a weird energy.

Or maybe I'm just projecting my over-excited mental state onto them.

I reach Ari and attempt to concentrate on work and nothing else.

"Hey, Ari," I greet her.

"Morning, boss."

"Listen, I had an idea last night to solve our calibration problem. What if we switched to a predictive method based on torque control?"

"You mean instead of using sensors?"

"Exactly. Use the dynamic and friction models coupled with the motor current to predetermine the user intentions."

"Why?"

"So that the inertia of the operator will stop messing our readings?"

"The operator." Ari's eyes widen. "The inertia, of course."

I'm about to ask how long it will take us to develop the new model when a burst of chuckling explodes at the nearby station. I didn't make that up. That's definitely abnormal behavior.

"Hey, what's going on?" I ask Ari. "Did something happen?"

Ari shrugs. "There's gossip going around that someone made a sex tape in the lab last night."

My cheeks drain of color while also flaming up at the same time.

"A-a s-sex tape?" My eyes dart to the ceiling where, sure enough, tiny dome security cameras dot the corners. Oh. My. Gosh! How did I never notice those?

"Yeah, someone heard from someone who overheard it from the security guards on duty last night talking at the vending machines. They've been trying to bribe K-2P all morning to tell them who it was, but so far, he hasn't budged."

They don't know it was me. Or Thomas. Or me with Thomas. Still, I panic. But I can't have a meltdown in front of the entire floor.

I do my best to keep my voice steady as I say, "Please, work out some projections on what it'd take to switch to torque control."

Ari eyes me sideways. "Are you okay, boss?"

I don't know what distress signals I'm sending, but it must be something if she's picked up on it. I'd better hide and not show my face around for the rest of eternity.

"Yeah, I'm super." I force a fake smile that I hope doesn't make me look like I'm having a stroke. "I'll be in my office if you need me."

I speed-walk across the lab and shut myself into the private space of my office. In a panic, I check the ceiling. No cameras here, thank goodness. Next, I take in the crooked desk that seemed so romantic last night and that now only screams reckless and stupid at me. Its helpless listing incriminating me all by itself.

How could I have let myself be so careless? I could lose my job, my reputation, everything I've worked for. My heart pounds in my chest as I attempt to come up with a plan to cover our tracks.

Does Thomas know? Who knows? Who's seen the video? Were our faces recognizable?

Oh gosh, oh gosh. I stripped right in the middle of the lab.

I'm pacing the office, hands in my hair, when the door bangs open and Garrett, face red, contorted in rage, accuses, "It was you, wasn't it? With *him*." The way he says "him" drips with hatred.

I play dumb. "I've no idea what you're talking about."

"The sex tape. It was you. I've seen the way you look at him, like a bitch in heat."

The violence of the words shocks me. "D-Don't be ridiculous," I stutter.

Garrett slams his fist on the door, making the glass rattle in its frame. "I'm not an idiot, Reese. Everyone is whispering about it."

The reaction is so unexpected I don't know how to react. I'm full-on panicking when Maria appears next to Garrett.

She takes in Garrett's angry stance, my shocked one, and asks, "What's going on here? Are you okay?"

I think she's talking to me, but Garrett answers her, spewing more venom, "No, I'm not okay. Unless you think our boss sleeping her way to the top is okay."

My jaw drops in shock as I stare at Garrett in disbelief.

Maria's eyes widen at his accusation before she glares at him and chides, "That's enough, Garrett. You have no right to make such accusations."

He scoffs and storms out of the room, leaving me reeling from his outburst.

"Reese, are you okay?" Maria asks as she steps into my office fully.

"I don't know," I reply. "Please close the door."

Maria does as I ask, and then she studies me, leaning against the closed door with her back.

I look at her. "What are the chances no one heard him say I'm the one who made the sex tape?"

Her jaw slacks. "Oh my gosh, it *was* you?"

I nod.

"Thomas?"

Another nod.

I'm expecting judgment, or scorn, or at least a disapproving look. But Maria's face breaks out into a huge grin. "Well, good for you."

"What?" I ask incredulously.

"I mean, it's not like you did it during work hours or anything. It's your personal life. And if I had a chance to nail such a hot piece of manly ass, I would." She waves at the surrounding space. "I wouldn't care much about the premises either. Sometimes passion can't be contained."

I'm floored. "But what about the implications for my job? My reputation? Everyone will say I'm a slut trying to sleep her way to the top. Garrett already did."

"Garrett's a jealous idiot." Maria shrugs. "Honestly, if people want to talk, they'll talk no matter what. And if you're good at your job, that's what matters in the end."

I stare at her, still reeling from Garrett's accusation but also comforted by her unexpected response. For a second, I even let myself believe everything will be all right.

But then there's another knock on the door and Lizzie comes in.

"What can I do for you?"

She hardly meets my gaze. "I need your signature on these mechanic parts orders." When she's done talking, her lips press into a hard, disapproving line.

I sign the purchase order and hand the documents back to her. "Thanks, *boss*," she says, the word "boss" definitely dripping with condescension.

"Did you hear that?" I ask Maria once Lizzie is gone.

"Hear what?"

"The way she said *boss*, like she despises me."

Maria tilts her head. "I didn't notice anything. You're projecting."

I'm about to reply when another knock resounds on the door, and I might very well lose it.

I definitely lose it when I say, "Come in," and Thomas walks into the room in a light-gray suit, looking like salvation and damnation all at once.

A bunch of contrasting emotions explode inside me: solace and despair, want and rejection, regret and longing, and a need to simultaneously claim and deny. I can't believe that everything has turned so upside-down in the few hours since we said goodnight.

Maria takes this opportunity to make things a thousand times more awkward by saying, "I'll leave you two to it."

She scoots out of the office and is about to close the door when K-2P angrily whizzes in. "Those nerds tried to hack me to show them my recordings from last night."

Thomas tilts his head. "I take it the cat is out of the bag?"

I point a finger at him, rage finally overpowering all other emotions. "Don't you dare make a joke about this."

He raises his hands, one of which is holding papers. "I wasn't about to."

"What's that?" I say, pointing at the documents.

Thomas closes the door before answering me. "HR forms, stating our relations of last night were—uh—consensual."

"Oh my gosh." I cover my face with my hands. "Everyone knows."

"No one knows."

"At least *someone* knows if they've already given you papers to sign. Who?"

Thomas drops the papers on my desk, taking a moment too long to reply. "Well, HR, obviously, the security guards who were on duty last night, the head of security and... my father."

I whimper. "Please tell me your father didn't see the video."

Thomas clears his throat. "Err..."

I finally collapse on my chair, hiding my head under my arms. "This isn't happening."

I sense the air shift and Thomas's presence next to me. "Would you like me to share the good news with you now?"

I lower my arms. He's perched on the desk next to my chair. "What good news?"

"My dad has agreed to move me out of Mercer Robotics."

A tiny spark of hope flickers inside me. "Are you serious?"

He beams at me. "Cross my heart."

"So, you no longer work here?"

His smile falters. "Yes, I do, but only for another six months. My father has asked me to stay on until he can present a new candidate to the board."

The flicker of hope in my chest is promptly extinguished by an icy draft, and I shake my head.

Thomas takes hold of my hands. "Why are you shaking your head? This is good news."

I pull my hands back. "No, it's not. Can't you see what your father is doing?"

Thomas's jaw tenses and he crosses his arms over his chest. "What?"

"He's rolling the ball into the future."

"And why would he do that?"

"He probably hopes we'll have either broken up in six months or gotten used to working together as a couple. It'd be easier for him to give us a special waiver to date than to pick a new CEO. But I can't be with you if you're here. Especially not after what happened last night."

"Are you serious? It's only six months."

"I *am* serious. People already suspect us, and I've been getting the side-eye all morning. My reputation is in tatters. Everyone in my team is gossiping about me."

"We can keep things on the down low at the office. I'll be moving on with my rotations to production soon and then I'll be out of Mercer Robotics for good."

"Not if your father has his way." I fiddle with a mechanical pencil. "I can bet you everything I have that in six months another reasonable request is going to come up. 'We still haven't found anyone for the job. Please, son, stay on a little longer.' And then it's going to be you becoming Interim CEO or some other scheme. Your father wants you here, and he's making sure you stay exactly where you are."

"I can make it extra clear to him that he only has six months and not a day longer."

"That's going to be useless; he's going to say yes now only to say no later."

"You're acting as if you know my father. He wouldn't do that to me."

"And you're acting like a boy who's afraid to stand up to his daddy."

The air suddenly turns thick as Thomas's eyes grow cold. He stands up, ferociously slow. "A man-child." His jaw ticks. "*Claro.*"

My jaw drops as I remember how his ex-girlfriend left him accusing him of being immature. And I just accused him of the same thing.

"Thomas, I—"

He raises a hand. "No, you made your point perfectly clear." Then he adds something in Spanish that I don't understand, but that sounds ominous enough, and storms out of the office, banging the door on his way out.

And I don't even care that the scene is probably going to fuel the office gossip. All I care about is the fact that I either have to quit my job or quit seeing Thomas, and I'm not sure I can do either.

"What did he even say?" I ask out loud.

"You don't want to know," K-2P offers from the corner where he's been keeping oddly quiet.

"And since when do you speak Spanish?"

"Thomas is teaching me."

"Teaching you?"

"Yes."

"Why?"

"Because I told him I wanted to learn it like a person and because he's a good man."

With that last scathing remark, K-2P goes to his station and, even if it's the middle of the day, he powers down just as another crack spreads down my heart.

37

THOMAS

I storm out of Mercer Industries with my head in a jumble. I get into my car and drive away, not even sure where I'm headed.

This morning I woke up the happiest man alive, and now all that happiness is slipping through my fingers like sand. No matter how hard I try to hold on to it, it's scattering in the wind.

It hurts to think that Reese believes my father is trying to pull my strings. My dad isn't a bad person, or a bad parent, but he's a ruthless businessman. Deep down, it hurts more that she might be right. That I might've been too naïve to see it.

Childish. Foolish. Not smart enough.

She's too much for me, I'm not enough for her.

She's no doubt already regretting what happened last night—at least the "in the office" part of it.

The thought slashes across my chest, cutting deep.

What if the backlash from the sex tape is enough to end our relationship before it even starts?

One thing Reese made crystal clear: if I stay at Mercer Robotics, we're done.

Should I go back on my word to my father?

I sure don't like the sound of that, but what's the alternative?

I grit my teeth and grab the steering wheel so hard my knuckles hurt.

As the skyscrapers of upper Manhattan come into view, I finally realize where I'm headed. My brother's office.

I park in his building's space reserved for guests and sit in the car, alone, in the semi-darkness of the underground garage, thinking.

What now? What do I do?

Do I really have to choose between my family and the woman I love? Can I stand to disappoint my dad? To confirm that I'm incapable of taking responsibility for the family business? That I don't deserve to be his successor?

And what am I doing in my brother's basement, anyway? Can't I solve a problem on my own without running to a responsible adult for help?

Yes, I can. I *will* solve my own problems. Reese deserves to be with a man. I'm not just going to sit here and feel sorry for myself.

I'm about to put the car into gear when a knock on my car window makes me jump.

I turn my head and find Gabriel on the other side, peering down at me with a curious expression.

He beckons for me to exit.

I get out of the car. My brother is standing there hands shoved into his suit pants, head tilted to the side, staring at me interrogatively. "When security alerted me my brother was about to pay me a visit, I didn't know what to expect." He raises one brow. "Then when you sat in the car for half an hour without coming out, I thought I'd better come to check on you."

I shrug, running a hand through my hair. "Just needed some me time to think."

Gabriel nods, understanding passing between us. "My parking

facilities are state-of-the-art and you can do all the thinking you want here, but perhaps you'd like to come up to my office instead?"

I hesitate, but then I know I can't keep bottling everything up inside. I nod.

Gabriel places a hand on my shoulder, a small smile forming on his lips. "Let me guess, women troubles?"

* * *

An hour and a half later as I drive home from my brother's office, I'm nowhere near closer to finding a solution. Gabriel confirmed I can't exclude the possibility that Dad, by postponing the decision, is trying to bend me to his will without me even noticing. But my brother also asked if I was ready for the consequences of a fallout with our father should I choose Reese over him.

What's Dad going to do? Fire me?

And even if he does, would that really be so terrible?

Except for the fact that I'd be out of a job, and no one would hire the son of a billionaire to do anything, I guess it wouldn't be the end of the world.

Now I finally understand why Gabriel resisted the easy path of coming to work in the family business with every ounce of will he had in him.

And maybe that's what I should do too, set out on my own. Grow up. Start a company.

To do what?

To make a difference in the world. To create something that I believe in, rather than just pleasing my father's shareholders. To be my own boss, make decisions for myself, and not have to live in the shadow of my father's legacy. No matter how easy and downhill that road has been, maybe it's time for a little uphill climb.

I stop at a red light, and a thought occurs to me. It's mere seconds, but the idea takes clear shape in my mind. And then I laugh because maybe, just maybe, the way for me to grow up is to go back to thinking like a child.

38

REESE

I had envisioned tonight to be a lavish affair with champagne flowing and a lot of we-can-finally-be-together sex. Instead, I'm alone, having a glass of not-so-good wine I picked up at a liquor store for the sole reason that it was pink.

I want to see Thomas, kiss him, hear his voice, have him tell me everything is going to be all right. I pick up my phone to call him or text him at least a thousand times, but every single time, I drop the phone back down because what am I going to say?

Either he quits, or I do. Thomas didn't seem very inclined to go against his father. And I've spent the best part of two hours looking for jobs online. All positions at director level like mine require ten or more years of experience in a managerial role. I've only been in mine for two. At Mercer Robotics, I got lucky. I started at entry level, but my boss recognized the potential in me in less than a year working together and then started grooming me to take over right away.

And the hard-ass engineers in my department had time to get to know me and trust in my capabilities before I took over.

But to go into an interview cold, with my young face and pink hair... they're going to take one look at me and think I'm joking.

I could go to a headhunter and have them cash in on my reputation. But even if by some stroke of luck, a company gave me the job, I know how hard it'd be to gain the respect of a new team who's never worked with me. The struggle it'd be to get older, more experienced people to follow my lead. Plus, the idea of leaving *my* people, *my* projects, is daunting. I don't want to lose them.

But I also don't want to lose *him*.

So, what?

Maybe I'll be so miserable at work from now on with all the gossip about that stupid sex tape that I'll want to quit.

That is if Thomas wants anything to do with me at all, considering how I hit him below the belt and threw his ex-girlfriend's words right back into his face.

He was so angry. No, worse, he was hurt and crestfallen.

What did I expect him to do, anyway? Choose me over his family's empire?

No one has ever chosen me. Samuel chose his family. My last boyfriend chose his pride. My father chose freedom from responsibility. And my mother chose herself. Maybe I'm not worthy of being chosen. And even this time, Thomas will choose his family, his billions, his legacy. Not me. It's never me.

And, honestly, I can't expect Thomas to throw all his privileges away after a single night of passion. Yeah, he said he loved me. But now, that love has to be tested against his loyalty to his family and his duty to uphold the Mercer name. And I knew that going in. I knew the risks, but I couldn't stay away from him. Not when he looked at me with those intense, gold-speckled hazel-green eyes that can see into my soul.

And now I can't love him openly, and I can't go back to not loving him.

It sucks. Everything sucks.

* * *

The next few days are equally horrible. Thomas doesn't show up at work. Half the office gives me the side-eye while Maria keeps a steady flow of overly sweet coffee drinks coming my way.

On Wednesday, Garrett hands in a transfer request to a different department. He comes into my office wearing a new suit. How do I know it's new? He tells me. Garrett informs me he wore it specifically to interview with the head of production to make sure his transfer to a department with better morality went smoothly. I approve the request without a moment's hesitation. Glad he'll be someone else's problem from now on.

Later that day, I'm sitting at my desk doing a budget review with Maria when an email from Garrett pops up in my inbox. The subject line reads "Goodbye Friends."

I turn to Maria, not sure what to expect. A final insult? A genuine goodbye?

Maria grabs the mouse and clicks on it. "Let's see what the toad has to say."

The message is basically a long passive aggressive goodbye.

Maria rolls her eyes. "What a total tool."

Garrett concludes the email saying he's attaching a photo of all of us together on Halloween and reiterating how sorry he is to leave, but also specifying how his values won't allow him to do any different.

I frown as I see the extension of the attachment is an mp4, a video not a photo.

"He sent a video?" I ask. "You think it was a mistake?"

Maria shrugs. "Open it."

She leans over my shoulder as I hit play, and we both gasp.

Garrett has appeared on screen, shirtless and flexing in front of his bedroom mirror like a bodybuilder.

"Feel that muscle!" Garrett growls to himself in the video, kissing his biceps. "Garrett, you handsome devil, you're a born leader! Rooooarrr."

Maria and I stare at each other, jaws dropped. We can't believe what we're seeing.

"Check out those rock-hard abs!" video Garrett continues. "Ladies, control yourselves!"

That's it. Maria and I completely lose it, doubling over in laughter. I have tears streaming down my cheeks. We're howling, and I have to pause the video to catch my breath.

"Oh my gosh, can you believe that?" I say between fits of giggles.

Maria wipes her eyes, still cracking up. "That was the greatest thing I've ever seen. He's even more delusional than I thought!"

K-2P waltzes next to us. "Told yah he was pretty big on self-esteem."

"Yes but this?"

We laugh hysterically as I play the video again. Garrett just gifted us the best goodbye present ever.

On Thursday morning, I'm sure I've hit rock-bottom when I bump into a security guard, and the poor guy takes one look at me and his eyes widen in recognition. Then he lowers his gaze to the floor and blushes from his neck to the tips of his ears. He must've been one of the guards on duty the night I desecrated the lab with Thomas.

But Friday morning, things escalate to a new level of horribleness when I arrive at work and find Monica, Nolan Mercer's personal assistant, waiting for me in the lobby.

She greets me with a tight-lipped smile and informs me that Mr. Mercer would like a word with me in his office.

This time I don't need K-2P to run projections to know that I'm either getting fired or going to face some serious repercussions for my actions with Thomas.

The ride in the elevator is tortuously slow and nerve-racking. When we reach the top floor, Mr. Mercer's assistant barely meets my eye as she gestures to the corner office. "He's waiting for you."

Well, that doesn't sound ominous at all.

Bracing myself for the end of my career, I approach the open door.

Contrary to my previous visit, the president of the group is standing this time, his back turned to me as he stares out of his giant windows.

I've barely made it a step into the office when he calls out, "Please close the door behind you, Dr. Campbell."

So he can murder me with no witnesses? I still do as he says and even push a squeaky, "Morning, sir," out of my lips.

He doesn't turn, or sit, or invite *me* to sit. So I stand awkwardly in the middle of his corner office as he talks.

"I have to confess that when I assigned my son to your division for the beginning of his training, this was not the outcome I had in mind."

I'm not sure what "*this*" means to him. The sex tape? Thomas wanting to transfer to another division? Something else entirely?

I keep quiet and wait.

Ever so slowly, Nolan Mercer turns to face me and his eyes widen slightly. I wasn't forewarned about this meeting, so I'm standing in front of him wearing an old pair of jeans leggings and a black hoodie with "robotic dogs still byte" slashed in white print across the front. In the elevator, I haphazardly pulled my hair into a bun but without a mirror, I'm not sure if I properly concealed all the pink tips.

The president of Mercer Industries is still studying me, inexorably silent. What is he thinking?

Should I talk? Apologize for defiling his lab? His son?

Maybe it's better if I keep my mouth shut.

Finally, after what seems an interminably long time, Nolan Mercer moves toward his chair and gestures for me to do the same.

Sitting while facing each other makes things a fraction less awkward, but I still feel like I'm sitting on a seat made of thorns.

"So, you and my son?" Mr. Mercer pierces me with his laser-blue eyes.

I concentrate as best as I can on containing the heat in my cheeks. But if he's really seen the video, it might be too late to show any kind of decorum.

When I still don't talk, he picks up an envelope from his desk, flipping it in his hands. The back side is blank; on the front side, a single word is spelled out in black sharpie: yes.

My heart jolts in my chest as I recognize Thomas's handwriting.

"Thomas came in here last night and asked me to answer one question honestly."

My brain whizzes with possibilities. What question? And is yes the answer his father gave him? What's inside the envelope?

Nolan Mercer stares at me expectantly, letting me know it's time for me to become an active participant in this conversation.

"What question, sir?"

"He asked me if, come six months, I was planning to hold him down with another request to stay on at Mercer Robotics."

My eyes drop to the yes written on the envelope, then latch back onto Nolan Mercer's blue ones.

"The hint came from you, didn't it?"

I see no point in denying it. "And now you're angry with me?"

Thomas's father doesn't answer right away. But when he does, his lips tilt up at the corners. "To the contrary, Dr. Campbell. I'm surprised by you—a little blindsided, even. But mostly intrigued. When I asked Thomas to join Mercer Robotics, I wanted him to step up, to take responsibility for something so that he'd be more ready to step into my shoes one day. I sure didn't expect him to fall in love and quit the family business."

Thomas told his father he's in love with me *and he quit his job*? The two revelations battle for attention inside my brain. I haven't heard from him in three days, I've no idea what he's thinking. Until a minute ago, I wasn't even sure he still wanted anything to do with me. But if he handed in his resignation and told his father we're serious, then... maybe... there's hope.

I must be gaping at Thomas's father like an idiot because he clicks his tongue. "Ah, I take it this is news for you, too. Guess I'm not the only one who gets to be surprised these days."

I swallow. "Why have you called me here, sir?"

If it's not to fire me and not to give me a roasting, I want to know what I'm doing here.

"Ah, engineers." Nolan Mercer shakes his head, dare I say almost benevolently? "Going always straight to the point." He sighs. "You're here because I wanted to have a chat with the woman who made my son finally take life seriously, and made him eager to make something of his many talents, even if it won't be in the family business."

"I'm not fired?"

Nolan Mercer actually chuckles at that. "No, Dr. Campbell, you're not fired. Mercer Robotics has already lost too many excellent resources to part with another one. And you're too precious to the department, anyway. In fact, I should probably let you get back to work. I've been told Bios Torc Solutions is on our heels about hand-guided programming."

Am I being dismissed? Seems like it.

I give him a curt nod. "Very well, sir."

I stand up, but instead of letting me go like last time, Nolan Mercer stands up as well and escorts me to the door.

"Dr. Campbell," he starts, then stops. "May I call you Reese?"

This conversation is getting weirder by the second.

At a loss for words, I simply nod.

"Very well, Reese. And I don't expect you to call me Dad any time soon, but maybe you can drop the sir?"

"Yes, S—err..."

"Nolan will be fine."

I nod again.

He smiles and then winks at me. "Looking forward to seeing you at family brunch on Sunday."

39

REESE

Nolan Mercer winked at me and then invited me to Sunday brunch. What does that even mean?

As I ride down in the elevator, I feel like I'm having an out-of-body experience. Surely what just happened didn't really happen. It can't have happened.

Nolan Mercer can't have just told me it's okay that I'm single-handedly responsible for making the heir apparent to the family empire renounce the throne and that there will be no consequences.

I take out my phone and call Thomas. Straight to voicemail. Is his phone off, or has he blocked me? Why would he block me if he loves me? If he told his father he's *in love* with me?

I barrel into the lab and talk to no one as I head straight for Maria's station. "I need your phone."

She turns to me with a perplexed blink. "Morning, boss."

I gesture impatiently for the phone.

Raising both eyebrows, she hands it to me. I copy Thomas's number from my contacts and press call. Voicemail again. He didn't block me. His phone is off. Why is his phone off? Is he okay?

He must be; his father saw him just last night and didn't seem in the least worried about Thomas's well-being. He seemed proud.

Thomas, Thomas, Thomas... what are you up to?

I give Maria back her phone with a short, "Thanks," and head into my office.

My first instinct would be to get out of here and go search for Thomas. But his father made it clear where my place is, exactly here making sure we beat the competition out of the park. And I don't want to push my luck by making a sex tape at work, then persuading the chief's son to quit, and also slacking off at my job.

As welcoming as Mr. Mercer—*Nolan??!*—appeared to be, I don't think I can get away with leaving the office in the middle of the morning to embark on a manhunt. Especially since I have no idea where to look.

So, I try to focus on work. But every time I glance over at the desk next to mine, where Thomas used to sit, all I can think about are his soulful eyes and the hurt in them the last time we saw each other.

* * *   ˙

Somehow, I make it through to the end of the day. As I get out of the office, the first thing I do is call Thomas. But his phone is still dead.

I go home, missing him.

I eat dinner, missing him.

And I sit on the couch staring at the black TV screen, still missing him.

Missing him is like a physical pain, it's a constant throbbing ache in my chest, a hunger that can't be satiated, a fire that can't be extinguished.

I can't sleep, I can't rest.

I'm a throbbing, burning mess.

I need something. A piece of him. Even something small would do. If I had a voice message on my phone, I could at least fall asleep listening to his voice. I could even do with one of his notes.

My brain snaps. Of course! The thing he left for me in my drawer at the office. I never checked it. And it's Friday night. I'm not waiting until Monday morning to find out what it is. In a complete sense of déjà vu—after all, going to the office after hours put me into this mess in the first place—I pull on shoes and a coat and practically run out of the house.

Outside it's raining and freezing but I don't care, I don't go back for an umbrella. I sprint toward the subway station, adrenaline pumping through my veins, turning me superhuman. There's a train already waiting on the tracks. I leap inside it a moment before the doors close.

I count the stops in my head, willing the train to move faster. When we finally reach the right station, I dash out of the train and take the steps two at a time, my heart jackhammering in my chest.

I burst into the office building, my breaths coming in quick gasps. The night guard looks up at me in surprise, but I ignore him.

My shoes squeak against the polished tiles as I hurry toward the elevators, pressing the call button impatiently. When the doors finally open, I jump inside and punch the button for the basement. One floor down, the elevator dings and I step out, running across the lab in a last mad dash toward my desk.

I reach my office, push the door open, and find Thomas inside, crouching next to K-2P.

40

THOMAS

The door to Reese's office bangs open, making me jump. But the temporary shock is nothing compared to the jolt of electricity that shoots straight through my spine as I spot her standing in the doorway.

Her hair is wet and plastered to her face, she's panting and breathless, and her expression is wild and desperate.

And she's never been more beautiful.

For a moment, I just stare at her—unable to think or move. All I can do is take in the sight of her, drinking in every detail.

"Thomas?" she asks, as if she can't trust I'm really here. "What are you doing here?"

I stand up and pat K-2P's dome. "It's Friday night, and I didn't want this guy to spend the weekend alone. I know he hates it."

Reese's face twists with something ugly and beautiful at the same time. For a moment, I think she might cry. Instead, she lets out a sound that is a mix of a strangled sob and a battle cry and launches herself at me.

When she barrels into me, I'm not prepared for the impact. I stumble backward until we crash against the metal blinds covering the glass walls of her office.

And then we're kissing.

Reese's mouth is determined, urgent, and fierce. Demanding.

Her hands are on my face, in my hair, pulling me closer and closer. My hands snake around her waist, joining in the effort of obliterating all and any distance between us.

My head spins with her scent, with the taste of her lips on mine. Every sensation is so achingly intense.

We kiss until we can't breathe and my lungs ache. Until our lips are swollen and bruised. Until I am so lost in her I don't know who I am or where I am.

The kiss ends softly as my arms tighten around Reese's waist, but neither one of us backs away; we just stand there with our foreheads pressed together, trying to find our breaths again.

Trembling hands find their way to my face and she cups either side of it, gazing up at me with eyes that are still fiery with emotion.

"I love you," she says. "I want you. Being without you has been like being trapped underwater with no air."

The words hit me like a physical blow. "It's over, baby, you don't have to miss me anymore. I'm here, I love you. I quit my job."

"I know." She hugs me. Squeezing me within an inch of my last breath. For someone so small she sure has a hell of a grip.

"*How* do you know?"

She looks up at me, an unsure smile on her swollen lips. "Your father told me. He asked me to call him Nolan, invited me to family brunch, and winked at me."

That pulls a smile from me. "Did he now?"

"What is family brunch?"

"A message to me."

"What message?"

"That if I'm not sure enough about us to bring you to family brunch, then I should probably reconsider my choices."

Reese frowns. "Your dad thinks you're making a mistake?"

"No, he's just telling me to be sure." I gently dig my fingers into her hips. "I *am* sure."

"And what were you waiting for before telling me? I've been dying here."

"I wanted to wait until tomorrow. I didn't suppose you wanted to discuss anything here at work, and I didn't want to ambush you after a long day at the office."

"That is the silliest thing I've ever heard. Ambush me, ambush me whenever you want."

"Oh, I plan on ambushing you a lot from now on, Campbell."

Her eyes go molten and her gaze drops to my mouth. "Well, in that case..."

She presses against me in a sensual way that has my head spinning again. But before she can kiss me I turn her in my arms and flip her around, pulling her back flush with my front. Then I lower my head to whisper in her ear, "What do you say this time we take this somewhere more appropriate and cut those poor security guards a break?"

I nip her earlobe.

She squirms against me. "You're not making the argument to wait a strong one."

That's when K-2P wheels in front of us. "How about I do? You can't make another sex tape in the office. Plus, my battery is running low, and I don't plan on exiting the room. So, either I stay here and recharge and watch whatever happens, or we all go to Thomas's place and I recharge in the privacy of my room while you two do whatever has you both so worked up in *his* room."

Keeping my arms tightly wrapped around her, I add, "My bed is enormous and soft, but if you're dead set on desk sex I—"

She turns around and pushes a finger over my mouth. "Stop talking before we make another scandal. Let's go home."

We lace our fingers and walk out of the office hand in hand, headed home—K-2P trailing behind us.

And tonight, home is more than just a place, it's a whispered promise of us, of a future together, of a new beginning.

41

REESE

Despite the heating in Thomas's car blasting hot air at max speed, I'm trembling by the time we arrive at his building. The adrenaline has washed out of me, and my soaked hair and clothes have caught up with me.

Thomas notices right away. While K-2P whizzes off somewhere in the apartment, presumably *his room*, Thomas gently drags me toward the bathroom, where he gets a bath started, filling the giant tub with steaming water. He undresses me next, down to removing my socks, but he stays mostly clothed, pulling off only his suit jacket and button-down shirt.

A shiver runs through me and I don't know if it's from the cold or from the sight of him bare-chested. Next thing I know, he's picking me up and gently lowering me into the tub.

My skin burns in protest for a second but then it quickly adjusts to the bubbly warmth. Just when I think I've gone to heaven, Thomas begins bathing me. He grabs a sponge and massages the sensation back into my toes, to then move up to my legs, torso, and arms.

"Mmm," I moan contentedly. "I don't think I'm ever going to take a shower again."

"No?" My eyes are closed, but I can hear the amusement in Thomas's voice as he asks, "Is it the giant tub or the personal bathing service?"

I peek up at him from under one eyelid. "Aren't you joining me?"

He shakes his head. "Not tonight, baby. Tonight, I'm taking care of you."

I'm about to protest, but then his deft fingers sink into my hair, massaging my scalp, and I lose all cognitive function.

By the time he rinses me off and wraps me in a towel, I'm limp.

"Better?" Thomas asks, offering me support with his body—his front to my back—and staring at me with a smile through the mirror.

"Mmm, getting there," I tease. "If I remember correctly, I was lured here with the offer of a huge bed and party favors."

His laugh rumbles up his chest and vibrates against my shoulders just for a second before he scoops me up into his arms.

I curl into his chest as he carries me out of the bathroom and to his bed.

He tenderly drops me onto the mattress, then takes off his pants and socks before finally climbing in next to me. He pulls me in close, nuzzles my neck, and whispers, "I've dreamed of having you in my bed since the first time you flashed me your underwear."

I cup his beautiful face. "And you've no idea how many times I wished I was brave enough to kiss you."

His eyes darken as he moves on top of me. Thomas rests on his elbows and gazes down at me, his expression more tender than I've ever known him to be. "No more wishes and no more dreams; from now on, it's going to be just us together in the real world."

And then he kisses me.

* * *

When I wake up the next morning, my brain takes a minute to be completely still and content before it explodes with questions.

What is Thomas going to do now that he quit working for his father? Is he going to regret leaving Mercer Industries? Will he resent me for it? What am I going to wear to Sunday brunch? Am I officially invited? And then, what did he put in my desk drawer? Every time I remember to check and get to the office with that sole purpose, we end up having mind-blowing sex instead. Not that I'm complaining.

Thomas groans next to me. "Cool your circuits, Campbell, you're disturbing me with your overthinking."

"Tell me you have a plan, that you didn't just quit your job on a whim and are going to resent me for it."

Thomas lifts one lid. "I have a plan. I didn't just quit my job on a whim and I won't resent you for quitting. Happy?" He closes his eyes again and snuggles into me. "Now can we go back to cuddling?"

Cuddling soon turns into more, and he distracts me for the good part of an hour. But the moment he tries to drop asleep on my chest again, I ask him, "What plan?"

"Do I have to sex you into silence again?"

I chuckle. "You can. But I will ask again once it's over, so unless you plan on sexing me all day long..."

He rolls off of me and pulls up on an elbow. "Is that a challenge, Campbell?"

The way he stares at me now, it's a challenge I wouldn't mind losing, but I also want to know he'll be okay in the new situation. "I just want to make sure you'll be as happy as I am. Can you tell me what the plan is? Then I promise you can sex me up all day."

Thomas sighs and rolls onto his back. "Ah, you drive a hard

bargain, Campbell. But since my plan requires your approval, we might as well discuss it. I just wanted to do a little more research before I presented it to you."

I've no idea what he might be talking about. "What plan?"

"And don't worry, if you hate it, there are a million other things I can do. A friend a while ago pitched me an idea for a start-up in smart urban agriculture, but I've passed because I still thought I'd spend the rest of my career at Mercer Industries, but now I'd be free to explore it..."

"Thomas, what's plan number one?"

He lets out a long-suffering sigh. Then, placing both his hands under his head, elbows wide, biceps bulging in a way that makes me regret not taking him up on his offer for all-day sex, he stares at the ceiling. "You know what the best part of being at Mercer Robotics was for me? Beside meeting you, I mean."

I shake my head because I have no clue.

"It was meeting K-2P." He tilts his head toward me. "He's brilliant, mostly I'm sure because he's an extension of your genius mind." Thomas taps my forehead with his fingertip. "And I've always considered it a pity he has to live hidden in your office like something you shouldn't be proud of."

He rolls fully onto his side now. "So that got me thinking, what would be the best application for him? And then I got an idea. As a kid, I would've given anything to have an intelligent droid like those you see in movies as a toy. And I did some research, and all the models on the market right now are crazy expensive, so what if we made an affordable one that every kid in America could have?"

"We?"

"I'd do all the work, build the company, the marketing, and so on... but the IP would be yours. We'd be partners. You'd still be working at Mercer Robotics but would have the final say in all technical developments for the AI. We could also leave the model open-ended so that older kids could code their own programs into it. It could be great for a lot of kids.

"And not just little hot nerds like you. I've read that interacting with a machine could be advantageous to kids on the spectrum to practice social skills in a safe environment. We could build specific modules catered to different learning disabilities..."

As he keeps talking, my heart swells in my chest. Just when I think I can't possibly love this man more, he goes and does something so incredibly sweet and smart and fantastic. My lips wobble.

Thomas takes in my distressed expression and frowns. "You're not talking."

I shake my head. I'm not talking because if I open my mouth, I'll start to cry.

"You hate the idea. If you hate it, don't worry, there are a million other things I can do."

I'm still shaking my head as I launch myself at him.

Wrapping my arms around him, I bury my face into his chest and sniffle. "It's perfect," I tell him, voice muffled by the bedsheets.

When I look up at him again, he's watching me quietly. Then he smiles. "Having a moment?"

I nod.

Thomas runs his fingers over my spine. "Why are you crying, babe?"

Wiping the tears from my face, I bury my head back into his chest. "You're too lovable."

Instead of mocking me, he cradles my face and pulls me up, gently brushing the hair away from my tear-stricken cheeks. "I take it you like the idea?"

"I love it, I love *you*." I stamp a kiss on his mouth.

"Good, now can we stop talking about work and get on with the all-day-sex plan?"

* * *

And so it goes that Saturday, we spend the entire day in bed, half the time making love, half the time planning functions and specifications for the toy version of K-2P.

On Sunday, Thomas brings me to one of those classy, old-fashioned buildings in the Upper East Side, where you need to be approved before you can buy. The elevator doors slide open, revealing the Mercer family penthouse. I step out hesitantly, gripping Thomas's hand as he guides me toward the living room. An onslaught of nerves surges through me, and I immediately feel underdressed in my simple jeans, sweater, and ankle boots.

"Everyone, this is Reese," Thomas announces, gesturing to me with a proud grin. "Reese, meet the family."

His mother, an elegant woman with kind eyes, immediately pulls me into an embrace. "So wonderful to meet you, dear."

"Thank you, Mrs. Mercer. It's an honor to be here."

"Please, call me Camila," she insists with a wink.

His father gives me a firm handshake, his gaze intense, assessing. "Reese. Nice to see you again."

"You too." I still have to keep myself in check not to add "sir" at the end of the sentence.

Thomas's brother, Gabriel—a darker, slightly more intimidating replica of Thomas, rises from his seat, giving me a nod. "Hey, Reese. I'm Gabriel." He gestures to the gorgeous brunette at his side. "This is my girlfriend, Blake." Then he pulls Thomas into a hug that more resembles a wrestling move than a welcoming embrace.

Blake grins, her nose scrunching up adorably. She's wearing black leggings and a fleece, even more underdressed than I am. I immediately like her.

"Hi, I'm Blake. It's great to finally meet you!"

"Finally?" I ask as we shake hands.

She smirks at me and leans in conspiratorially to whisper, "Yep, that one has been moping about you non-stop since the day you guys met."

Thomas, freed from the hello wrestling hold, bumps shoulders with me. "What are you ladies whispering about over here?"

I turn to him, slightly slack jawed that this gorgeous man has not only chosen me over a family empire, but was moping over me. Since. Day. One?

Blake saves me from having to answer. "I was just telling her not to worry if you and your brother fight. It's completely normal and a sign of your affection for each other."

"Enough with the formalities," Thomas's father calls, clapping his hands. "Now, let's eat!"

The aroma of maple syrup and sizzling bacon envelops me as I take my seat at the long dining table. Blake and Gabriel are seated across from me and Thomas, their fingers interlaced over the white linen, and his parents at the opposite ends of the table.

Despite my initial anxiety, the conversation flows effortlessly, and I feel oddly at ease among the Mercers. Especially with Blake in front of me, making all sorts of funny faces and covert comments.

"Everyone," Blake speaks up suddenly, "Gabriel and I have some news to share." She glances over at Gabriel, who nods with a grin.

"Go on," Camila urges, excitement in her eyes.

"We're expecting!" Blake exclaims, her face beaming. "The baby's due in mid-July!"

"Congratulations!" I say, genuinely thrilled for them.

"Congrats, you two!" Thomas chimes in, not looking overly surprised. He turns to me and winks.

"A grandchild?" Camila is half-shocked, half-tearful.

"The family's growing fast." Nolan's mustache bristles with approval. "Let's toast."

As the conversation moves toward babies and parenting advice, the spotlight shifts from me to the ecstatic parents-to-be. The pressure of being the newest member at the table dissolves, replaced by the joy of celebrating new life. Who would've thought that meeting my boyfriend's billionaire family could feel so... normal?

Then, over coffee, Thomas and Gabriel get into a brawl about who's more awesome at some space game on the Xbox and their father has to separate them by blowing an air horn while Thomas's mom tells me and Blake to cover our ears. Seeing a family worth billions of dollars act in such a cozy, laid-back way is a shock all on its own. Not to mention that when we leave after lunch, Nolan Mercer winks at me again.

And on Monday morning, I arrive at the office extra early, before anyone is there. I go alone as K-2P is now officially part of MC Toys—MC for Mercer Campbell, the new company Thomas is starting. In the lab, I calmly stride toward my office and once inside, I sit at my crooked desk. Then I open the first drawer on the right.

Inside, I find a little wrapped package with a blue note stuck on top.

I have more where this came from in case you want to keep on coming back, Campbell.

Thomas, x

I unwrap the package and find my favorite white chocolate candy bar from Italy, which they don't sell in the States. Giggling like an idiot, I hug the candy bar to my chest and make a silent promise to Thomas: *Yes, I will be coming back for more. More chocolate. More Love. More you.*

EPILOGUE
REESE

I can do this. The aisle is only twenty yards long. The altar is not that far.

No reason to panic.

And the ceremony is small, with only family and close friends.

That's easy.

It doesn't matter that one of the close friends will probably be the next president of the United States, or that family means the boss of the boss of my boss is here, right?

"Don't be nervous," the wedding planner whispers next to me. We're standing hidden in a cove of trees, out of sight of the outdoor reception setting, waiting to make our entrance.

"Nervous?" I turn to her, clutching the flower bouquet in my hands for dear life. "I'm not nervous. What makes you say that?"

She pointedly stares at my death grip on the unfortunate floral stems. "Then why are you trying to strangle that poor flower arrangement?"

The flowers are already dead, by any standard, but I force myself to unclench my fingers and give some circulation back to my knuckles. Then I smile like a lunatic, promising the wedding planner that I'm fine.

I concentrate on the soft organ music playing in the background, keeping my gaze trained on the green grass under my fancy new shoes. After six months of dating Thomas, I should be used to the bubble wrap that comes from dating a billionaire. Or to the fact that I work for his father—*many levels* below him. And I mostly have. Now I can handle family brunches like a pro, but a wedding? That's a different story.

When the chords shift to the song preceding the bridal march, the wedding planner nudges me. "You're first after the flower girl."

As if I didn't know already.

Nora, the maid of honor's stepdaughter, struts out of our hidden cove in her tulle dress, projecting a hundred times more confidence than I can summon.

Then it's my turn.

"Chin high and one foot in front of the other," the wedding planner prompts. "Keep on the white carpet so that your heels won't sink in the ground, and you'll be fine. You can do it."

Of course I can. I've been walking since I was one. I'm very proficient at walking. Well, maybe not in sky-high heels like the ones I'm wearing today. But I practiced my runway walk, I can do it. Deep breaths.

"You're out in three, two, one..."

The wedding planner ushers me out from behind a huge oak trunk, and just like that, I'm standing in the middle of the outdoor wedding setting, all eyes on me. But I only have eyes for the man standing next to the altar, one step down from the groom.

Thomas smiles, and suddenly all worries fly out the window. I no longer care if the people gathered in this garden control half the country's GDP. Or that one *or more* of them will be president one day.

I float down the aisle, eyes glued to the best man, who can't take his eyes off me—smoldering, indeed.

I reach the flower gazebo, doubling as an altar, without stumbling, but my heart still does a little somersault when Thomas winks at me.

The maid of honor, Marissa, who's sporting a baby bump similar in size to that of the bride, is next. And then the bride.

Blake looks resplendent in a flowing white gown, her long, dark hair cascading down her shoulders in glorious waves. She isn't wearing a veil, just a small crown of white flowers resting delicately on top of her head.

The ceremony flies by. The vows are a little bizarre, but totally romantic. Gabriel promises to love and to cherish his bride and to never lift a finger should she get in business trouble. An inside joke? From Blake's bright smile, the bride seems to appreciate the pledge. And a few people in the know, including Thomas, chuckle along.

Gabriel also promises to never let Blake go to sleep without hearing "I love you" at least once, no matter how tired or grumpy he might be. It's sweet and makes me smile. And to always make sure that she is never without her favorite brand of ice cream in the freezer, which garners a laugh from the crowd.

In return, the bride promises to always be his partner, to constantly keep him on his toes, but also to allow Gabriel the occasional romantic kidnapping. Again, Thomas and the maid of honor chuckle at the inside joke.

Then the rings are exchanged, and the ceremony is over in a flurry of confetti and joyous tears.

Thomas is by my side in seconds. "You look like a dream in that dress," he whispers in my ear. "I can't wait to take it off you."

My toes curl in my pumps and heat rises to my cheeks.

"Don't blush so much," Thomas mock-chides. "Or everyone will know I'm talking dirty to you."

I give him the side-eye. "Then stop talking dirty to me."

He grins. "Impossible."

We make our way to a different area of the resort where the reception is being held. The venue is simply stunning—a lush garden, with fairy lights woven through the trees, and tables adorned with flowers of every color. Soft music floats through the air, and guests are mingling, sipping champagne, and nibbling on delicious canapés.

As we approach the table with our seating arrangement, Marissa and the bride are already sitting there, complaining about the third trimester being the worst, while their men do their best to make sure they're as comfortable as possible.

In my short time dating Thomas, I've gotten to know his brother and sister-in-law a little. I see them every Sunday at brunch, and I've enrolled in one of Blake's ballet for beginners classes at her gym, but I don't know Marissa and her fiancé that well.

I take my seat next to Thomas and smile at the two women. "Did you guys plan to get pregnant at the same time?"

"No." The bride beams back at me. "This is very much an accidental baby."

I didn't know that. For obvious reasons, we never discussed the conception story of the baby while at brunch with Thomas's parents.

The maid of honor caresses her belly. "This baby, on the other hand, was very much planned. It was the paternity that was accidental." She stares up at her fiancé, the other groomsman in the wedding party, John, and they share a look so sizzling I'm afraid the flower arrangement between them might catch fire.

I stare at them, unsure what to say.

Marissa turns to me, explaining, "I was supposed to get pregnant with an anonymous donor, but the IVF clinic I was getting treated at accidentally used John's sample."

"Wow." My eyes bulge. "Is that how you guys met?"

"No." Marissa smiles. "He made me fall for him in high school, then broke my heart, and then disappeared for the next sixteen years, only to get me accidentally knocked up with his baby two weeks after coming back into my life."

John grins, raising his hands. "The knocking up wasn't technically my fault. But I'm not complaining." He glances at me and Thomas. "How did you guys meet?"

Thomas flashes the table a smug smirk. "Her droid invited me in on her having a striptease in her office."

The whole table chuckles, and then Gabriel asks, "This is the same droid you're going to mass produce?"

Thomas nods. "We're going to get both of your babies a prototype as soon as they're born. We should be on the market next year and the pre-sales are already amazing."

My chest swells with the familiar sensation of overwhelming love and pride, and I squeeze Thomas's hand under the table. He's been working relentlessly hard to bring together our toy company. And it's amazing all that he's accomplished in such a short time.

"What about you guys?" I ask the bride and groom. "I don't think I ever heard how you met."

The groom takes a sip of champagne and then unleashes a smile on the table as devastatingly charming as that of his younger brother. "She bad-mouthed me in the press."

Blake scowls. "I gave the press *factual* statements, and then he thought it appropriate to barge into my office uninvited and mansplain to me all the reasons I was wrong."

I smile. "Uh-huh, I take it the mansplaining went well. What did you do?"

Blake's smirk is feral. "I sent him to have a pizza to cool down and reflect on the error of his ways."

"Best pizza in New York," Gabriel declares, and the whole table laughs.

The rest of the wedding banquet is just as easygoing. All my earlier tension at the start of the ceremony now seems completely unjustified.

After I finish a giant slice of wedding cake, we dance and drink more champagne. I lose the bouquet to one of Thomas's cousins, and console myself with a slow dance in the arms of my gorgeous boyfriend. I don't need to catch a bunch of dead flowers to know we'll get married someday. The music picks up and we dance, and dance, and dance until we collapse back at our table. It's late, some of the guests are already leaving, and my feet hurt. But soon, as much as I don't want to get up again, I have to excuse myself to go to the bathroom.

"Don't forget your bag," Thomas says, handing me my clutch.

"I don't really need it. I'll be back in a sec."

"Take it," he insists. "In case you need to powder your nose or something."

Is he implying my nose needs powdering? Frowning, I take the clutch from him and head to the bathroom.

After a quick visit to the toilet, I stand in front of the wide restroom mirrors to assess my reflection. My nose looks just fine. My lipstick, however, could use a retouch.

I open my clutch, searching for my lip gloss, and find a blue note instead.

My heart rate immediately picks up.

I'm dating a pickpocket.

How does he manage to always sneak notes in my bags without me ever noticing? I find them at the oddest moments, sometimes totally inappropriate instances, but whenever I read one of his messages—be they sweet, funny, or outright indecent—my heart flutters, then I smile like an idiot as thrills zap through my body. And today is no different.

With my fingers itching with anticipation, I unfold the blue note.

Room 873, don't make me wait.

Oh, so today he went for *casually* indecent.

Without returning to the reception—the party is over anyway—I rush through the hotel lobby and head straight for the elevators.

The ride up is unbearably slow, and when the elevator doors open on the eighth floor, I rush down the hall, my heart pumping.

When I reach the designated door, I find another blue note stuck on the outside.

Knock, then close your eyes.

I raise my fist to the door and close my eyes a heartbeat before knocking. I'm ready for whatever is waiting on the other side, for slipping into this never-ending dream my life has become since Thomas stole my very heart and soul.

And then the door opens...

Strong, warm hands gently grab mine, pulling me into the room.

Thomas leans in to whisper in my ear, "Keep your eyes closed."

The hairs on my arms stand to attention as he sneaks past me to close the door. Then he's hugging me from behind, placing his hands over my eyes and awkwardly prompting me forward. We shuffle-walk, doing our best not to stomp on each other's feet, until Thomas pulls me to a stop.

He drops his hands from my face. "You can open your eyes now."

Flowers fill every surface in the room in all shapes and in every shade of pink. Roses, azaleas, begonias, lilies, hydrangeas, and many others whose names I don't know.

I don't even have time to admire their beauty before a giant blue question mark made of Post-it notes snags my attention to the back wall.

I turn to Thomas. "What is this?"

"Go read," he prompts me with a look on his face that's part adoration, part mischief, and part eagerness. "Start at the center."

I go to the wall and pick up the note that ends the curl on the upper part of the question mark.

I love your scowls

I beam, picking up the next note and reading them one after the other.

Almost as much as I love your smiles

But what I love the most

Is when you can't help smiling at me

Even when you're trying to scowl

Your intelligence challenges me

Your humor delights me

Your body inflames me

My cheeks sure are flaming right now.

Your strength and your resilience astound me

In your arms, I find a rare kind of peace

I love you, despite you saying you prefer the prequel trilogy of Star Wars *to the original movies*

I chuckle at that.

Really? I mean, Han Solo, Leia? Come on, Campbell

I'm downright laughing now, but my heart rate has also picked up a certain speed.

But you love your villain origin stories, and I can live with that

In fact, I want to live with that

Every day

For the rest of my life

Reese Campbell, you've stolen my breath, my heart, my soul from the very first day I met you

Tears well up in my eyes.

I'm in love with you

I want to grow old together

I pick up the last note.

Turn around

Thomas is behind me, down on one knee, cradling a tiny jewelry box in his hands. Inside, propped on a soft velvet lining, an engagement ring topped by a giant pink diamond shaped like a football. The gem glints under the overhead lights. But not even the perfect diamond sparkle can compete with the intensity of Thomas's eyes on me now—smoldering more than ever.

"Marry me," he says simply, his voice raw with emotion.

"Yes." I drop to my knees on the soft carpet and hug him, burying my face in his neck. "Yes."

Thomas pulls back slightly, a goofy smile on his face. His hands shake as he takes the ring out of the box.

As Thomas slips the ring onto my finger, I can't help but grin. "You do realize this means you're stuck with my extravagant movie opinions for life, right?"

His laughter rings out, warm and genuine. He pulls me closer and I end up sitting on his lap on the floor. "Oh, so next, you're going to tell me *The Hunger Games* prequel was better than the original movies?"

"I'm not *that* extravagant."

"No, you're extraordinary," he says, suddenly serious. He cups my cheeks and brushes wayward locks of hair away from my face. "And I'm the luckiest man alive to have you as my future wife."

I might die if I don't kiss him now, and so I do. And as we embrace, surrounded by a sea of flowers and love notes, I know this is just the beginning of our forever.

ACKNOWLEDGMENTS

Thanks to all of you who have been clamoring for Thomas to have his story written since meeting him in the first book in the series, *Not in a Billion Years*.

A book about him wasn't initially planned, but Thomas is one of those characters that gets under the skin and demands attention. I developed a major writer's crush on him in book one, and I suspect you did, too, if you're reading this. Anyway, thank you for pushing me to write this book. I hope it delivered all the swoons, that you fell in love with Thomas a little more, and will want to keep him as one of your favorite book boyfriends. I will.

Thanks to my editor, Rachel Faulkner-Willcocks, for always making my stories the best they can be. Thank you to Candida Bradford and Susan Sugden for helping to improve my prose.

Thank you to the production team at Boldwood Books for their incredible formatting skills. And to the marketing team for helping me put this book in front of as many eyes as possible.

Thanks to readers and reviewers for all your nice comments and pretty posts, or simply just for reading my stories.

And finally, thanks to my family for their constant support.

ABOUT THE AUTHOR

Camilla Isley is an engineer who left science behind to write bestselling contemporary rom-coms set all around the world. She lives in Italy.

Sign up to Camilla Isley's mailing list for news, competitions and updates on future books.

Visit Camilla's website: www.camillaisley.com

Follow Camilla on social media:

instagram.com/camillaisley

tiktok.com/@camilla.isley

facebook.com/camillaisley

x.com/camillaisley

bookbub.com/authors/camilla-isley

youtube.com/RomanceAudiobooks

ALSO BY CAMILLA ISLEY

The Love Theorem

Love Quest

The Love Proposal

Love to Hate You

Not in a Billion Years

Baby, One More Time

It's Complicated

The Love Algorithm

WHERE ALL YOUR ROMANCE
DREAMS COME TRUE!

THE HOME OF BESTSELLING
ROMANCE AND WOMEN'S
FICTION

 WARNING:
MAY CONTAIN SPICE

SIGN UP TO OUR
NEWSLETTER

https://bit.ly/Lovenotesnews

Boldw∞d

Boldwood Books is an award-winning fiction publishing company seeking out the best stories from around the world.

Find out more at www.boldwoodbooks.com

Join our reader community for brilliant books, competitions and offers!

Follow us
@BoldwoodBooks
@TheBoldBookClub

Sign up to our weekly deals newsletter

https://bit.ly/BoldwoodBNewsletter

Printed in Great Britain
by Amazon

45427880R00155